THE
SWAMP
GUIDE

A FLORIDA KEYES MYSTERY

THE
SWAMP
GUIDE

A FLORIDA KEYES MYSTERY

Carl and Jane Bock

ABSOLUTELY AMAZING eBOOKS

ABSOLUTELY AMAZING eBOOKS

Published by Whiz Bang LLC, 926 Truman Avenue, Key West, Florida 33040, USA.

The Swamp Guide copyright © 2018 by Carl and Jane Bock. Electronic compilation/ paperback edition copyright © 2018 by Whiz Bang LLC. Cover photo by Carl Bock. Author photo by Carol Helzer

For information contact:
Publisher@AbsolutelyAmazingEbooks.com

ISBN-13: 978-1945772818 (Absolutely Amazing Ebooks)
ISBN-10: 1945772816

This book is dedicated to those heroic individuals working for the restoration and protection of the Everglades and Florida Bay, two of the most endangered ecosystems in North America

THE SWAMP GUIDE

A FLORIDA KEYES MYSTERY

CHAPTER 1

The day of the red hat and blue shoes began like any other, but it marked the beginning of a long hard time while we tried to figure out what happened to the woman who was wearing that hat and those shoes on the day she fell off the edge of the earth. I might have quit the crime-fighting business altogether if I'd known how much the case was going to stink up my life. After all, it was just a sideline. I was supposed to be a fisherman.

George Lancaster and I met for an early breakfast that day at the Hogfish Grill, like we often did before connecting with our clients. George is a fellow swamp guide, and one of my best friends. Everybody calls him Snooks. He's a canny angler no matter what the prey, but he and his namesake have some sort of a special relationship. He can sniff out a snook's hidey-hole when none of the rest of us even has a clue.

The combined aromas of frying bacon, buttermilk pancakes, and fresh coffee hit me as I walked into the little restaurant. The place was full of fisherman, chatting optimistically like they always do in anticipation of a fresh day on the water. Snooks already was at the counter, having coffee. He'd saved me the seat next to his, and ordered for both of us – an egg sandwich with bacon for me, three eggs over easy with a big pile of hash browns for him. He pivoted on his stool when he saw me coming. "Morning, Sam. What's new at Sawyer's Backcountry Charters?"

I slid in next to him. "Kind of an easy day, I hope. My guy wants to throw flies for mangrove snappers and bring home dinner. Apparently the wife has been after him about it. I'm thinking we'll fish a couple of the local keys and see what happens. Any suggestions?"

Snooks is in his early sixties and has me by a good twenty years. He's spent most of his adult life angling up and down the Florida Keys, and nobody knows the skinny water better than he does. The guy is a gold mine of tips and know-how.

He fiddled with the rubber band holding a little gray ponytail that only partly concealed his advancing bald spot. "You might try either Clovis or Ranger. The moats around those keys are plenty deep. 'Course the biggest snappers will be tucked way back under the mangroves, so your guy had better know what he's doing. Otherwise you'll spend the whole day getting him unhooked from the branches." He paused while the waitress, a thin dark-haired woman in her fifties, came out from the kitchen with our food. "Oh, and one other suggestion. You might bring some live shrimp and spinning gear in case those snappers are feeling picky."

"Thanks, but we've fished together before. He's pretty good with the fly. I think we'll stick to that approach. What's on your schedule?"

I swallowed some coffee and watched while Snooks scooped his eggs up on top of the hash browns and worked his fork around mixing the whole thing together. He took a big bite, chewed, swallowed, and wiped the grease off his chin with a paper napkin. Snooks is one of those lucky souls who can eat like a horse and stay thin. He stands only a couple inches shy of my six feet, but I probably outweigh him by sixty pounds.

Snooks forked in two more bites before he got around to answering my question. "Got a fella wants to go deep into the everglades, try for some snook and redfish, maybe a young tarpon."

"And you'll be taking your canoe?"

"Yep. The usual routine. The tide's gonna be good. I just hope the mosquitoes and the no-see-ums behave themselves."

We both specialize in taking clients back into parts of Everglades National Park where boats with motors are not permitted. We strap canoes to the side of our boats for the ride across Florida Bay, then tie up to a convenient mangrove and paddle our clients on from there. It's a tricky business, and not for everybody. The days are long and sometimes the bugs are awful. But the fishing, the wildlife, and the scenery make it all worthwhile, especially for a hardcore client.

Snooks is strictly a fisherman, while I cater to people with a wider range of interests. Usually they want to fish, and I'm pretty good at that – not as good as Snooks but getting better thanks to him. Some of my clients want to see birds instead of fishing. I can do that too, because of a background in zoology. And then sometimes I have people who just want to get paddled out into all that empty, where they can enjoy the scenery and escape whatever it was they fear or resent or don't want to think about, if only for the day.

Remote parts of the everglades are beautiful and haunting, and a trip out there can be its own reward, even without the fish or the birds. But the glades hold their share of danger as well. Snooks and I had learned this the hard way, and we always were properly cautious. Even so, we weren't prepared for some bad things that were about to happen.

We were about three-quarters finished with breakfast when a man I had never seen before came in and took a seat at the far end of the counter. He was tall and heavy-set, at least six-five, with a flat face, unruly blond hair, and beady blue eyes. He glanced at Snooks and favored him with a nod. Snooks barely nodded back, and then muttered something under his breath that I didn't catch.

"Who is that guy?"

"That's Reuben Fletcher. Surprised you haven't seen him before, 'cause he's a guide like us. Sort of."

I took a bite of breakfast sandwich and drained the last of my second cup of coffee. "What's that supposed to mean?"

Snooks snorted a half-laugh. "Reuben's a world class jerk. He follows me around all the time, and then he butts in when I find the fish. It drives me nuts. And there's rumors he doesn't always pay attention to things like size and possession limits."

"Has he ever been caught?"

"Not that I know of. He drives a 22-foot Pathfinder with a dark blue hull stripe. If you see him out on the water, go someplace else." Snooks shoveled in a last fork-full of hash browns and spun around on his stool. "Let's get the hell out of here before he comes nosing around. I'm tired of dealing with that guy."

CHAPTER 2

"You're the captain, Sam. I'm just a passenger. So you decide. How much time do we have?"

Marshall White was a whole lot more than just a passenger. A bespectacled banker from Boston, he was a long-term client who had proven himself a damned good fly fishermen – a real "stick," in fact. That's what swamp guides call somebody who knows how to handle the equipment – to make the fly go where it is supposed to go with minimal disturbance to the water.

But he was right. It was my call. The waters around Clovis Key already were shallow, and the tide was falling fast. We'd tried several other spots earlier in the day, without much luck: only two mangrove snappers in the live well, both just a bit over the ten-inch size limit. They would be delicious, but it wasn't nearly enough for a decent meal for Marshall and his wife.

So I decided to go for it. We probably had about an hour before my eighteen-foot Hell's Bay skiff would be in trouble. Like nearly all the keys scattered across Florida Bay, there was a moat of relatively deep water surrounding Clovis. The trick was getting in there and then getting back out. I raised up my 70-horse four-stroke Yamaha outboard and used the trolling motor for the last hundred yards. Once safely into the moat we began working our way counterclockwise around the key, looking for shady spots with overhanging mangroves.

The day was clear and calm. A dense stand of

mangroves grew like a hedge all around the perimeter of the key, forming a rich green band that separated a cloudless blue sky overhead from the clear emerald water between my boat and the island.

There were lots of fish, and Marshall knew just how to reach the biggest ones. He cast with a sidearm motion that kept his fly low to the water. Sometimes he even made the fly hop a couple of times after it landed, like skipping a stone. This allowed him to lay his offering well back under the mangrove canopy where the big fish were tucked in.

After about forty minutes we had five good snappers in the boat, and he'd only snagged up once. A remarkable feat. We were just about ready to go, but Marshall was still up on the bow reeling up his line when he pointed to a little sandy cove about fifty yards ahead of us. "What's that?"

At first I didn't see anything. "What's what?"

"I don't know. It's something red, right up on shore. Looks like it could be a hat. Let's go take a look."

I wasn't sure we had time and said so. "And anyway, what's so interesting about a hat?"

"I don't know, it just looks odd, that's all. Not like something a fisherman would wear. Why don't you troll on up there? I'll make one cast, try to snag it with my fly, and then we leave. We can be out of here in five minutes."

"Okay, but you only get the one shot. We don't want to spend the night out here waiting for the tide to come back. You can't imagine what the bugs are going to be like once the sun goes down."

One shot was all he needed. What Marshall White

retrieved was an old straw hat, dyed red, with plastic yellow flowers attached to the band. Marshall laughed as he brought it on board and unhooked his fly from the brim. "Looks like the Red Hat Society has been to Clovis Key. I wonder what the hell they were doing way out here?"

I'd never heard of the Red Hat Society, but for some reason Marshall knew all about it. He explained they were groups of women, often of the senior citizen variety, who always wore red hats and purple dresses and had adventures together.

"Want to keep it?"

Marshall shrugged. "Not particularly, but now that we've got it I suppose we should. There's enough litter around here already."

I stowed the hat in a hold up under the bow along with the life preservers, and then forgot all about it. It was only much later that I learned where it had come from, and why it had nothing at all to do with the Red Hat Society. The actual owner had experienced an adventure all right, but it was not the kind a Red Hat Lady or anybody else would have chosen.

CHAPTER 3

Snooks came by after work that day to bum a beer. He did that a lot because it was a standing invitation. I would happily trade a whole six-pack for just one of his tips. On this particular day he'd found a place where the tarpon had started to roll. He'd also spotted a pair of bonefish, two of a dwindling number that still inhabited the Keys. It was good information, and a real bargain in trade for a couple of beers.

We were out on my deck, enjoying our Yuenglings and watching some white-crowned pigeons picking fruits out of the poisonwood trees across the canal from my house. I live on Lower Matecumbe Key, which is part of the village of Islamorada, in one of those developments where all the lots are waterfront because of a network of man-made canals. My uncle Fred built the house back in the early 1970s, at a time when people of modest means came here mostly to fish. He and my aunt had no children, and he left the place to me when he died.

The whole neighborhood is changing now that the Keys have gotten popular with people whose pockets are way (way) deeper than mine. Today my little wooden house on stilts is squeezed in between high-end homes going for a million plus. I probably could burn my place to the ground and still get half a million just for the lot.

The afternoon was drawing to a close and the angled rays of a fading sun lit up the mangroves along the canal in a yellow-green glow. Snooks and I were on our second rounds. I could tell something was bothering him, because he wasn't being his usual talkative self.

"How did it go out there?"

He said, "huh." Then he scratched at a loose piece of skin on top of his sunburned right ear and kept quiet.

"Huh what?"

He stirred, uneasy. "Turns out I had a real googan today. It was a miracle he even got into the canoe without falling overboard. And then it seemed like half his casts went up into the mangroves. I kept telling him the fish were mostly in the water."

"Did he get better?"

"Maybe a little, but still it was a long damned day." He took another sip of his beer, and sighed. Then he started fiddling with his ponytail, which I had learned from experience meant he was thinking hard about something.

Googan is a term guides used for fishermen who are not just inept, which is forgivable, but who also are too ignorant or arrogant to admit it, which is not. I knew that Snooks was a patient man, like all guides who are any good.

"So that was it? Just the googan?"

He shook his head and set his empty beer bottle down on the little glass-topped table in front of us. "It was something else."

Why was I having to pry it out of the man? "Well...?"

"On the way out we paddled past this really big crocodile laid up on a sandy point. I'm guessing she had a nest full of eggs somewhere close, because she didn't look happy to see us."

I wondered how Snooks could tell a happy croc from an unhappy one. To me, their expressionless gray faces might just as well have been carved in stone. Sometimes their mouths were open, revealing all sorts of big teeth, but I was pretty sure even then they weren't smiling.

I was tired of prompting Snooks so I just stayed quiet and sipped my beer. It took about another thirty seconds.

"It was a pair of blue shoes. They were lying right there in the sand next to the croc."

I put down my beer and turned in his direction. "Oh yeah?"

"But that wasn't the worst part. There were feet in the shoes."

CHAPTER 4

The everglades aren't what they used to be. Experienced guides can still find the fish and the birds, but nobody pretends it hasn't changed for the worse. Nobody, that is, except for some developers and agri-business moguls and their political henchmen. The glades have always depended on fresh water flowing from north to south, right down through the central part of the state and out into Florida Bay. A mix of fresh and salt water is the magic elixir that brings life to the glades. But that same fresh water has the inconvenient habit of flooding things like golf courses and neighborhoods and fields of sugar cane, and as a result the whole system has been jerked around in the name of progress. By now there is no easy way of getting all that ecological toothpaste back in the tube without ruffling some very wealthy and powerful feathers.

In light of the fading guide business, and largely because of a degree in zoology, I have developed a small side career as a private investigator and expert witness. Specifically, I'm pretty good at identifying things like fur or feathers or scales that might be evidence in cases involving poaching or the sale of contraband wildlife. This in turn has gotten me involved with law enforcement, especially in Everglades National Park. They let me take the training classes required of incoming law enforcement Rangers. I was licensed to carry, although my Glock forty-caliber had never actually left the house.

Given my experience with the Park Service, not only was I startled by Snooks' revelation, I naturally had questions.

"After you spotted those shoes, what did you do about it?"

He looked rueful. "We left."

"That's it? You just left?"

Snooks fiddled with his ponytail. "Yeah, my client was scared shitless. Told me to get the hell out before he barfed. So that's what we did."

"But you called the Park police afterwards, right?"

Snooks took a last sip of his second beer, set the bottle back down, then shook his head and gazed out across the canal. "I screwed up, didn't I?"

He had, but I didn't see any point in beating him up about it. What's done was done. "Did you get the coordinates?"

He shook his head again. "Nope. The GPS stays back in the boat, not in the canoe."

"Could you find it again? The place with the shoes and feet?"

"Sure. 'Course they might be gone by now."

I'd thought of that. "I still think we need to get over there. There might be other evidence around. It's probably too late for today, but we can meet up first thing in the morning. I assume you're available."

"Yeah I'm available, but do the Park Rangers have to find out?"

I wasn't sure what he was talking about. "Find out what? If the shoes are still there, or anything else, then I'll give 'em a call."

"Yeah sure, I get that. But do they need to find out I already was out there and didn't do anything about it?"

We had come to the crux of the matter. Snooks had just asked me to cover for him.

People still ask me why I didn't call the cops right then and there, tell them the whole story, and just hand off the whole matter. In hindsight my life would have gone a lot simpler if I had done exactly that. All I can say is that Snooks was a friend, and he'd come along at a point in my life when I needed one. And besides, maybe the shoes would be right where Snooks had first seen them. Maybe it would all work out.

So we made our plans, agreeing to take my boat and canoe and leave the dock at first light the next morning. Snooks said he had another client lined up, but he'd find a substitute guide.

CHAPTER 5

People come to the Florida Keys for lots of reasons. For many it is the terminus of a lifelong southward drift to escape the cold or the past or, more often than you might suppose, the law. U.S. Highway 1 is the only road connecting the string of islands to the mainland. They call it the Overseas Highway, and the last stop before you're not even in the country any more is Key West. Some people refer to it as Key Weird, but I expect that's less about any criminal element than it is about the kaleidoscopic mix of residents and visitors to the island. One time I accidentally went down there on St. Patrick's Day, and I didn't figure it out until this guy came running down Duval Street wearing nothing but a big sparkly green hat.

The fact is that things could get creepy anywhere in the Keys, because the bad guys spread themselves out along the whole length of the archipelago, from Florida City on down. There were any number of ways a pair of occupied shoes could end up next to a crocodile out there in the glades, but I couldn't think of any that weren't ominous.

Unlike many swamp guides, I remain partly tethered to the mainland. My wife Katie lives up at our condo in Fort Lauderdale, where she teaches plant science at the Florida Institute of Science and Technology. I was on the faculty there myself, teaching vertebrate zoology, until three years ago when they kicked me out. Actually it was sort of a mutual decision.

I really liked those students and colleagues who shared a passion for the natural world. But the mind-numbing committee work and endless petty squabbling were awful. I just couldn't play the game. They say that academic politics are especially nasty not because the stakes are so large, but because they are so small. The department chair, whom I actually liked, once told me about a colleague who came in to complain that his annual raise was $100 dollars less than the guy down the hall. The chair said she took out her wallet, handed the man five twenties, and told him to get the hell out.

As much as I had grown to dislike certain aspects of life as a teacher and scholar, leaving the mainland and my wife had been hard. Some of Katie's friends from Fort Lauderdale still haven't forgiven me. What happened that made an over-educated forty-year-old run off to a little conch house in the Keys and play fisherman? There were no easy answers.

I tried to get up to Lauderdale as often as possible, and Katie sometimes spent weekends in Islamorada, but that had been happening less frequently in recent months. It did not take a genius to figure out that our marriage was starting to fray at the ends.

Katie could have moved down to the Keys permanently, but we never really talked about that. In the first place, her tolerance for the minutia of the academic life was greater than mine. And besides, it would have been next to impossible for her to pursue her passion without access to some expensive equipment that wouldn't fit into our budget, let alone inside my little house in Islamorada. She taught introductory plant science and advanced courses in forensic botany. That's the use of plant evidence in criminal investigations, and it also happened to be her main research interest.

So I kept on living down in the Keys, guiding fishermen and the occasional birdwatcher, while Katie stayed up in Lauderdale teaching and working with law enforcement. About the only common ground in our lives, besides a diminishing number of conjugal visits, was when criminal cases came along that required identification of both zoological (me) and botanical (her) evidence. I didn't know it yet, but Snooks' discovery over in the glades was going to be one of those times.

CHAPTER 6

Snooks and I met at my dock at 6:30 the next morning. Our destination was Cape Sable, the southern and westernmost point on the Florida mainland. It would have been a 40-mile straight line boat ride from my house, except you can't actually get there following a straight line. Florida Bay is an extension of the Gulf of Mexico, tucked in between the Keys and southern coast of Florida proper. The bay actually is complicated mosaic of small mangrove islands, shallow shoals, and deeper basins. Critical to overwater navigation are a limited number of channels crossing the shoals and connecting the basins. Weaving your way through these channels is tricky. It was a lot harder back before the advent of GPS navigation devices, but even now you have to know what you're doing. For sure it is no place for the guides who specialize in taking clients out into the Atlantic. They drive macho boats capable of handling the deep blue water and all the big fish that go with it, but they aren't worth crap in the shallows of the backcountry. I didn't particularly like some of the blue water guides I'd met over the years, but I probably was just jealous because their equipment was bigger than mine.

Swamp guides are a humbler lot, and we drive smaller craft with minimal draw. Things still can go wrong. More than once I found my way into a shallow bay embedded deep in the mangroves, wonderfully full of snook and redfish and tarpon, only to discover at the end of the day that my escape route had dried up as the tide began to fall. They have a saying down here about swamp guides: unless you've been aground, you haven't been around.

~ ~ ~

We loaded up a cooler with ice, drinks, and snacks, along with my portable GPS unit and a radio by which I could contact Park personnel when the time was right. Then we strapped a canoe to the starboard gunwale of my flats boat and headed out.

Snooks insisted on bringing his favorite fly rod and an old salt-encrusted vest stuffed with leaders and flies, "just in case." I frowned but didn't push it. It seemed unlikely we'd be doing much fishing, but you never knew.

The day started out clear and relatively calm, with only a slight wind blowing out of the southwest. Things were timed so we could make our way into the backcountry with the help of a rising tide, which then would turn and help push us back out in the afternoon. Or that was the plan, anyway.

I drove down my canal at idle speed, and then opened things up once we got out into the Gulf proper. By 7 AM we had passed the Buchanan Keys and wiggled through a couple of channels into Rabbit Key Basin. We left the basin via the Iron Pipe Channel and made our way north through two more cuts before heading west along the Florida coastline toward Cape Sable. Once we had arrived at the cape, we turned north into the East Cape Canal and followed it up into Lake Ingraham. By the time we tied up to some mangroves and transferred into the canoe it was nearly eight o'clock. Snooks guessed we had about a mile of paddling ahead of us, back into the no-motor area where he had found the blue shoes the day before.

The place was so thick with mosquitoes and no-see-ums you had to keep your mouth closed to avoid inhaling an early lunch. But we'd lathered up ahead of time with an insect repellent strong enough to dissolve the plastic parts of polarized glasses if you weren't careful. Between the repellent, long sleeves, and masks that covered our faces, the clouds of hungry insects were tolerable.

The first leg of the canoe trip took us up a narrow creek squeezed in between overhanging mangroves. The bugs were all over us in there, but they let up as soon as we broke out into relatively open water. A rising tide made paddling easy.

As usual, the place was full of birds. A half-dozen roseate spoonbills flew west overhead, their pink plumage bright against the morning sky. A pair of yellow-crowned night herons and four common egrets fed on a shallow flat that was slowly disappearing before the tide. Soon the rising water would make things too deep for easy wading, and the birds would give way to schools of mullet and their predators, including redfish, snook, and lemon sharks. We spotted two medium-sized crocodiles sunning themselves on shore, but Snooks said we weren't there yet. Instead, he pointed to another a narrow channel leading off to the north.

"We go though there until we come out into the next lake, and then we turn left. We're looking for a sandy point about three hundred yards down the shore, along the south side. The shoes and feet should be lying at the end of a fallen tree trunk, assuming they stayed put overnight."

CHAPTER 7

We got lucky, if that is the right word, because the shoes were right where Snooks said they'd be. We eased the canoe up on shore and looked around for company. The winds were calm, and it was dead quiet except for the call of a kingfisher coming from someplace farther back in the glades.

The shoes were simple canvas affairs, faded blue, with rubber or plastic soles that once could have been white. They were about eighteen inches apart, one upright and the other on its side, laying on dry land about ten feet above the current water line. This was fortunate. Any lower down on the bank and the tide would surely have swept them away overnight.

It was a grisly sight. Socks sticking up out of the shoes were frayed at the ends and stained a dark reddish-brown. Flies swarmed everywhere, no doubt busy laying their eggs on the rotting flesh inside. The shoes themselves seemed oddly in motion. I pulled a pair of binoculars out of my daypack for a closer look, and figured it out. Even from the back seat in the canoe I could see the pulsing masses of maggots.

Snooks took off his battered old Boston Red Sox ball cap and scratched at the bald spot just above the point of origin for his ponytail. "What happens now?"

"Now we take a GPS reading, and then I get on the radio."

"I don't see any sign of that crocodile. Should we get out for a closer look?"

"Two good reasons for not doing that. First, this could be a crime scene, so we don't want to disturb it with things like our footprints."

He nodded. "Sure. I get that. Not that I wanted to go up there anyway. You said there were two reasons?"

"Uh huh. Take a look behind us."

About fifteen feet off shore a pair of eyes the color of yellow-brown mud had poked up out of the water. They were flat and unreadable, but the long row of shiny wet scales following about eight feet behind left no doubt as to their identity. I knew something about the biology of crocodiles, including the fact that the females could be defensive around their nests. If this gal *was* in fact a gal, and if she had eggs buried nearby, we could be in trouble. There are virtually no known cases of American crocodiles attacking humans, but this did not seem like the right time to find out just how far they could be pushed.

It was a quandary, because I didn't want to just paddle away. If the croc had already eaten the wearer of those shoes, maybe she was saving the feet for a mid-day snack. And if there had been a crime committed here, the last thing Park Service Rangers would want is for that big old girl to eat what remained of the evidence.

Snooks kept staring at the crocodile. "What are we gonna do?"

"I think we stay right here in the canoe. You make a lot of noise in the water with your paddle if that croc starts coming ashore. I'll fire up the GPS, and then contact Park Headquarters with our location."

I found our coordinates, and then got on the radio. I was looking for a Ranger named Mike Nunez. We had worked together before, and I both liked and trusted the man. Snooks had dropped the ball the day before, and I was anxious to keep him out of trouble if possible. Even if Mike figured things out, he owed me a couple of favors, so I thought he might be more inclined to let my friend off the hook than would some other Park employee.

The dispatcher was able to patch me through to Mike, who by good fortune was on patrol just north of the marina at Flamingo, the closest point by boat to our present location. I told him about the shoes and the crocodile, but left out the details of how and when they had been discovered.

Understandably, he had lots of questions. "Did you say a pair of shoes?"

"Roger that. And they're occupied."

"By what?"

"By feet, I imagine." I knew it was a smarty remark. "We haven't really checked on that."

"Why not? And anyway, how did they get there, and how did you happen to find them?"

A lurking crocodile gave me all the excuse I needed to put Mike off for the moment. "She's big, probably female, and maybe getting defensive about a nest. How soon can you get here, or should we just grab the shoes and whatever else we can find, and get the hell out?"

"No, please don't do that. You have coordinates? I can be on the water in about fifteen minutes."

I gave Mike the reading off my GPS. "You got a good flats boat or a canoe? We're in a real skinny spot, and the tide's about to fall."

There was no answer, but the message was clear enough. Mike Nunez did not need advice on how to get around in his own backyard.

CHAPTER 8

Evidently the "no motor" regulation did not apply to National Park Rangers responding to emergencies, because forty-five minutes later Snooks and I picked up the sound of an outboard, approaching fast from the southeast. Ten minutes later Mike emerged out of the mangroves onto our lake, spotted us and waved, and turned in our direction. He was driving a little 17 foot Maverick, and he was alone.

He beached his boat next to my canoe and cut the engine. I followed his eyes toward the shoes, but his first question wasn't about that.

"Where's the croc?"

I hadn't noticed, but she was gone. "Guess she took off."

Mike shook his head. "More likely just sank out of sight. We need to move fast on this."

With that he picked up a backpack and a large caliber rifle, and stepped out of his boat onto the shore. Mike stood about four inches short of my six feet. He had straight dark hair, black eyes, and a long trunk and a barrel chest that he'd inherited from his mother, who was full-blood Seminole. I knew Mike and his family had stayed tight with the tribe. I'd seen him in his dress uniform, including the regulation Smokey-the-Bear hat. Between the hat and his robust upper body, Mike actually looked a lot like the legendary fire-preventing ursine.

Mike invited us to join him in searching the area.

"I'd like to wait for a full forensics team, but I don't think we have that option because of the croc. I'm gonna need your help."

Snooks did not look thrilled, but I understood. "You bet. What would you like us to do?"

"For the moment just stay here by the boats and keep an eye out for our reptilian friend, while I check the area for footprints and take some photos. Then we'll expand the search and put anything we find into evidence bags. I've got gloves for all of us."

It seemed longer, but Mike finished his preliminaries in about fifteen minutes. There still was no sign of the crocodile, nor had Mike found any human footprints. At Mike's invitation we gathered around the shoes and crouched down for a closer look. I could see no distinctive markings such as a logo that might have told us something about their brand or style. Up close there was an odor like sweet rotting fruit, and the maggots crawling in and out made for a gruesome scene. Mike and I had been there before, but it must have been a brand new experience for Snooks. He lasted less than a half-minute before he stood up, shouted, "Jesus, I'm gonna hurl!" – and bolted for the nearest clump of mangroves.

Mike apparently had been waiting for an opportunity to get me alone. "So how did you guys happen to find this anyway? Just out fishing or birding?" He paused while we both listened to Snooks tossing up whatever he'd had for breakfast. "Where are your clients, and how come I saw only one rod in the canoe?"

There was no easy way out, let alone an honest one,

so I just fessed up with the real story of who had found the shoes and when. "I'm sure he's sorry, and I hope you can let it go. I think he sort of panicked. And anyway, it looks like no harm done, right? The shoes were still here this morning."

It sounded lame because it was. Who knew what other evidence might have disappeared overnight from the crime scene? Assuming it was a crime scene, which wasn't my call in any event.

Mike didn't get a chance to respond, because at that point Snooks came staggering back out of the bushes, pale and sweaty. "Sorry about that."

Mike said "no problem" but nothing else, which I took as a hopeful sign.

Naturally, we started with the shoes. Mike took a pen out of his pocket and poked around the top of the shoe that was sitting upright.

"Can't tell for sure because of the decay, but I don't see any sign of a clean cut here."

I thought about the crocodile. "More like something chewed it off rather than sliced it off?"

"That would be my guess. But the forensics people will make that call when the time comes."

Mike pulled an extra-large evidence bag out of his pack, picked up the shoe and dropped it carefully inside. The mate of the pair had been lying on its side, and when he righted it we both noticed a handful of plant leaves stuck around the laces. The vegetation impressed me as out of place somehow, like it didn't belong in mangrove country. But it also looked familiar.

Mike poked at the leaves with a pair of tweezers he

had extracted from his shirt pocket. Then he held one up for my inspection. "Do you recognize this?"

"Maybe. I'm not really a plant expert, but I know a lady who is."

He nodded and grinned. "That's why I asked. Tell you what we're gonna do. We'll split this sample. I'll keep half for the Park record, and you take half for Katie. Will you be going up to Lauderdale any time soon?"

"That can always be arranged."

Once we had the shoes and their contents bagged-up, we started a broader search of the whole area. For all we knew there could be more body parts around. Snooks drew crocodile watch while Mike and I did the actual exploring. We worked outward from the shoe site in circles of increasing circumference, checking the ground and vegetation for anything that looked suspicious. It took nearly an hour before Mike was satisfied.

The good news was the crocodile never showed up. The bad news was that nothing else did either.

Mike stretched and shrugged and gathered up his pack and weapon. "I'll get a bigger team in here tomorrow, or maybe this evening if I can round 'em up, and then we'll expand the search. But it doesn't look like there's much more to find. This is a strange one for sure. Just those damned shoes, and nothing else. Strange."

"You keep saying that. But I agree. Makes you wonder if the croc ate all the other evidence. I can't imagine how those feet could have gotten way back here all by themselves."

"Yeah, well, we'll have to see. Mean time, I'm gonna block off the access channel with crime scene tape at the point where you tied up your Hell's Bay. You might spread the word that this place is off limits until further notice."

Something was worrying me about the whole setup. If the croc had eaten whoever used to be in those shoes, and done it recently, might her stomach not contain critical evidence? And was that the reason Mike had brought along his rifle? It was a tricky issue for both of us. I knew Mike well enough to understand he shared my passion for conservation. He'd be no more anxious to take a prime breeding female out of the Park's crocodile population than I would. The species was uncommon and still protected as 'threatened' under the Endangered Species Act.

But I had to ask the question that must have been on both our minds. "Are you gonna need to get inside that croc's stomach?"

He looked out on the water and gave me a simple two-word answer.

"What croc?"

Then he turned away and walked back toward his boat.

I got the message.

The whole time Mike and I had been talking things over, Snooks had been fidgeting around, like there was something he wanted to say but wasn't sure if he should.

"What is it?"

"Well, uh, while I was watching out for the croc a couple of really big redfish tailed in the calm water over there against that far shore. And I was wondering, uh... since I brought my gear, if, you know, we might..." He trailed off, probably realizing he was skating out onto thin ice. Or at least he would have been if we ever got any down here.

Mike Nunez, bless his heart, let the guy off the hook. "Sure, go ahead. Just stay away from this place, and be sure to put the crime scene tape back up where you found it before you leave."

Like I said, Mike is a good guy.

CHAPTER 9

By all rights we had no business fishing that day. Snooks must have known he'd dodged a bullet after neglecting to report a probable crime scene. But what the hell, we were there and so were the fish, and Mike had said it was okay. The tide was falling fast and pretty soon we'd be high and dry. There was no time to waste.

I watched as he strung up an old 8-weight Elkhorn fly rod he'd gotten years ago somewhere out in Colorado.

"Now I'm gonna tie on my special killer redfish fly."

"What's that?"

"It's a chartreuse and white Clouser Minnow, size two-ought."

"Isn't that your special killer fly for just about everything? Didn't you tell me it even worked on crappie that time you went out to west Texas?"

Snooks tightened the knot connecting his leader to the fly, then bit off the tag end and spit it out. "Well yeah, but somehow it just feels right on this particular occasion."

Ignoring Snooks' fishing instincts nearly always turned out to be a bad idea. "Well okay then, that works for me."

We launched the canoe and set out for the other side of the lake. Because redfish are bottom feeders, they spend a lot of time with their noses down in the mud. This means in shallow water their tails necessarily spend the same amount of time sticking up out of the water. Out of gratitude or guilt, or maybe both, Snooks volunteered to paddle while I sat in front, watching out for telltale tails, so to speak.

We were more than half way across the lake when I spotted a fish, moving slowly but steadily from our right to our left, about twenty feet off shore. Patches of muddy water showed where the fish had been feeding. Based on the size of the tail, which periodically appeared and then submerged, this particular redfish was a big one.

Snooks was full of advice, like he'd forgotten I was a fellow-guide instead of a client. "That fish looks big enough to keep, in case you're interested."

I shook my head. "No, that's all right. I prefer to practice catch-and-release on canoe trips. These backcountry spots are rare and precious. I like to keep them that way as much as possible."

"Good. Me too. Just thought I'd mention it." He kept paddling until we got within easy range, which for me was about fifty feet. Then I stood up to cast. Things can get wobbly standing up in an ordinary canoe, but mine had a pair of special pontoons attached to the gunwales that gave us plenty of stability.

I had just finished stripping off enough line to get started, when Snooks offered more advice. "A redfish might not be intelligent in any human sense of that term, but one thing it knows for sure is that a little baitfish should be trying to get out of its way. The last thing you want to do is cast your fly beyond the fish and then strip it back like the bait is swimming right toward it. Bound to spook it that way."

I already knew this, but decided played along. Snooks' ego had taken enough of a beating for one day. "Then what should I do? If I cast short, the fish might not even see the fly."

"What you want to do is cast beyond but well to the left of the fish, and then bring the fly back so it passes by at just the right distance in front of its nose."

It was up to me to decide what the right distance might be. Too far out, and the fish might not see the fly at all. Too close, and it would look like the supposed prey was chasing the predator. Tricky business.

For once, it all worked perfectly. My cast was on target, and the line and leader made a reasonably soft landing. The fish kept moving slowly right to left, apparently unperturbed and unaware. Then she spotted the fly, surged forward, and ate. There was a big muddy swirl as soon as I set the hook, and the fish immediately broke for deeper water. My reel sung as I held on and applied as much pressure as I guessed a twelve-pound test leader would tolerate.

Redfish are strong and deliberate fighters, given to powerful no-nonsense runs. I've heard fishermen say things like, "this guy has real shoulders" when they were fighting one. That particular image has never quite worked for me. Fish with shoulders? What redfish do have are sturdy well-muscled bodies better suited to deep powerful runs than to any sort of fancy acrobatics.

At first this particular fish lived up to expectations, as she ran straight and deep out into the lake away from the shore. Then suddenly my line went slack. At first I though the fish had gotten away, but I soon realized she was still hooked up but had begun swimming directly back toward us. I scrambled to take up slack line in order to remain tight to the fish. It was a real struggle, and I ended up paying more attention to my gear than to what was happening out in the water.

It was only when Snooks shouted, "Holy shit!" that I looked up, just in time to see a big gray dorsal fin cutting through the water. It was a lemon shark, about twenty yards behind the redfish and closing fast. It must have been at least a six-footer, given the distance between its dorsal fin and tail. My fish was fleeing for its life. Snooks grabbed his paddle and began to slap the water in hopes of distracting the shark, while I kept gathering fly line and drawing the redfish in toward the boat as fast as I could.

We got lucky, me and Snooks and that big redfish, but it was a close call. The shark spun away about ten yards out, just as I finished pulling my catch in beside the canoe. I reached down and gently pulled her up over the gunwale. Snooks snapped a quick photo, and then we put her back in the water. I estimated her at thirty to thirty-five inches, and somewhere between eight and ten pounds.

There was no sign of the shark, but I held on to her tail just in case. This also gave me a chance to work the fish back and forth, helping aerate her gills so she'd be better prepared to defend herself should it become necessary. She was tired from the fight, and the last thing I wanted to do was release a weakened fish in front of a hungry predator.

That redfish did something smart when I finally let her go. Rather than swimming out into the lake, she just tucked up under the canoe and held there, slowly finning in place. This gave her time to re-oxygenate her depleted muscles, and perhaps also to determine where the lemon shark had gone. After about two minutes I looked back down in the water, and she was gone.

"Thank you Snooks, that was great. Now I think we'd better get the hell out of here."

Snooks pointed back over his shoulder. "But I think I just saw another fish tailing farther up the lake, and..."

I shook my head. "Yeah, but look at the tide. Can you imagine what could happen if Mike Nunez came back this evening and we were sitting here stuck in the mud?"

"Is he gonna do that?"

"He thought maybe. More likely tomorrow, but we better not take the chance."

CHAPTER 10

When Snooks and I got back to the dock the first thing we noticed was a woman sunbathing up on my deck. She had a straw hat over her face, but a pair of long, shapely, and well-tanned legs looked very familiar. It turned out Katie had left school a half-day early for a surprise weekend visit. She must have packed in a hurry, because she apparently had forgotten the top half of her bathing suit. This became obvious when she sat up to see who was coming. She waved at us with her right hand and held the straw hat in a strategic place with her left. "Hey guys. How was your day?"

I decided to reserve the details for later. "It was interesting, wasn't it Snooks?"

Snooks seemed to be having trouble deciding what to do with his eyes. He managed an unintelligible mumble and then got busy unloading the boat. He also had the good sense to decline my invitation to come up for a beer. "I'd better get back. Got a client tomorrow who wants to try for some permit off the Arsenicker Bank, and my boat's not ready."

As soon as Snooks left, Katie stood up and dropped the hat. Then she walked to the edge of the deck and leaned out across the railing. Katie is tall at five-feet eight inches, and otherwise slim, but she has full soft breasts that do interesting things whenever she bends over. It had always been a turn-on for me, and I scampered right up the stairs to give her a hug.

"Maybe we'd better go inside before the neighbors get too excited."

Katie laughed. "Probably a little late for that."

"Let's go indoors anyway. I collected some plant evidence today, and I need your help."

Once inside, Katie disappeared into the bedroom and came back out wearing a pair of denim shorts and a white cotton shirt tied up across her midriff. Her shoulder length black hair hung loose, framing an oval face dominated by large dark eyes that reflected her Italian heritage. We kissed, but only briefly, before she stepped back and frowned. "Aren't you glad to see me?"

"Of course I am. Why do you have to ask?"

Katie took a deep breath and let it out slowly. There was something about the look in her eyes that I didn't like. "Oh, let's see. You and Snooks come back from a fishing trip, and there's a topless woman sunbathing up on your deck. Snooks leaves right away because of course *he's* figured things out. But then all you want to do is talk about some plant evidence? *Really*?"

At first I couldn't think what to say. "Sorry" sure wasn't going to cover it. Katie just stood there silently with her arms folded across her chest.

"I thought maybe we'd get the plant stuff over with before ... oh hell, you know."

She kept glaring. "Know what, exactly?"

"I was just surprised to see you is all. It threw me for a loop. You must know I've missed you."

"I've missed you too. Why in hell do you think I'm here?"

"So can we start over?"

Katie dropped her arms to her sides, cocked her

head a little to the left, and shrugged her shoulders. "Sure. How?"

It wasn't much, but it was a start. "How about a hug?"

This time she might even have grinned. "How about a shower instead? You don't smell that great."

"Together?"

"Okay."

Now we were getting somewhere.

~ ~ ~

An hour and a half later I got out of bed, pulled on a clean pair of jeans, and went out to the kitchen to get us each a beer. Katie emerged a half-minute later wearing an old khaki fishing shirt of mine, and apparently nothing else. We had solved none of the world's problems, and certainly not our own, but at least I felt married again. I hoped she did too.

We sat together on an old saggy leather couch in the living room that was positioned to afford us a view out onto my deck and across to the mangroves lining the other side of the canal. It was nearly dark now, and there was no wind. Through the open window I heard a bird screech somewhere off to the west, probably one of the yellow-crowned night herons that lived in the neighborhood, getting ready for an evening hunt.

The time had come to tell Katie about my day's adventure. She had lots of questions, which I answered as best I could. Once she was up to speed I handed her a plastic bag with the plant material we had collected from beneath the blue shoes Snooks had found back in the glades. "Mike Nunez hopes you can identify this. It looks familiar to me, but I can't say exactly why."

She took a pull on her beer, then held the bag up to the light provided by an old brass floor lamp at her end of the couch. After examining its contents from several angles, she laid the bag down on the coffee table in front of us, and turned in my direction. "I can't be absolutely certain until I get it back to the lab, but this looks like water hyacinth. And you say this came from over by Lake Ingraham? Isn't that salt water up there?"

"Uh huh. Why? Is that important?"

"Could be." Then she got professorial on me. "Water hyacinth is the common name for *Eichhornia crassipes*. It's a floating aquatic plant, but it only grows in fresh water."

"So there's no way it could have gotten to that spot back in the glades by itself?"

"Not likely. I'll have to check the literature on that. As I recall, water hyacinth can tolerate brackish water for a time. But there's no way a whole plant could survive very long in the part of the Everglades where you found this one."

I had been hoping the plant had a narrow distribution, which might then give us a clue as to the origin of whoever had been wearing those blue shoes. "Is it rare?"

Katie shook her head. "Far from it, unfortunately. The species is native to South America, but by now it has spread all over the place, including much of the southeastern United States. It's popular with gardeners because it has beautiful purple flowers, and much of the spread is attributable to escapes from backyard fishponds. The thing has become a real pest in some places, clogging up waterways and displacing native vegetation. There's no way to tell where this one came from."

This wasn't the best news, but it wasn't all bad either. "At least we know our victim, assuming there was one, must have been in or near fresh water at the time he or she died, right?"

"Seems likely. And we both know there aren't a hell of a lot of such places down here in the Keys."

"Okay, that's good then. I'll let Mike Nunez know about your tentative identification, in case it helps with their investigation."

"And I'll get back to you with a positive ID once I'm back up in Lauderdale."

Katie took another sip of her Yuengling, and set down the bottle. "And now can we get on with other matters?"

"I thought we just did that."

"We did, and now I'm hungry. You know that always happens."

"Unfortunately there's nothing worth eating in my refrigerator, so we're gonna have to go out."

"First time that ever happened."

CHAPTER 11

Our destination once we made it out of the house was a local watering hole on the ocean side called the Safari Lounge. I liked it for a bunch of reasons. It was close to home, they sold a good drink for a fair price, and it was a handy place to catch up on local gossip. Their bar food was okay, but we usually opted instead for some great Cuban food at a nearby restaurant called Habanos. The Safari Lounge/Habanos combo had become something of a tradition for Katie and me when she was in town, and for Snooks and me the rest of the time.

We took the five-minute drive over in Katie's silver Prius and parked about halfway between the bar and restaurant, next to a line of blue water charter boats tied up at the local marina. Then we walked over to the steps leading up into the bar. Like lots of structures on the oceanfront, the Safari lounge had been built up off the ground as a protection against storm surges during hurricanes.

From the outside, the Safari Lounge looked like an ordinary brown wooden building with a pitched roof. The inside was something else. A large four-sided bar filled the center of the main room, with a small bandstand and pool tables on the side opposite the ocean. Large windows lined the other three walls, affording a great view of the Atlantic. A striking internal feature of the Safari Lounge was the high angled ceiling from which there hung an assortment of stuffed African wildlife. Because of this distinctive feature, the place had become known among locals as the Dead Animal Bar. They sold t-shirts adorned with drawings of the animals, along with the bar's motto: "Where the Extinct Meet to Drink."

It made for an interesting cross-cultural experience to drink a Margarita under the watchful eye of a rhinoceros staring down from overhead, but that is what we decided to do. We took two empty stools and I waved to the bartender, an attractive forty-something woman named Flora Delaney. Flo, as she preferred to be called, had medium-length brown hair that she kept pinned up out of the way, and a broad open face centered on a pair of striking green eyes. Her short Bermudas revealed enough of a pair of well-muscled legs to make things interesting, but tonight she was wearing an extra large Safari Lounge t-shirt that seemed almost deliberately baggy.

Flo came right over to take our order. In addition to being a very good bartender, she also was a valuable source of all kinds of useful information. If you wanted to find out how the wind was going to blow during the coming week, or whether the yellow-tailed snapper were on the bite out at the Tennessee Reef, or which local politico had just been caught (again?) with his or her hand in the cookie jar, Flo was your gal.

While she put ice in the blender to make our margaritas, I surveyed what remained of the night's crowd. There were several familiar faces, but one that stood out belonged to a man wearing a loud Hawaiian shirt and too much gold jewelry. He had a ruddy complexion, a high forehead, and thinning brown hair combed straight back. I recognized him as Pete Donovan, the owner of Pelican Pete's Emporium.

The Emporium was a crowded rambling affair that catered mostly to tourists, especially those with tastes that ran to cheap and tacky. There were bumper stickers, window decals, and a seemingly endless assortment of plastic insulated coffee and beer mugs. If you wanted a pink flamingo for your front lawn, Pete had 'em in three sizes. Then there were the t-shirts, most of which fell at the upper end of the sleaze scale. They said things like: "Sun and sand? Hell no, I came for the sex," or "Stop staring at my itty bitty titties."

There were rumors Pelican Pete Donovan had other things for sale that stayed behind the counter or in a back room. Drugs, of course, but also contraband wildlife items like turtle shell jewelry and boots made out of crocodile hide. It was in this context that the Florida Fish and Wildlife Conservation Commission once had asked me to sniff around the place. Pete showed me one small item he had behind the counter. It was a tortoise shell pendant that I recognized as coming from a hawksbill hatchling, one of the endangered species we have down here in the Keys. The pendant had a little hole in one end that somehow didn't look new, like it had been bored out a long time ago.

Other than the one pendant, I'd gotten nowhere. It was enough for a raid on Pete's establishment, but that had turned up empty, very possibly because somebody had tipped him off. He'd gotten away with only a small fine, claiming the pendant came from someplace in the Caribbean. Nevertheless, Pelican Pete and his operation stayed right up there on the Fish and Wildlife radar, and they'd asked me to keep an eye out.

Pete was huddled in conversation with a man I did not recognize who was sitting on the adjacent bar stool. I asked Flo if she knew who he was. She finished pouring our margaritas, then glanced over and shook her head. "Never seen him before."

Being the nosy sort, I caught Pete's eye across the bar and waved. He acknowledged with just the briefest nod before turning quickly back to his companion. Given our history, it was no surprise the man wasn't happy to see me.

There was an ancient popcorn machine in a back corner of the Safari Lounge. It gave me an excuse to walk past where Pete was sitting on the way to get Katie something to eat, and to attempt a conversation with the man.

"Evening Pete. Good to see you."

He looked up from his beer only reluctantly. "Oh yeah, hi Sam. How are ya? How's fishing?"

"Pretty fair, but not great. How's business?"

"Oh, you know, some days are better than others. Sort of like fishing I guess."

I really wanted to meet the man sitting next to him. There were rumors that Pete had dealings with suppliers of black-market items, and I thought this guy might be one of them. He was a black-haired fat man perhaps in his mid-sixties, so pale it looked like he never went out in the sun. It was the sort of thing you noticed in the Keys, where most people spent a lot of time outdoors. Because Pete made no move to introduce us, I did it myself.

"Hi. Sam Sawyer." Then I stuck out my hand.

The guy looked uncomfortable as hell, to the point where I wondered if he was going to shake back or even make eye contact. He finally did both, but his watery brown eyes held mine only for an instant, and the handshake that followed was limp and moist. He never said a word.

I delivered Katie her popcorn, and it wasn't two minutes later that the pale fat man called for the bill, and then he and Pete went out the door into the night. I noticed the man had used a credit card to settle their tab, which gave me an idea. This was going to get tricky, but there was something about Pete Donovan's buddy that made me want to get a look at his credit card receipt. There didn't seem to be any other way except to ask Flo straight out if I could have a peek. I knew I was putting her on the spot, but at least by now we were alone in the place. I was going to have to trust her, and it would have to be mutual or the whole thing could go badly for both of us. But I knew Flo well enough to count her as a friend. It seemed worth the risk.

I told Flo that Pete was under investigation by the Florida fish and wildlife people (true), that I was a paid consultant (also true), and that I suspected the man with Pete might be one of his suppliers (just a guess, but possible). Then I asked if I could take a peek at his bill. She gave me a look that said I'd just called in every favor she owed me now or might ever again. But she went over to the cash register and wrote something on a piece of paper. Then she came back and handed it to me. It said "Hector C. Morales."

"Thanks, Flo."

She shrugged and went back to wiping down the bar. "Never did like that Pete Donovan anyway. Something shifty about the guy."

I stuck the note in my shirt pocket and paid our tab with an extra big tip. Then Katie and I left for our dinner over at Habanos. She had beer-battered shrimp and a dinner salad, while I had the churasco steak with a side of fried green plantains. The food was great. Katie ate all of hers, but she wasn't talking much, and between bites she kept looking past me out the window at the darkened waters of the marina. I tried several times to get a conversation started, but it didn't happen. Finally I asked her what was wrong.

She finished a last bite of shrimp and crumpled up her paper napkin. "Uh, ... nothing. Why?"

"You seem sort of distracted tonight."

"Yeah, sorry. Guess I am. Next week's gonna be complicated."

I wanted to ask what sort of complications, but something told me to hold off. We had the whole weekend ahead of us, and I didn't want to spoil it by risking another confrontation like the one we'd had earlier that afternoon.

Katie declined the offer of coffee, so I paid the bill and we left.

CHAPTER 12

I fished with a client for eight hours the following Monday. We went way out in the Gulf looking for cobia and tripletail, but we didn't find any. It was one of those days.

There was a phone message from Katie on the landline when I got back. "Just tried your cell, but guess you're out of range. Anyway, I had a look at that plant sample under my scope and compared it with some specimens from our herbarium. You can tell Mike it's water hyacinth for sure. Love ya. Bye."

I called Mike Nunez with the news, and he had questions.

"And your Katie says that plant, water hyacinth, it doesn't normally live in salt water?"

"Right. At least not for long."

"I think I've seen it on reservation land around here, but I guess only in fresh water. And you said they sell it in nurseries because of the purple flowers?"

"Right."

"But it grows wild all over the place in south Florida?"

"Right again."

"I wish you'd stop saying that. If I had some of this wrong, maybe that plant would turn out to be more of an actual clue."

"Yeah, well at least we know it probably didn't get out in there in the glades all by itself."

"Good point, Sam. Whoever wore those blue shoes

probably brought the plant with them."

I could think of one other possibility. "Or some third party brought both the shoes and the plant, in which case there might be more evidence. Did you get back to the site? Did you find anything else?"

There were vehicle noises in the background, and I realized that Mike must be on the road. At least five seconds passed with no response, and at first I thought we'd lost the connection.

"Sorry. Had to deal with a left turn in some traffic. Anyway, you asked two questions with different answers. As I think you probably know, when we get a case like this it gets turned over to the Investigative Services Branch of the Park Service. I called their office as soon as I got back to headquarters after our little get-together out there last Friday. Their agents showed up the next morning, and we did a team search at the site the same afternoon. Scoured the whole area."

"What did you find?"

"Not a damned thing."

"What about the croc?"

"No sign of her either."

"So what happens next?"

"The Investigative Services folks have got the shoes and the feet at their lab, but I haven't heard back. I'll give 'em a call about the water hyacinth, and then we just wait it out. These things can take time. But before I let you go, how was the fishing?"

I laughed. "Got one nice redfish, thanks. Oh, and thanks too for letting my friend off the hook. Snooks felt real bad about the whole thing."

"Yeah, well, he should have. But no harm done I

suppose. Be talkin' to ya."

After Mike hung up I called Katie to thank her for the rush job on the hyacinth. She didn't answer on either the landline or her cell. I left a message in both places and wondered what she was up to on a Monday evening. Probably giving a lecture or something.

I was about to grab a beer out of the fridge and stick a frozen pizza in the oven, when I remembered something from the previous Friday night. One rule I have tried to follow in my investigative work is to stick with just one contact person in each relevant agency if at all possible, just to keep things simple. It also helps if they get along, which isn't always the case among people working for different branches of law enforcement. Fortunately I had found three individuals whom I both liked and respected, and who seemed to feel the same way about each other. For the National Park Service that was Mike Nunez. For the Monroe County Sheriff's Department it was a detective named Stella Reynard. And for Florida Fish and Wildlife it was Dave Ackermann. Dave was the guy who had asked me to poke around Pelican Pete's Emporium, and I thought he might like to know about the man named Hector Morales who had been buying Pete Donovan drinks at the Safari Lounge.

Dave was new to the area, an avid fly fisherman who'd grown up in the northeast. The first time we met he described himself as "the only Jewish game warden in the South." This may or may not have been true, but I liked the guy right off. In addition to our dealings with Pelican Pete, he'd hired me a couple of times to go fishing. His excuse was that he needed to get to know this area. I knew better, but a client was a client and I wasn't surprised when I discovered that he was a damned good angler.

Dave picked up on the first ring, said he didn't mind being interrupted after hours, and thanked me for the information. He'd never heard of a Hector Morales, but said he'd check it out. "In the mean time, it happens that tomorrow is my day off, and I'm wondering if you might be available."

He didn't need to say for what. I had no clients scheduled for the next day, and I'd planned to spend it cleaning up my boat. But that could wait. "Sure. What did you have in mind?"

"Oh, I don't know. Who's eating right now?"

"You mean with a fly?"

"That would be my strong preference."

Snooks had reported last week that Spanish mackerel were still active out in the Gulf. I knew a couple of spots where we might be able to get into some good-sized schools. Dave liked the idea, and we agreed to meet at my dock at 7:30 the next morning.

I was ready for another routine day on the water. I probably should have known a boat ride with a game warden could take unexpected turns, even if it was his day off.

CHAPTER 13

Dave Ackermann showed up fifteen minutes early, holding a mug full of steaming coffee in one hand and a canvas satchel in the other. I was curious about the satchel.

"What's in there? I've got all the right gear for both of us."

He grinned and explained, "I'm sure you do, but this isn't fishing stuff. They like me to carry the badge, a radio, and a sidearm even when I'm off duty. Just in case something comes up. Oh, and if possible we should fish today in state waters, not in Everglades Park. That way I'll have jurisdiction."

"Can do, I suppose, though it does leave out some of my favorite spots."

Dave laughed. "That's good isn't it? Now it won't be your fault if we get skunked."

"What does that mean? I'm the guide. It's *always* my fault."

"Not if I won't let you go where you want, right?"

"Yeah, yeah. Just get in the boat, okay?"

They have a rigorous fitness requirement at Florida Fish and Wildlife, and Dave was a good example. He stood about six-two but he couldn't have weighed more than 190 pounds, and from his appearance nearly half that was in his upper body. It made for an intimidating presence, which must have been useful at times given his job. But he had a broad open face that softened the effect. Today he wore a ball cap advertising Disney

World of all things. It only partly covered a full head of curly light brown hair.

I'd already loaded everything in the boat except a cooler with ice and drinks. Dave helped me with that and then we both got on board. I'd stowed a couple of spinning outfits on the boat in addition to my fly rods, and Dave spotted them as soon as we got settled. "What's that about? I thought we were fly fishing for mackerel today."

"We are. Those are for just in case."

"In case what?"

"In case we see a tripletail and he won't eat the fly. We're also gonna go by the bait shop at World Wide Sportsman on the way out and pick up some live shrimp, in addition to a couple blocks of chum."

"And here all along I thought you were a purest."

"Have you ever eaten tripletail?"

"No."

"Then don't go all righteous on me. I don't do it very often, but they're the absolute best seafood you've ever eaten. Assuming we get lucky. Tripletail aren't all that common."

"Fair enough. Oh, and speaking of luck, I've already had some with that name you gave me last night."

"You mean the guy I saw with Pelican Pete at the Safari Lounge? That was fast."

"Ain't computers wonderful? I have a way of tapping into the department's data bases from home, and the name Hector Morales popped up in a couple of places."

"In what context?"

"Two, actually. Turns out he owns a pet store up in Miami that specializes in reptiles. We suspect he may have been responsible for turning loose some of the first pythons that showed up in the Everglades."

I knew that escaped pythons were multiplying like rabbits in south Florida, to the serious detriment of native wildlife. But I'd always thought the releases were from individual owners who got spooked when their cute little pet snakes got too big to handle. "How did you get the goods on him?"

"Apparently we didn't. The case is still open."

"You said there were two things?"

Dave nodded. "Yeah, the other has to do with crocodiles. He sold two hatchlings to a woman who happened to be an undercover agent for Fish and Wildlife. We thought we had him on that one for sure, because the DNA showed they were the American species."

"But he still has the store?"

"Yeah, his defense was that he thought they were alligators, which are legal if you have the necessary permit. Some damn-fool judge bought it, and that was that."

~ ~ ~

We took my boat up the coast to Worldwide Sportsman, where we got our bait and then headed west out into the Gulf of Mexico. I knew a couple of spots about fifteen miles from home where some bottom structure attracted large numbers of small fish. These in turn often drew in the larger predators including mackerel, cobia, and sharks.

It was a clear day with little swell, which made for

a comfortable half-hour boat ride to the first of my hot spots. Unfortunately, another boat already was anchored up by the time we got there – a new-looking Pathfinder with a dark blue hull. There were two guys on board, and one of them was fighting a fish off the stern. Based on the bend in his rod, I could tell it was something big. The other man was tall and had lots of blond hair sticking out from under his cap. He had a gaff in one hand, like he was getting ready to pull something on board that was too big to lift with the line.

I waved, and the man with the gaff waved back. Then I asked Mike if he wanted to stay and watch or just go on ahead to my other spot.

"Let's watch. We're trained always to watch."

I cut the motor and let my Hell's Bay drift with the tide. In a little while something odd happened. Most fishermen like to show off their catch, but when the time came the men in the Pathfinder pulled whatever they had around to the side of their boat opposite us, so we couldn't see what they were doing. Shortly after that the man with the gaff hauled something big and dark up over the gunwale. Then the fisherman dropped his rod, picked up a club and swung it down hard, three times in rapid succession.

Apparently that was enough for Dave. "Let's get over there. I don't like the looks of this."

I started up the Yamaha and steered toward the Pathfinder at idle speed. When we got within about twenty yards Dave asked me to put it in neutral but continue drifting in their direction. Both men obviously had seen what we were doing, but it was the big blond who spoke up.

"Say gents, we don't mind sharing a good spot, but aren't you getting a little close?"

Dave cleared his throat. "Actually, I'd like to see your fish."

"Maybe later, okay? We'd like to get our bait back in the water before the tide quits."

"No sir, we're coming in now. I'm with Florida Fish and Wildlife. I need to inspect your catch, take a look at your licenses, and maybe do a boat safety check. It shouldn't take long and you'll be back to fishing in no time."

It turned out Dave Ackerman was all wrong about that. As soon as we got close enough, I recognized the blond man as Reuben Fletcher. He was the guide Snooks had warned me about at the Hogfish Grill a week ago, and his client had just caught and killed a goliath grouper. This particular species, which could reach hundreds of pounds, had become so rare in the Keys it was illegal even to lift one out of the water for a photograph, let alone keep one.

Fletcher and his client pretended they didn't know anything about goliath groupers, claiming instead they had caught some sort of big fish they had never seen before and wanted to take it home for dinner. There was a chance that might have worked for an ordinary fisherman, but there was no way it was going to work for a guide. Dave took his time doing all the necessary paperwork, and made a big point of writing down the registration number off the Pathfinder "just in case you gentlemen forget your court dates." Then he confiscated the grouper and told them to go home. The client glared at Reuben the whole time, like it was all his fault. Reuben glared at me, like it was all mine. I couldn't wait to tell Snooks that his least favorite guide likely would be going out of business for a while.

~ ~ ~

After the incident with the goliath grouper had ended, Dave and I headed east to the second of my favorite mackerel spots, which was an old sunken boat. We set up on a falling tide whose current immediately drew our chum out into a steady stream behind my skiff. This would be essential to attract the fish. A gentle wind blew from north to south, but it wasn't strong enough to interfere with Dave's ability to throw the fly a respectable distance.

In other words, conditions were perfect.

Except that nothing happened.

Whole schools of baitfish quickly packed in behind the boat and began eating the chum. They must have been happy, given all that food and the apparent absence of any predators. But it was the predators we had come for, and after an hour of nothing I could tell that Dave was starting to get restless. He'd made lots of great casts, with all sorts of different fly patterns, and I'd even thrown a couple of live shrimp just to see if it made any difference. It hadn't.

We were just about to pack it in and maybe look for a different spot, when all hell broke loose. Dave had thrown a red-and-white Clouser about forty feet behind the boat and hadn't even started his retrieve when the line went tight and his reel began to sing. He hung on as the fish quickly stripped off all ninety feet of his fly line and kept going. I could tell it was a big fish by the speed of the run and the bend in Dave's rod, and by the fact that it took him a good five or eight minutes before he got it back within twenty feet of the boat.

The fish seemed to have calmed, but I cautioned Dave to be careful. "Keep a tight line and be ready for another run. Those Spanish mackerel can fool you into thinking they're done, when actually they're just resting up for the next round."

"How do you know it's a mackerel? We haven't even seen the thing yet."

He had a point. "I don't know for sure, but the location and time of year are right, and so is the behavior of that fish."

It turned out I was correct on both counts. It was a Spanish mackerel, and it was good for another strong run before Dave managed to get it up next to the boat. He was about to reach down over the side and grab the fish, when I caught him just in time.

"Careful there! Mackerel have nasty teeth. I've still got the scars to prove it."

"What do you want me to do? You want to handle this?"

"You said this was an educational trip, right? She's all yours. Just be sure to get hold of the fish behind its head, and keep your hands away from her mouth. Then lift her up into the boat."

"Couldn't we use the net?"

"We could, but lots of times the fly and leader get all tangled up that way, and it ends up being more trouble than it's worth. Just be careful, and you'll be fine."

Dave did as he was told, and laid the fish against a

ruler that was taped to the inside of my hull. It measured twenty-nine inches – nowhere near a record, but still a fine catch. He held it up for me to photograph, turning it so the late morning sun lit up the silver-blue back and white flank peppered with bright golden spots. Then he used pliers to extract the fly from its jaw, and released it back into the water.

Mackerel like to run in schools, and I had learned from experience that a fighting fish already on the line could attract others. Presumably they were trying to find out what all the excitement was about. I encouraged Dave to get his fly back in the water as quickly as possible.

Things happened even faster than I expected. Dave had laid his fly rod down while he was attempting to untangle a knot in his line. He'd accidentally dropped the Clouser over the side, and another fish came out from under the boat and grabbed it before he even had a chance to pick up the rod. Dave scrambled to get things under control, and then held on as his second hook-up of the day did its mackerel thing.

Over the next hour Dave caught and released a half-dozen more fish, including one cero mackerel, a less common species that differed from the Spanish variety by having a golden line running the length of the body in addition to the spots.

Something unusual happened just before the tide went slack. By this time Dave had invited me to join him as an angler. It was not something guides normally do, but he was a friend and he'd already caught plenty of fish, so I agreed.

I was playing a good-sized mackerel when my fly

line got wrapped around the trolling motor. I was fumbling around trying to get things untangled, and not paying any attention to my fish, when suddenly Dave shouted "Holy Cow!" I looked up just in time to see a commotion in the water and then right beneath it a big brown fish began swimming away.

Cobia are wide-bodied predators that superficially resemble sharks. This one must have spotted my mackerel flailing around, assumed it was injured, and moved in for the kill. My line went tight and I could feel the telltale throb of a truly heavy fish. At first I thought the cobia must have gotten hold of my Clouser, and that I was hooked up to a fish whose size and strength likely were beyond the capacity of my eight-weight fly rod. But after a few seconds everything went slack and the fish was gone. There was a weight on my line, but it wasn't moving.

It turned out that cobia and I had been playing tug-of-war with a mackerel, and the outcome was a tie. The cobia swam away with the posterior half, while I got the rest. Once I had it on board, Dave grabbed his camera and took a photo of me holding up the front half of the mackerel. Its lower jaw was still attached to my red and gold Clouser minnow, and there was a jagged bloody cut where the back half of the fish should have started.

"Well, Sam, it looks like the old catch-and-release may not be an option for this one. What do we do, just feed it to the fish that are still out there?"

I laughed and shook my head. "No, I have a better idea. Mackerel are great eating, especially if you smoke 'em. And I have a special recipe for smoked fish dip you're gonna love. The front half of this guy's going home with us."

That cobia must have frightened off what was left of the school, because we never got another hit. After about forty minutes of fruitless casting, I decided it was time to make a move.

"You ever caught a snook?"

Dave shook his head. "Nope. Wouldn't mind, though. Got something in mind?"

"The best snook water is back in the Park, but I do know a place on the ocean side we could check out. And it's not far from home, so if nothing happens we won't have wasted much time or boat gas."

"Let's go for it."

The wind stayed calm and we had a smooth ride back. The spot I had in mind was a little bay tucked into the back side of Long Key. I drove under the Channel Five Bridge, and then made a right turn into the bay. As soon as we rounded the corner I spotted a big offshore boat poking around the edge of the mangroves, about 200 yards away. It was a gray Yellowfin with twin black Mercury outboards.

Dave asked me to cut the engine. Then he pulled a pair of binoculars out of his bag. "Something about that doesn't look right."

"I agree. For one thing that boat's way too big for the shallow water back there. They must be tearing the hell out of the sea grass. What do you want me to do?"

"Move in their direction, but keep it slow, like we're just a couple of curious fishermen."

I dropped the Hells Bay down to idle speed, while Dave continued looking through his binoculars. "From what I can see, there's two guys aboard, one at the wheel and the other at the stern. They don't seem to be fishing and I don't even see any gear. But the guy in back is doing something, maybe with a gaff? It's still too far for me to tell."

"Must be our day for two guys and a gaff. How do you want to handle this?"

"Let's go in casual. Then if something's going on, I'll pull my badge."

"So am I officially deputized, or wardenized, or whatever you call it?"

Dave laughed. "Something like that. But you just drive the boat and let me do the talking when we get there."

I continued south, keeping it dead slow like Dave asked.

We hadn't gone more than fifty yards when a shot rang out, and then I saw one of the guys pull something big and gray up over the transom of the Yellowfin.

Dave still had his binoculars up.

"What happened?"

"I'll be damned if they didn't just shoot a crocodile, or maybe it was an alligator, but there aren't supposed to be any alligators out here in salt water, right?"

"That's my understanding, but you're the wildlife officer. What now?"

"Just pick up your speed a little."

It had gone silent in the other boat, and nobody was moving. When we got within thirty yards Dave asked to borrow my camera. He took several photos, and then apparently decided it was time to start a conversation. "Hey gents, what's up? Any trouble?"

One of the two men in the Yellowfin was bigger and

older than the other. He did the talking while the younger and smaller one fumbled around in the bottom of the boat like maybe he was trying to hide something.

"No, no trouble. We're huntin' alligators. Just bagged us a good one too."

Apparently Dave decided to suck them in as far as he could before revealing just whom they were dealing with. "Don't you need a special trapping permit for that?"

"Sure, and we got 'em too. Not that it's any of your business."

"You're wrong about that. There's two things you should know. One is that alligators mostly live in fresh water, so what you've got there most likely is a crocodile. And they happen to be endangered. And the second thing, even if it is a gator, you're not allowed to hunt them anywhere in Monroe County, which is where we are."

Then he pulled out his badge. "And sorry, fellas, but I'm a state wildlife officer and we got a problem here. We're coming along side for a look-see. I want you to stay put and not try anything stupid."

We should have seen it coming, but even if we had it probably wouldn't have made any difference. As soon as the two guys figured out what was happening, they fired up their twin Mercury 350s and gunned it out across the flats. Their boat was dragging bottom and churning up a big plume of mud, but it kept moving. I pivoted my Hell's Bay in pursuit, while Dave stood in the bow and shouted for the men to stop. He had his sidearm out by now, but he wisely made no effort to shoot. There were all sorts of downsides to getting into a gun battle with somebody packing a bigger weapon with a longer range.

There was some good news, because the two guys in the Yellowfin made no effort to shoot either. The bad news was that it wasn't long before they had plowed their way out into deeper water, and their boat took off at a speed I knew my little flats skiff could never match. The last we saw of their boat it was disappearing out into the Atlantic.

Dave told me to back off and drop the pursuit. "No way we're gonna catch 'em. And I'm not sure we wanted to anyway. No telling what those guys might have tried. The last thing I'd want to do is get a civilian and his boat all shot up over a poaching incident. Still, it pisses me off. Did you get the registration number off that boat?"

"No, did you?"

"Nope. I didn't even see the tag. Maybe they'd removed it or had it covered up or something. What about a description of the two men? I should make some notes before our memories start to fade."

"Again, I'm not sure, because we didn't get all that close before they took off. The big guy at the wheel looked to be in his forties maybe? Clean-shaven as far as I could tell, and he was wearing a pair of those rubberized coveralls favored by commercial fishermen. I think they were gray or off-white. The smaller guy was in jeans and a yellow t-shirt. They both wore ball caps, but I couldn't see any logos or anything. What about you?"

Dave shrugged. "Pretty much the same, I guess. Not much to go on. But I've never seen a gray Yellowfin like that one before. Can't be all that common. I'm gonna get on the radio and call it in. Maybe one of our folks or the Coast Guard will spot the thing and pull 'em over. I sure would like to know what they've got in the back of that boat."

Once Dave had finished his call, I restarted the Yamaha and we headed for home. There had been plenty of excitement for one day, especially the finale, and maybe I needed to relieve some tension. In any event, just after we got back on the bay side of the Channel Five bridge I started to laugh, which understandably annoyed Dave.

"What's so damn funny?"

"Oh nothing, really. Just that it seems like my whole life is about crocodiles these days."

"Yeah, that and a goliath grouper. Must be our day for endangered species. But what about crocodiles in particular?"

I probably did owe the man an explanation. "One thing you already know about is Pelican Pete Donovan, but there's a lot more."

Then I told him about Snooks Lancaster and his gruesome discovery up in the Park. We drove back to my dock in silence, but I could almost hear the wheels turning inside Dave Ackermann's head.

CHAPTER 14

I didn't think much about blue tennis shoes or crocodiles or even goliath groupers for the next three days, because a client had roped me into entering a bonefish tournament down in Key West. We ended up tied for fourth place, along with the other sixteen teams that didn't catch a single fish the whole time. In our case, we didn't even see one. The night of the awards banquet, which we skipped, I got a call from Mike Nunez. He said there had been developments in the shoe case, and then he asked if we could get together in person because he'd rather not talk about it over the phone.

"Sure. When and where?"

"I'm really tied up in the Park right now, and I was wondering if you could come up here. You can be on the clock."

This meant I could charge my standard $100 per hour consulting fee including travel time. We agreed to meet at a well-known fruit and produce stand called 'Robert Is Here,' which was on the mainland up in Homestead and not far from the entrance to Everglades National Park. The place had a reputation for world-class milkshakes made from all sorts of exotic fruits, and that was what we planned to do for lunch.

Mike already was in the parking lot when I got there about 11:30 the next morning. We ordered our shakes and took them to a picnic table out in back of the place. He got the coconut-guava special, while mine was dragon fruit and papaya. They were delicious as usual. We made small talk as we drank our shakes, and after about ten minutes I began to wonder why Mike wasn't getting to the point. We had worked a number of cases before, and I'd never seen him the least bit hesitant about talking business.

Finally, my curiosity got the better of me. "What can you tell me about those shoes and feet? I assume that's why we're here."

He put down what was left of his shake, cleared his throat, and then looked around like he wanted to make sure nobody was within earshot.

"Okay, here's the deal. But I want your assurance that all this stays confidential."

"Of course, Mike, it always does until you say otherwise."

"Good. Our team of Special Agents has been working hard, but so far we only know two things for sure. First, the feet are those of a woman. Second, the shoes almost certainly were made in Cuba."

"You mean for export?"

He shook his head. "Our trade arrangements with Cuba aren't that great, and in any event the shoes are of such poor quality it's unlikely their government would allow them to be exported."

"But it could be some sort of black market deal, no?"

"Possible, but again unlikely. Apparently our team checked with other government folks who keep track of this sort of thing, and to their knowledge shoes like that have never shown up in the U.S. except under one circumstance."

"What would that be?"

"That would be on the feet of immigrants."

"So your working hypothesis is that the woman was Cuban, and maybe an illegal immigrant?"

Mike shook his head again. "That's *their* working hypothesis. Not necessarily mine."

I was beginning to get the picture. "You have a different theory? What about the woman herself? Wouldn't an ID resolve this?"

"They took DNA of course, and it's been analyzed. No matches have turned up, but as you know it's sort of like looking for a needle in a haystack unless you have an idea who the victim might be."

"What about missing persons?"

"We thought of that. But again nothing turned up. There are no recent unsolved cases in south Florida that seem to fit. We even gave out basics of the case to the press, in hopes a witness might read about it and come forward."

He handed me a one-page press release. "You can keep that. It got us lots of coverage in the papers and on T.V., but so far it hasn't produced any new leads."

"Assuming the woman was an immigrant from Cuba, how in the hell did her feet and shoes end up way out there in the glades?"

Mike shrugged. "No idea."

"What about the water hyacinth that was stuck to one of the shoes?"

"Yeah, thanks again for that identification. The team thinks it fits with their overall hypothesis."

"How's that?"

"Apparently that plant is just as common in Cuba as it is in Florida."

"So the theory is that this woman, an unidentified and therefore probably illegal Cuban immigrant, came ashore with water hyacinth stuck to her shoe, and then somehow she ends up dead out in the 'glades? Maybe because she got eaten by a crocodile?"

"That's about right. Or she could already have been dead before the crocodile got involved. No way to tell for sure with just the shoes and feet to go on."

I drained the last of my milkshake and set the empty cup down on the table. "What happens next?"

A family of four walked by, milkshakes in hand, looking for a place to sit in the shade. Mike waited until they had passed before he replied. "Technically the case stays open, pending identification of the victim. But the team of Special Agents has written their report and gone home. As far as they are concerned, the case is now in mothballs."

"What about Immigration and Customs Enforcement?"

Mike shook his head. "Our agents checked with them. The I.C.E. folks don't seem all that interested either."

"So just another unidentified dead Cuban immigrant, case closed?"

"Something like that."

"But you feel otherwise?"

Mike nodded. "Maybe."

"Any particular reason?"

"Nothing specific I can put my finger on. I just think there's been a bit of a rush to judgment here.

Could be related to budget cuts. You know the Park Service is hurting right now. But for me, there's just too many loose ends."

"Like?"

"Well, it's like you said. How did that woman, or at least her feet and shoes, get way over here in the Park? Nearly all Cuban immigrants come ashore on the Atlantic side."

He had a point, and I sensed we had come to the crux of the matter.

"What would you like me to do? I assume we're here for more than just milkshakes."

"You interact with all sorts of people, and I'd like you to keep your eyes and ears open. Ask around. Has anybody heard of a missing woman, Cuban or otherwise? Everybody knows there are undocumented workers all up and down the Keys. Something could happen to one of them and it wouldn't necessarily get reported to the authorities."

That seemed simple enough. "Sure, I can do that."

Mike rose to leave. "Thanks, Sam, but there's one little catch. At least for now, this is off the record, just between the two of us."

"But if I start asking around about a missing woman, what am I supposed to say when people want details?"

"Just give them the minimum. Use the press release as your model. But when I said this is just between us, that's not what I meant."

"You mean I'm off the payroll?"

"Hope you understand. Officially, this little get-together never happened." Mike tossed his empty milkshake container in the trash and headed for the parking lot. "Say hi to Katie, and stay in touch."

He didn't wait around long enough for me to accept or decline his offer. But what the hell, it wasn't like he'd ask me to do anything risky.

Little did I know.

CHAPTER 15

So I started asking around – clerks, waiters, neighbors, fellow guides, even a guy selling bait out of the back of his pickup – did anybody know, or had anybody heard about a missing woman?

For three days it went nowhere. Then a client gave me four nice mangrove snappers we had taken off the Arsenicker Bank, and I invited Snooks to join me for a 'cook your own catch' dinner at Habanos. Lots of restaurants in the Keys included this option on their menus. You bring in the fish, already cleaned and filleted, and tell them how you'd like them prepared. Then they add the side dishes and serve it all up at a reduced price. My favorite styles at Habanos were beer-battered and blackened.

Snooks readily accepted my invitation, with the condition that he buy us a couple of brews at the Safari Lounge ahead of time, following the usual pattern.

The place was crowded when we got there, but we found a pair of empty stools on the south side of the bar. Flo came right over with a pair of Yuenglings. Then Snooks spotted a client seated at a table over on the ocean side. "That guy is one of my regulars, a retired oilman from Tulsa. He's a good customer, so I need to go schmooze. Back in a bit."

I didn't recognize Snooks' client, a distinguished looking man with a deep tan and a full head of carefully-styled silver hair. But I knew the man sitting with him. It was Ed Grimes, a sometime client of mine.

Ed was a little guy, barely over five feet, with an oversized bald head and rimless bifocals. He was wearing a green polo shirt over tan Bermudas cut short enough to reveal a pair of knobby knees that I could see under the table.

We exchanged waves.

Ed was a real estate developer from Palm Beach. He didn't look the part, but he must have been damned good at it because everybody said he was loaded. Ed liked to fish, but his real passion was birds. He was one of those people who would go anywhere to add a new species to the list of varieties he had personally observed. He once told me about the summer he'd flown all the way to some remote island in the Aleutians just to see a hawfinch. He said it was a species normally confined to the Old World, but apparently one of them had wandered across the Bering Sea far enough to become eligible for Ed's North American life list.

One time I paddled Ed Grimes back into the everglades on a birding trip, and it had been a strange experience. The purpose was for him to "get" (his term) the swallow-tailed kite, an uncommon bird of prey that I had seen before, deep in the mangroves. It took half the day, but as soon as we'd spotted one he was ready to leave. Apparently that kite, or any bird for that matter, no longer was interesting once he'd checked it off on his list. Most of my birding clients were not like that at all, and I had to wonder if Ed had any real appreciation for the natural world. It seemed like he counted birds the way other people collected stamps.

As soon as Snooks headed off with his beer to join

his client and Ed Grimes at their table, I caught Flo's eye and waved her back over. I could see that she was busy, and she must have noticed my glass was still almost full, but she came anyway.

"Hi Sam, what's up?"

"Got a quick question, if you've got a minute."

She gestured back over her shoulder but did not break eye contact. "Pretty busy tonight, but it should be okay for the next little while. Let me know if you see anybody waving an empty glass in the air."

I said I would, and then I caught her up on the glades incident.

"Yeah, I saw that in the paper. Pretty weird, but what does it have to do with me?"

"Probably nothing, but you see and hear a lot, and I was just wondering. Has anybody said anything about a missing woman? Or maybe one of your regular customers hasn't been around lately?"

I knew it was a long shot, but there was nothing to lose.

She shook her head. "No, can't say as I have." Then she snapped her fingers. "But now that you mention it, I haven't seen Mabel for a while."

"Mabel?"

"Yeah, you know, that old gal who comes around selling cut flowers?"

"Guess I must have missed that. Has she gone missing?"

"I wouldn't say that necessarily, because she only comes in here maybe once a week. It's just that I haven't seen her now for about a month, which is unusual."

"Does this Mabel have a last name?"

"Not that I've ever heard."

"What else do you know about her? Does she live around here?"

"Gee, Sam, I thought you were better connected than that. No, Mabel comes here in some kind of little rowboat. She ties up at our Marina, hawks her flowers both here and over at Habanos, and then leaves. Never says much. Never even has a drink."

"Where does she come from?"

"I've only heard the stories, so this is second hand. But you know about Schwimley Key, right?"

I knew Schwimley was a privately-owned island completely inside the boundaries of Everglades National Park, about five miles northwest of Islamorada. It was some sort of inholding dating back to the very beginnings of the place. I wasn't sure of the details, but apparently the owners had refused to sell it to the government when the Park was being established. Today it just sits there, off limits to fishermen or campers or anybody else. The water is so shallow around the key that even the best flats boat could get stuck, and as a result the Park had closed off the whole area to the public.

"Sure I know about Schwimley. But nobody lives there, right?"

Flo started to say something when a man came up to the bar right next to me. It was the retired Tulsa oil exec, holding three empty beer bottles. "Sorry to interrupt, but any chance we could get some refills?" He pointed back to the table where Snooks and Ed Grimes were looking expectantly in our direction.

Flo apologized and said she'd be right over.

Before he went back to his table, the oilman turned in my direction and stuck out his hand. "Name's Bryce Wickstrom. Mr. Lancaster over there says you're a guide too. Maybe we can go out some time." We shook and I said something about Snooks being the best there was. The last thing I wanted to do was butt in on his business.

I thought that might be the end of it, but Flo was back in less than three minutes, and she hadn't forgotten about Mabel. "The rumor I heard was that she might live out there on Schwimley."

I was incredulous. "But how could that be? I thought the whole area was off limits."

"I have no idea, and like I said, it's just a rumor. I do know when she comes in here she usually smells kinda bad, like maybe she doesn't get a bath all that often."

"What does she look like?"

"Oh, about my height, maybe in her mid to late sixties. Gray stringy hair worn too long for somebody her age. She always wears baggy nondescript clothes, except for the hat and the shoes."

"What about them?"

"For the last year or so, she's been wearing this red straw hat and a pair of blue tennis shoes. Kind of a weird combination."

It was then I remembered the hat Marshall White had snagged with his fly out at Clovis Key two weeks earlier. It was still in my boat, forgotten until this moment. "Does the red hat have a band around it with yellow flowers?"

Flo nodded. "I thought you said you didn't know Mabel."

"I don't, but I might have run into her hat."

"Are you gonna tell me about that?"

It was a close call. "I probably shouldn't at this point."

She didn't like that and I wasn't surprised. "Well fine then. I gotta get back to work. I am supposed to be the bartender here and not just a fount of knowledge for snoops like you." It sounded grumpy, but she gave me a little half-smile at the same time, so things probably were still okay on the Flo front.

It fit, and I started to wonder. If this Mabel person lived alone on an isolated key, and rarely came to the mainland, she was just the sort of person who wouldn't necessarily be missed. At least not for a while.

It was time to bring Mike Nunez up to speed. I walked outside to a little patio area with tables and umbrellas where the smokers usually drank, and gave him a call. He answered right away and listened while I told him the story about a woman named Mable who lived on Schwimley Key, who might be missing, and who always wore blue tennis shoes and a red hat with yellow flowers on the band.

"I get it about the shoes, but what does a red hat have to do with anything?"

"It turned up all by itself on Clovis Key. One of my clients found it. It's still in my boat, because until just now I had no reason to connect it with your case."

"Huh. You better bag it and get it to me the next time you have a chance."

"You bet. And I think we need to get out there to

Schwimley Key and take a look around."

"You're right. Sounds interesting. But I can't go for the next couple of days. We're all tied up in some sort of training session about international terrorism. Why don't you go ahead? I'll put the word out to our Rangers you might be on Schwimley and not to worry if they see a boat tied up nearby. I assume you'll be taking your canoe?"

"That's probably the easiest way to get onto the island."

"Good. Just be sure to let me know what you find, okay? And I don't have to tell you not to disturb anything."

I went back inside, got Snooks' attention, and pointed in the direction of Habanos. He waved to tell me he'd gotten the message. Then he pushed back from the table he'd been sharing with Ed Grimes and Bryce Wickstrom, shook both their hands, and headed for the door. We met on the outside stairs and walked over to the restaurant together.

~ ~ ~

Snooks and I enjoyed our snapper at Habanos. Afterwards, over coffee and a couple of flans, I asked him if he'd ever heard of a woman named Mabel who came around selling flowers and who might live out on Schwimley Key.

"I've seen an old lady selling flowers around here, but I didn't know her name was Mabel and I've never heard of anybody living on Schwimley. Why?"

I filled him in on what Flo had just told me, including the part about the blue shoes and red hat. "Mike Nunez asked me to go out there and take a look.

Want to go along? I'd like to have you stay with my boat and keep an eye on things while I go ashore in the canoe."

Snooks fiddled with the rubber band holding his ponytail. "Guess I should, under the circumstances."

"What circumstances?"

"I'm the guy got you tangled up in this whole mess in the first place. But I can't go tomorrow. Me and Bryce Wickstrom just made a date to chase a school of permit rumored to be hanging around the Ninemile Bank."

I couldn't have gone the next day in any event, because later that night I got a call from Ed Grimes. He subscribed to something call the Rare Bird Alert, a service that sends out information about unusual sightings. Somebody had spotted an American flamingo over on Lake Ingraham, and he wanted me to drive him over there the next morning. Flamingos used to be common in southern Florida, but not anymore. This was a rare chance for Ed to add a new species to his life list. He didn't want to fish but he wanted to get out there early. And he was willing to hand over $600 for what probably would be only a half-day's work. Ed wasn't necessarily my favorite guy, but the pay was good and I hadn't had a lot of work lately. I decided whatever awaited Snooks and me out at Schwimley Key, it could keep, at least for a day.

CHAPTER 16

Ed Grimes showed up at my dock an hour before daylight. He was carrying a fancy pair of Zeiss ten-power binoculars and a camera on a tripod attached to a monster telephoto lens. I loaded Ed and his gear in my boat and we headed off. I had navigated across Florida Bay in the dark before. It wasn't easy and it wasn't fun, but Ed insisted we get an early start because, "that flamingo could be long gone by first light."

Ed usually was a chatty guy, but on this morning he apparently didn't want to talk, which was fine with me because I had my hands full keeping track of our route. Nighttime navigation across the Florida Bay would have been damned near impossible before the advent of GPS devices. As it was, I had to wear a head lamp to avoid driving over lobster and crab pots before we got into Park waters, and also to pick up the white channel markers that showed the way through narrow passages on the way over to Cape Sable.

We had one close call, and it was all my fault. We were about half way to the Cape when I picked up a vertical white object, shining in the light from my headlamp. I thought it was a channel marker and so naturally I steered my boat in that direction. Everything seemed fine until we got within about a hundred feet, and then suddenly Ed shouted "Holy shit! That's a bird!"

In the dark I had mistaken a great white heron for

a channel marker. The bird had been hunting in about six inches of water, and we'd have run aground for sure if I'd kept going. I turned hard left, raising the motor and gunning it at the same time as the heron rose into the air and flew away. We churned up a little bottom before I managed to get my skiff back into the channel. Tearing up the sea grass was a big-time Park Service no-no. But it could have been a lot worse. At least I didn't have to get out and push my boat.

Things proceeded normally from there. The sun had just cleared the eastern horizon when we started our run back into Lake Ingraham, an expanse of open salt water separated from the rest of Florida Bay by a narrow strand of mangroves. Experts say the whole thing likely will blow out with the next big hurricane, but for now the lake remained a well-protected mix of shallow water and mud flats. The place was ideal for wading birds including, apparently, the occasional flamingo.

The word must have gotten out among the bird watchers of south Florida, because we were not alone. At least a half-dozen boats already were cruising up and down the lake by the time we got there, and the number kept growing as the morning progressed. I recognized a couple of fellow guides as soon as it got light enough to know who was who. Based on all the waving and, "hi, how are ya?" exchanges, it seemed like Ed knew many of the birders as well.

We were about half way through a falling tide, and the place was full of birds. I recognized good numbers of white ibises and tricolored herons, along with both snowy and common egrets and lots of little shorebirds that were hard to identify. But there was no sign of a flamingo. We'd already made three passes up and down the lake, and Ed and I were about to give it up, when somebody began shouting down toward the west end. We hustled over there and, sure enough, there was a single tall bird standing on a shallow flat. It had the unmistakable profile of a flamingo, glowing red and pink in the morning sun.

Everybody had their cameras and notebooks and tape recorders out, including Ed. All the boats were jockeying for a better position, and one of them must have gotten too close, because suddenly the bird rose up off the water and flew north over the mangroves and out of sight. I said something about that being too bad, and that we could have followed the bird into the no-motor zone except I hadn't brought my canoe. But Ed shook his head and said it didn't matter because he'd already "gotten" the bird for sure, and now we should just go on home. His life list had grown by the requisite amount, and apparently that was that.

We were just about at the end of the canal connecting Lake Ingraham with the rest of Florida Bay, when Ed tapped me on the shoulder and asked that I bring my skiff down to idle speed. The wind had come up, I was anxious to get home, and I really didn't want to slow down. But money talks. Apparently he wanted to say something before we got out into open water where conversation would be nearly impossible over the noise of the outboard and the slap of waves against the hull.

I put the motor in neutral and let us drift. "What's up?"

"First thing, I want to thank you. That was a great trip for a great bird. Never thought I'd get one."

"No problem."

Ed laughed. "Well, I guess it could have been if we'd chased that white heron any farther up onto the flats this morning!"

"All right then, all set? I'd like to get back in time to run a couple of errands."

"One other thing before we go. Earlier today, back there on the lake, were we anywhere close to the spot where they found those blue shoes with a woman's feet inside?"

"Pretty close. Did Snooks Lancaster tell you about that?"

Ed shook his head and looked puzzled. "No, I heard about it on T.V. It was all over the news. Why Snooks?"

"Because he and I were the ones who made the original discovery."

"Jesus! Any idea who she was?"

"Not yet. We're still looking."

CHAPTER 17

It was two days before Snooks and I were able to clear the decks for our reconnaissance of Schwimley Key. In the meantime I'd gone on Google Earth and taken a bird's eye peek at the place. It had the usual fringe of dense mangroves around the perimeter, but the interior was more sparsely wooded with large well-spaced trees that I couldn't identify from the air. Something that looked like a pond dominated the middle of the island, and next to it was the unmistakable outline of a small house or cabin. If there was a boat tied up somewhere, I could not find it, nor were there any other signs of human activity.

We had planned to leave early, but I couldn't get the Yamaha to start until about the sixth try, and even then it was running way rougher than normal. Snooks wondered if maybe we should cancel, but I decided to go ahead. After all, it was only about five miles and we could always use the trolling motor to get back if we had to.

We anchored at the edge of the shallow water along the south side of the island, after a boat ride that took longer than it should have because of my sputtering outboard. Our plan was to have Snooks stay with the skiff while I got in the canoe, went ashore, and explored the interior of the island. If somebody came along Snooks would explain that he'd been having engine trouble on the way out to the Rabbit Key Basin, that the problem was now fixed, and that he was about to head back to Islamorada. We had our phones with us, the signal was strong, and Snooks would let me know when he was coming back, if it came to that.

I loaded the canoe with a backpack filled with my camera, a pair of binoculars, a notebook, and some plastic evidence bags left over from previous cases. I also took a canteen of water, a couple of apples, and a bottle of high-powered mosquito repellent, just in case.

I began by paddling around the whole perimeter of the island, which took about forty-five minutes. Most small keys have a deep water moat around them, but the one around Schwimley was unusually shallow, and no more than six feet wide. The fringe of mangroves looked impenetrable for the most part, but there was a small stretch of open sand on the west side where two large crocodiles basked in the sun. I had just about decided the beach was going to be the only place I could go ashore, with or (hopefully) without the crocodiles, when I spotted a narrow channel of open water on the east side where someone obviously had cut away the mangroves. I paddled over to the opening, and headed inland. The overhanging branches were low and hard to get under, but after the first twenty feet it opened up. An old green rowboat was tied up at the head of the canal. The craft was no more than ten or twelve feet long, and it had an ancient 10-horse Johnson outboard attached to the stern.

I pulled my canoe up on the mud next to the rowboat, swung the pack over one shoulder, and got out. It was quiet except for the chatter of some birds in the trees above my head, and the hum of a thousand mosquitoes that were busy figuring out if I was breakfast. If Mabel actually lived here, she must have been one tough old lady.

A narrow path led from the head of the canal toward the interior of the island. I followed the trail as it wound through an open stand of mature poisonwood and gumbo-limbo trees, until it stopped at the doorstep of a small cabin. Just beyond the cabin was a pond that I estimated at maybe one hundred yards in diameter. The right side of the pond was covered with a mat of floating vegetation that I recognized as water hyacinth, and next to it on shore was a well-tended flower garden. Two small crocodiles lay motionless half way out of the water on the far bank.

The cabin itself was little more than a crude shack. The walls consisted of vertical wooden planks that looked like they had been bleached by a century of sun and stained by a thousand rain showers. The front wall was taller than the back, and the sloping roof was covered in a layer of tarpaper that looked a lot newer than the structure itself. A rusted stovepipe emerged from the roof along the back edge, and a pair of four-panel windows flanked the wooden front door. An outhouse stood off in the woods to my right. There were no power lines.

There also was no sign of life. I called out 'hello in the house' and waited for a response. Nothing happened. Then I tried the front door, which was unlocked. I stepped inside.

The cabin had only one room, sparsely furnished but tidy. Shelves along the wall to my left were filled with an assortment of canned goods and other non-perishables like bottled water and breakfast cereal. A cot along the back wall was drawn up close to an old-fashioned pot-bellied stove. A square wooden table sat in the middle of the room, along with a single straight-backed chair. Above the table a Coleman lantern hung suspended on a wire attached to the ceiling. A second lantern sat atop an old wooden armoire in the back right corner. The doors were open, and I could see a variety of clothes hanging inside. There were three pairs of shoes at the bottom, but none of them was blue.

If this was the place that Mabel lived, which seemed likely, I wondered where she did her cooking and where she tended to matters of personal hygiene, limited though they might be. These questions got answered when I walked back outside and around the far side of the cabin. A mirror hung on the wall, and underneath it stood a four-legged wooden bench with a rusted granite basin on top. Next to that was an aged outdoor barbecue with a can of starter fluid and a bag of briquettes underneath. There also was big freezer chest, like the kind people take on camping trips. Powerful odors of decay wafted up when I opened the lid. The contents included two blocks of cheese, a half-eaten package of lunchmeat, the remains of a dozen eggs, and a quart of milk, all variously putrefied. Two bags of ice had long since melted away, leaving perhaps two inches of water in the bottom of the cooler.

Everything about Schwimley Key was surprising, but especially the pond. Obviously it was fresh water, given the hyacinth, and such things were very rare in the Keys. In fact I only knew of one other such place, down on Big Pine, and it was man-made. I wondered if Mike Nunez or anybody else knew about it. One thing was for sure: the pond made things much more livable on Schwimley Key, which could have been the reason the owners had refused to sell it to the Park Service in the first place.

I wondered what Mabel did for money. Her groceries and clothing hadn't fallen out of the sky. Based on the size of her garden, which I subsequently walked over to investigate, the flower business could scarcely have been enough. Was there something else? And what about Mabel herself? Who was she and where did she come from? A background check would be almost impossible without a last name, and nobody seemed to know what it was.

I collected up items that I thought might contain DNA, including some of the canned food, a bar of soap, and a hair brush. Then I photographed both the inside and exterior of the cabin, as well as the surrounding landscape including the pond. A longer walk around other parts of the key might have turned up some interesting things, but it was time to leave. Somebody might come along, and it could get complicated for Snooks even with our contingency plan.

For now, I'd seen enough. Mike Nunez needed to get out here, along with a crime scene crew. If the feet in the blue shoes had been Mabel's, then there must be some of her DNA around the island that could be matched up. Maybe there was good evidence on some of the items I had collected, but if not there were people more expert than me who would know what to do. A DNA match wouldn't tell us who or what had killed Mabel, or why, or even how. But it would be a start.

I was packing up getting ready to leave when

something bright caught my eye in a poisonwood tree next to the cabin. It was a small bird, flashing brilliant red and green plumage as it moved through the foliage dappled with sunlight. By the time I got my binoculars out, it was gone. Given the colors and the size, my first thought was that it must have been a hummingbird. But something about it wasn't right. There was another possibility that better fit what I'd seen in that brief glimpse, except that particular bird had no business at all being in the Florida Keys.

~ ~ ~

The canoe ride back was uneventful until I rounded the southern tip of Schwimley Key and discovered that my Hell's Bay had caught fire. Smoked billowed up from the stern, and flames engulfed the outboard. Snooks was jumping around doing something, but it was too far away to tell. I paddled furiously in his direction and was about half way there when the black smoke and flame disappeared in a big white cloud. It turned out Snooks had been looking for the fire extinguisher, and then he had found it.

By the time I got to the boat Snooks had the fire under control, but both he and my Hell's Bay were a mess. I pulled along side and asked him what the hell had just happened. He was holding his hands behind his back, looking more rueful than injured.

He offered an explanation that was reasonable enough. "I decided to tinker around with your outboard to figure out why it ran so rough on our way out here. I took off the cowling, checked the fuel line and fiddled with the wiring. Stuff like that."

"How did the fire start?"

"When nothing seemed wrong I decided to crank it over and see what happened. That's when the whole damned thing blew up."

"Are you all right?"

"Yeah, I guess. My hands got a little singed."

He held them out for my inspection. The backs of his hands were bright red, but at least they weren't black. Nevertheless Snooks was burned and there we were stuck out in the Gulf with nothing but a trolling motor. At least we were still afloat. I thought about calling the Coast Guard for a rescue, but decided by the time they got organized we probably could be back at the dock on our own. I got on my cell and called an ambulance instead, and asked them to meet me at the house.

One hell of a mess.

CHAPTER 18

By the time we had limped back home the ambulance already was there, along with a Monroe County Sheriff's Department cruiser. I recognized Deputy Stella Reynard, who was standing on the dock along with two paramedics – a man and a woman, both in their twenties. We got Snooks out of the boat and into the back of the ambulance. The paramedics took a look at his hands and one other place on the side of his nose. They said that a couple of burned spots were borderline between first and second-degree, and these needed immediate attention. They strongly recommended an ambulance ride up to the hospital in Tavernier.

Snooks shook his head, said he was fine, and then he complained about how much it was going to cost him for the ride. Probably his health insurance wasn't that great, assuming he had any at all. I reminded him there was a local foundation that provided financial assistance to fishing guides who became disabled for any reason, and they probably could help out. He muttered something about not being "some damned charity case," but then he shut up and went along. The last I saw of him before they closed up the back of the ambulance, I thought he looked just a little bit relieved.

I wanted to follow the paramedics up to the hospital in order to give Snooks a ride home, assuming they let him out any time soon. But Stella stepped in, said there wasn't a rush, and that we needed to talk. It sounded more like an order than a request. We had worked two different cases together over the past eighteen months, both involving the illegal pet trade, and I had come to both respect and like her. So I said sure, and why didn't she come in for a cup of coffee. She accepted my offer and followed me upstairs as soon as the ambulance had departed.

Stella took a seat at the kitchen counter while I made coffee. She cut a fine figure in her departmental uniform. She was tall, about five-ten, with high cheekbones, close-cut curly black hair, and a flawless café-au-lait complexion. I knew she had been born and raised in New Orleans, and that her first job in law enforcement had been with that city's police department. I also knew she'd escaped to south Florida in the months immediately following Hurricane Katrina, when there had been some serious trouble in the department. She'd never volunteered anything about the particulars, and I knew better than to ask.

Stella was all business when it came to her job, and I was not surprised she didn't wait for me to finish up the coffee before getting down to it.

"What were you and Snooks doing out there? I didn't see any clients in your boat."

I knew this was going to get tricky. "We, uh … I guess you could say we were on a little scouting expedition." By now the coffee was ready. "Cream? Sugar?"

She shook her head. "No, black is fine. So how come this little scouting expedition took you out next to Schwimley Key?"

She must have seen the surprised look on my face,

because she didn't wait for an answer. "You know, Sam, when you get on your cell phone these days, a person on the other end can pick up your exact location if they have the right know-how. And in this case that happened to include the 911 operator you called to request the ambulance."

"And let me guess. It all got relayed on to the Sheriff's Department along with the paramedics, right?"

Stella took a swallow of her coffee and set the mug back down on the counter. "Yep, and the Coast Guard too." She took another swallow and let that sink in. "They were kinda pissed you didn't call them in the first place, since marine accidents are supposed to be in their bailiwick. Oh, and let's not forget the Park Service, since you were in their waters when your boat blew up or whatever it was."

So much for my semi-secret reconnaissance of Schwimley Key. Now everybody up to and including the Coast Guard was going to be on my case about it. I was lucky there hadn't been a half dozen more people waiting on my dock when I brought Snooks in, all of them rightfully grumpy.

Obviously there was nothing left to do but fess up. And anyway, Stella had earned it. "So you got the call, and then you kept everybody else off my dock?"

She laughed at that. "Right. But it wasn't easy. It only worked because I gave my word they'd get the full story as soon as I did."

"Soon, as in right now?"

"This isn't a social call, Sam, your fine coffee not withstanding. So yeah, right now would be good."

99

I started by asking Stella if she had seen the flier from the Park Service about a missing woman. She said she had. Then I told her about Snooks' discovery of the blue shoes, and about my conversation with Flo at the Dead Animal Bar about a possible missing woman named Mabel, who was rumored to live on Schwimley Key.

By now Stella had finished her coffee and declined a refill. "You took it upon yourself to go out there alone instead of notifying the proper authorities, of whom there are many including me?"

"No, that's not right. I asked Mike Nunez about it, but he said he couldn't go. That's why Snooks and I went by ourselves. Maybe I should have asked you, but to tell the truth I thought it might be a waste of your time. I mean suppose this Mabel person had been there, which seemed likely, then the whole thing would have been pointless."

"But she wasn't there?"

"Nope."

"And the island was unoccupied?"

"I didn't say that." I helped myself to a second cup, and then described for Stella Reynard what I had found, including the food, soap, and hair brush that I had just brought home.

"You need to give me that stuff. It could be evidence."

"Shouldn't I give it to Mike Nunez, so the Park people can do DNA comparisons with the contents of the shoes?"

"I'll make sure that happens, and I'll fill him in on the details. You need to understand that this whole thing is about to become a multi-agency investigation, assuming there's been a crime."

I was beginning to get the picture.

At this point Stella excused herself, went out to her cruiser, and came back in with a tape recorder. Then she asked me to tell my story all over again, for the record. Once we had completed that task, I thought maybe we were through and I could go check on Snooks. But I was wrong. There was one more thing that Stella wanted to hear about – my boat.

"What does any of this have to do with your boat catching fire?"

She had me there. "Probably just a coincidence. I can't see any obvious connection. We were having engine trouble on the way out, and Snooks took it upon himself to tinker with the outboard while I was exploring the key. That's when the fire started."

"You have any idea how it happened?"

"Not really. With him being burned and all, my priority was just to get back home. I – that is, *we* – should ask him about that I suppose."

"I intend to, because maybe it wasn't just a coincidence."

"How's that?"

Stella gave me a look, because she knew I was smarter than that. "Maybe somebody didn't want you getting to Schwimley Key in the first place."

CHAPTER 19

Stella and I stood at the edge of my deck, looking down on the burned-out remains of my Hell's Bay skiff. The outboard was completely fried, probably a total loss, and the poling platform above it probably would need to be replaced. But thanks to Snooks' quick action with the fire extinguisher, I remained hopeful that the rest could be salvaged.

"I need to impound your boat, Sam. I know you're anxious to trail it up to the nearest repair shop so you can get back in business, but that's gonna have to wait."

"How long?"

"Not sure. I'll have one of our forensics guys come down and take a look, hopefully tomorrow. He might bring along a mechanic from the Coast Guard. They're really good at this sort of thing. Then it all depends on what they find. If it looks like your little accident was nothing more, you should have it back in a couple of days."

"And if they find something suspicious?"

"Well Sam, that's another matter. We'll probably have to impound it and bring in more experts, most likely an investigator from FDLE."

"FD – what?" It was an acronym I'd never heard before.

Stella grinned. "Sorry. That's the Florida Department of Law Enforcement. Sort of like our state FBI. Either way, you will get your boat back, I promise. Although from the looks of it, I'm not sure it's fixable.

You have insurance?"

"I do, but I hate to think about the deductibles."

"How big?"

"Can't remember."

"Bet you're gonna find out."

Just then my cell phone chirped. It was Snooks, and he was ready to come home. Apparently it wasn't as bad as the paramedics had thought.

"I've got some bandages on my hands and nose, and the docs say I need to come back in a couple of days for a follow-up. But for now, I'm ready to get the hell out of this place. Any chance you can come and get me?"

Definitely good news on a day when I needed some. "Be right there, my friend. Just sit tight. You still in emergency?"

"Yeah. I'm stuck out in the lobby reading a year-old *Time* magazine, so please hurry."

Stella Reynard was glad to hear the news about Snooks' burns, and asked if she had to put crime scene tape around my boat before she left. "Or can I trust you to leave the damned thing alone until we get back here?"

"It's all yours, I promise."

It was getting late in the day, and the light was fading fast. We both turned at the sound of a tarpon splashing somewhere up the canal, and I caught a twinkle in her dark eyes. Was it about the fish or about my promise not to go near my skiff? I couldn't tell. I may have said this already, but Stella is a class act. The Monroe County Sheriff's Department is lucky to have her.

~ ~ ~

One nearly universal characteristic of swamp guides is that our boats are better than our cars and trucks. They look better, they run better, and usually they're lots newer. My land-based transportation was a '98 Jeep Grand Cherokee with more than two hundred thousand miles on it. Frequent runs back and forth to Lauderdale were responsible for most of that. The Jeep had once been silver, but it had long since morphed into a sort of mottled gray with rusty spots around the edges. Snooks said that wasn't all bad, because a car that looked like a piece of crap wasn't as likely to get stolen. I think he was just trying to make me feel better.

Northerners believe their winters make things tougher than we have it in sunny Florida. That may be true for the people themselves, but for their stuff, not so much. The killer down here in the Keys is the salt air. Anything that can rust or corrode or get brittle does it twice as fast as it would someplace inland, no matter how cold or rainy the climate. Hardly anybody drives the tread off their tires down here, because the rubber oxidizes and starts falling to pieces long before they have a chance. Things like plumbing fixtures rust themselves shut in no time. And as for fishing gear, the headache never ends. We've all learned the hard way to rinse off our rods and reels after every trip, but even then they don't last very long. And when some googan client dunks his reel off the side of the boat for the third time in a day, sometimes it's easier just to throw the thing away and get a new one.

But I loved that old Jeep, and somehow it kept running in spite of its shabby appearance. Certainly

Snooks had no complaints when I used it to rescue him from the hospital emergency room. A ride was a ride, and he was glad to get out of that place. Not that the doctors and nurses weren't helpful. He had lotions and gauze bandages he was supposed to keep over the backs of his hands and for one little spot on his nose. Worst of all, he was under orders to rest and stay indoors out of the sun for at least ten days. Then he was supposed to come back in for a follow-up, when they would let him know if it was okay to go back to work.

Snooks was not a happy camper, but on the drive back to Islamorada we came up with a plan. I was an intact guide without a boat, while he had a boat that he couldn't use. We agreed I would take his clients and mine fishing, using his skiff, and we would split the fees. It wasn't ideal for either of us, but it was a whole lot better than nothing.

Snooks snapped his fingers. "And say, that reminds me. I was supposed to take Bryce Wickstrom out tarpon fishing tomorrow. In fact, he called my cell while I was in the waiting room back at the hospital."

"What did you tell him?"

"That I couldn't go because of what happened. You want me to call him back, and maybe set things up?"

"Sure. But how much did you tell him about what happened today?"

"I told him that you and I were out by Schwimley Key, that you were off exploring the island in a canoe when your boat caught fire, and that I got burned trying to put it out. Was that a mistake?"

"Probably not. Go ahead and make the call."

Snooks made the arrangements, and Wickstrom

agreed to be at my place by 6:30 the next morning.

Once we had the deal with Bryce Wickstrom set up, I decided to tell Snooks about my get-together with Stella Reynard. He was anxious to learn more about what I had found on Schwimley Key, since we really hadn't had a chance to talk about it earlier. I'd already told the story to Stella, twice including the one for her recorder. Telling it a third time in one day was sort of a drag, but Snooks deserved at least a summarized version considering what the whole episode had cost him.

After recounting events of the day, I had some questions for Snooks. "Any idea what happened to my boat? Like why it was running rough, and how it caught fire?"

He fingered the bandage on the side of his nose and winced a little. "Wish I did. I took the cowling off and did a quick inspection, but nothing seemed broken or even loose." Then he hesitated a bit. "But there was this smell of gasoline, and I probably shouldn't have tried turning it over. Looks like I screwed up again. Just not my week, Sam. Sorry."

"Go easy on yourself, Snooks. I probably would have done the same thing. I'm just glad those burns are going to be okay. But you should quit poking at your nose like that."

We were almost back to his house when Snooks remembered something else. "Did you happen to see that Yellowfin circling around while you were out in the canoe?"

This was a startle. "No. I must have been on the interior of the island by then. Was it gray and did it have twin black Mercury outboards?"

"Yep. Or at least I think so. It never got real close."

"Could you see who was on board?"

"Not to recognize. But there were two of them. Looked like men."

"Did they try to help when they saw the fire?"

Snooks shook his head. "No. They'd already left. For some reason I got the impression they weren't glad to see me."

"Did they have a canoe on board?"

"No."

Those two clowns Dave Ackerman and I had caught poaching crocodiles out by Long Key probably were the same ones Snooks had just seen out by Schwimley. But what were they up to? There was no way in hell they were going to get that big Yellowfin close enough for a landing, unless they planned on wading ashore.

I was still thinking about the gray Yellowfin as I turned west off the Overseas Highway and followed an unpaved road a short distance back into the mangroves. The road ended at the edge of a narrow canal, where an old houseboat was tied up to a sagging wooden dock. We had arrived at Chez Snooks. The walls of the houseboat were horizontal wooden planks painted pale blue. Some of them were warped and most were peeling. A dented tin roof added to the general run-down appearance. The transom was built to support an outboard motor, but it was empty. Snooks owned a home that floated, if just barely, but it no longer went anywhere. I had been inside his place on occasion and had found it surprisingly tidy and functional in spite of the bedraggled exterior.

An old beater Toyota pickup was parked next to the dock, the once-red paint job having long since faded to a dirty pink with rust spots. An eighteen-foot Dolphin skiff sat on a trailer next to the pickup. Unlike everything else here, the fishing boat looked relatively new and in prime condition, the deck and hull gleaming white and spotless in the afternoon sun. Even though Snooks lived on a canal, he had no ramp or lifts for taking his boat out of the water. Instead he kept it on the trailer and met clients at a nearby marina where he could hose it off at the end of the day.

I backed up my jeep into position and we hooked up his trailer. Then I got back behind the wheel, waved to Snooks as he ducked inside his little houseboat, and headed home.

The first thing I did when I walked in the door was check the landline for messages, but there weren't any. It had been five days since Katie's weekend visit, and we had not spoken since. I'd left messages on at least two occasions, and she'd left me one about the water hyacinth, but otherwise nothing. I was starting to get angry, and also a little worried. Maybe tomorrow I would call the university just to make sure everything was okay, even if she wouldn't return my calls.

CHAPTER 20

Fishermen are drawn to tarpon because they get really big and because they put on such a spectacular acrobatic fight after they've been hooked. There is nothing like the sunlit flash of a leaping tarpon to get an angler's blood pumping. The challenge is getting to that point.

Sometimes tarpon will eat, but lots of times they won't. If the water is too cold they usually just loaf around in the sun trying to warm up, which is one of the reasons tarpon fishing gets better in the middle of the year. But I've seen whole schools of tarpon on the prowl, when the season and conditions are right, and even then they'll ignore your offering like it's not even there. It may have to do with experience. A hundred-pounder might be fifteen years old, which means it has seen a thing or two, especially in waters like the Florida Keys that are full of fishermen. Tie on the wrong fly or move it the wrong way and they'll probably swim right on by. Cast a shadow or slap the water with your line, and they're gone.

I hoped that Bryce Wickstrom understood all this as we headed down to my dock the next morning and prepared to set out in Snooks' eighteen-foot Dolphin. I'd splashed his little boat the night before, and tied it up beside my blackened and forlorn Hell's Bay. It was still early, barely six-thirty, and nobody from the Sheriff's Department had showed up yet to do the preliminary forensics Stella Reynard had promised.

Hopefully by the time we got back from fishing they would have come and gone, and maybe I could have my boat back.

Wickstrom couldn't help but notice things as we stowed our gear on the Dolphin. "Snooks told me about your accident. Sure am sorry. Any idea how it happened?"

"Not really. I was out of the boat at the time, doing some exploring in my canoe. Fortunately Snooks was there to put the fire out or it might have been a total loss." I left out the part about how the fire started.

"I understand he tried to crank it up, when the whole thing went boom."

Just how many details of our trip had Snooks shared with the man? I made a mental note to ask him about it. "That's about right. Now, are you ready to go fishing?"

Bryce Wickstrom had brought his own high-end Sage graphite rod, and in all other ways he looked the part of a well-heeled fly fisherman. He sported a Patagonia canvas hat, polarized wrap-around glasses with magnifier inserts, and a Simms guide-weight fishing vest full of all sorts of odds and ends we probably weren't going to be using. The only peculiar thing about his equipment was an ancient Hardy Brothers reel that looked like it had seen much better days.

"You sure about the reel? I'd hate to lose a fish on account of it."

"I'm sure. This is my lucky reel. I've had it since I was a kid, and I never go anywhere without it."

"It looks older than you."

"It is. But like I said, it's my lucky reel, and a family heirloom."

"Fair enough, I suppose. It's your trip."

He also insisted we take nothing but fly gear, and that was fine with me as long as he knew the odds. It was mid-April, still a bit early for tarpon prime-time.

"I can easily bring spinning gear, and Snooks gave me some live crabs he had left over from an earlier trip. Sometimes bait will do the trick when the fish are being picky."

Wickstrom shook his head. "No, I've caught plenty of tarpon on bait in my life, and even a few on lures. But Snooks says you're the man when it comes to getting 'em on the fly, which I haven't ever done."

Coming from Snooks, that was a real compliment. "Ever tried?"

"A couple of times, but I wasn't much good at it because I'd had no experience with a ten-weight rod."

"But now you have?" This could be important.

"Yeah. I took a class, so now I think I'm ready."

Snooks had given me a tip the night before. A couple of days earlier he'd seen some fish moving along the edge of Ninemile Bank out on the gulf side. That would be our first stop. Then maybe later we'd try the so-called "Yellow-brick Road" just off Islamorada's Atlantic coastline. Sometimes whole schools of fish traveled south along there in shallow water, and it would be easy to see them coming with the afternoon sun at our backs. Maybe we'd get lucky. Maybe the wind would stay calm, there would be no clouds to block the sun, he'd make the perfect cast, and maybe a fish would eat. That was a lot of maybes, but that's why they call it fishing and not catching.

The ambush strategy for hunting tarpon usually makes for a lot of down time while you wait for a fish to come along. This in turn presents opportunities for conversation, assuming both the guide and the client are so-inclined. I hoped this would be the case on that particular day, because I wanted to learn a little more about Bryce Wickstrom. Snooks said he was a retired oilman from Oklahoma, and that he'd been down in the Keys for some little while, mostly to fish. But I was curious to discover how they had found each other, and more specifically how Wickstrom and my bird-watcher client Ed Grimes happened to be drinking together the other night at the Safari Lounge.

I used my push pole to tie us up in a likely spot on the gulf side, and then stood up on the stern platform for a better view. There were no clouds and almost no wind to disturb the surface. Distant mangrove islands shown bright green in the morning sun, which was at our backs and already high enough to provide excellent visibility down into the clear blue water off to our north. Any tarpon working its way down the flats in our direction should be easy to spot. I rigged up Wickstrom's leader with a purple and brown crab imitation of my own design, and asked him to stand up on the bow with his ten-weight rod at the ready. For the moment there were no fish.

After fifteen minutes of nothing a roseate spoonbill flew overhead, and I seized the opportunity. "Nice looking spoonbill, isn't it?"

Instead of looking up, Wickstrom gazed down into the water. "Where? I've never caught a spoonbill before."

So much for the bird-watching connection.

I decided to take the direct approach. "I noticed you with Ed Grimes at the Dead Animal Bar last week. Have you known each other long? He's a client of mine, but he's more interested in birds than fish."

Wickstrom kept watching the water ahead. "Didn't know that about Ed."

That was the end of our conversation about Ed Grimes, because just then I spotted a dark object, maybe a hundred yards out, moving south along the bank in our direction.

"There's something up there. Could be fish, and it looks like more than one."

"Are they tarpon?"

"Probably. Get yourself ready."

Wickstrom wanted to know if he had time to make a practice cast, and I said yes if he hurried up about it. He stripped off some line and made a beautiful throw, settling the fly gently on the water least sixty feet in front of the boat. Then he retrieved the line and coiled it up at his feet on the prow of the boat. He held the rod in his right hand and the fly in his left, ready to cast. The man clearly knew what he was doing.

It turned out there were three of them, moving deliberately along in single file. The lead fish was the biggest, a good hundred and twenty pounder, and I suggested that Wickstrom try for it. He waited until the fish was maybe a hundred feet away and then made his cast. A perfect throw would have been one that dropped the fly far enough ahead of the approaching fish so that it would have time to sink to the right depth to intercept the tarpon just as it arrived. That was exactly what happened, except the little crab imitation sank about three feet short of the fish.

The lead tarpon swam right on by, but the second one – it might have been eighty pounds – turned out and made a rush for the fly. I thought for sure it was going to eat but instead it stopped, maybe ten inches short. Then it turned away, got back in line, and swam off with the others. It was one of those close calls that all tarpon fisherman have experienced, and all too often.

Bryce Wickstrom set down his rod, took off his hat and pulled a red bandana out of his hip pocket. He wiped the sweat from his forehead and ran his other hand back across his full head of silver hair. Then he turned to me and shrugged. "What did I do wrong?"

"Nothing that I could see. Everything looked fine. Nice gentle landing to your line and leader. Maybe not exactly on target, but that shouldn't have mattered. It was obvious that second fish spotted your offering. Could have been the wrong fly I suppose."

There was nothing left to do but set up again and wait. At least it gave me a chance to find out a few more things about Bryce Wickstrom. I learned he had been born and raised in Tulsa, the only child of an oil baron. He'd gone to work in the family business right after graduating from the University of Oklahoma, and eventually had become its president and CEO. He was a lifelong bachelor, now semi-retired, presently staying in a long-term rental down in Marathon. He'd met Snooks by accident one morning at the Hogfish Grill.

I was coming to appreciate Wickstrom's qualities

as a fisherman, not the least of which was patience. Unlike some clients I have taken out, he did not complain about the lack of more fish, or suggest that we pack it in and go home. But after about an hour and a half with nothing in sight, I was the one who suggested we try another spot. I untied Snooks' boat from the push pole, stowed our gear, and we got underway. Forty minutes later we were anchored up on the Yellow Brick Road, after crossing under the Channel Two Bridge to the Atlantic side and working our way northeast past the Caloosa Cove Marina.

Another boat already was there, about midpoint along the good stretch of water. Courtesy among guides and others who know the tradition says you don't tie up in front of another fisherman and risk intercepting the path of any oncoming tarpon. Since I knew the fish likely would be coming from the northeast, we anchored southwest of the other boat, leaving a couple of hundred yards between us. In theory this should have given the fish time to settle back into a rhythm after they had passed the first boat. I remembered what Snooks had told me about Reuben Fletcher, and I was glad he wasn't there to cut in front of us. Dave Ackerman had called two days earlier to tell me the Fish and Wildlife Conservation Commission had permanently pulled his guide's license.

I changed over to a steel blue Puglisi fly that was supposed to look like a baby mackerel. There was no particular reason except to try something different. Wickstrom made his practice cast, collected up his line, and we waited. Again.

About fifteen minutes later my cell phone chirped.

I recognized the number for Stella Reynard, pushed the right key, and said hello.

"Are you alone?"

"No."

"With a client?"

"Yes."

"Can he hear?"

"No; not set up for it."

"Good, then you just listen and I'll keep this simple. My guys had a look at your Hell's Bay. Finished up about an hour ago."

"And?"

"And they just can't tell. They figured out the point of origin of the fire was someplace on the upper unit of your outboard. But the damage was so extensive that any evidence of tampering is long gone, assuming there was any."

"What happens now?"

"Now you get your boat back. But officially the case is still open."

"All right. Talk to you later."

If Bryce Wickstrom had any curiosity about what that was all about, he had the good sense not to ask.

We went back to fishing in silence.

Another half hour passed when I heard a shout, followed by the sound of a fish breaking water. The boat ahead of us had hooked up to a nice-sized tarpon and it was a jumper. Sometimes they are, and sometimes they're not. Most fishermen hope they are just for the show, even though the risk of a break-off is highest when the fish is out of the water. The guide in the other boat had unhooked from his anchor, and he was following the fish as it settled down and headed out into deeper water. He waved to get my attention, and then pointed back over his shoulder, telling me there were more fish in the group and the rest were headed our way.

There were at least seven fish in the school. If they held a steady course they were due to pass by no more than forty feet off our port side. I told Wickstrom to drop his fly in front of the group, and then to begin a slow retrieve once it had sunk to the proper level.

It worked. The lead tarpon charged the fly and ate. Wickstrom set the hook hard, and the fish was on.

The first few seconds were tricky because the tarpon immediately broke the surface in a cart-wheeling leap. Wickstrom bowed forward toward the jumping fish, thereby shortening the distance between himself and his prey and reducing the chance the tarpon would come tight on the line and break off. As soon as the tarpon splashed back into the water Bryce stood back up and set the hook three more times in quick succession. The initial bow and following hook-sets were essential moves if we were to have a chance of landing the fish, and Wickstrom did it all just right. Whoever had given him lessons must have known what they were doing. I learned later that it was Snooks. No surprise.

It took nearly an hour before we got that big old tarpon up to the boat, by which time we had followed it well out into the Atlantic. There had been a half-dozen more jumps, interspersed with powerful steady runs, but the line and leader held and my little Puglisi fly stayed buried in its jaw. Even Wickstrom's old Hardy reel managed to stay in one piece.

Based on length and girth I estimated the fish weighed perhaps one hundred and thirty pounds, a true fly-fishing trophy. We took some photos, moved the exhausted fish back and forth in the water several times to oxygenate its gills, and then let it go. Wickstrom wanted to lift it up out of the water while I took a photo of him holding his catch, but I said no. I reminded him it was against regulations to bring any tarpon out of the water that weighed more than forty pounds. The risk of damage, especially to the gills, was just too great.

When we got back to the dock I noticed right away my Hell's Bay was still tied up in the same spot. Bryce Wickstrom must have noticed too, but he didn't say anything. We got busy unloading Snooks' little Dolphin. Then he wrote me a generous check and thanked me for "the experience of a lifetime."

I thought the man was leaving, but instead he pointed to a bench on the dock. "Can we talk a minute?"

I said, "Sure, would you like a beer?"

"That would be great, thanks."

I went up to the house and brought back two Yuenglings. We sat down beside each other, and Wickstrom cleared his throat. "So where were you when your boat caught fire?"

"Out near a place called Schwimley Key."

"What were you doing out there anyway?"

"Oh, I do a little investigative work for the Park Service, and they asked me to take a look for something on the island."

"Did you find it?"

"Possibly. But if I may ask, why the interest?"

"No interest, really. I just wondered how much time you had available for guiding."

"You mean instead of working for the Park Service?"

"Something like that." Bryce took a big swallow of beer and set the bottle down on the bench between us. "You proved today that you're a damned good fisherman, Sam, and I'd sure like to go out again. But if people keep trying to burn up your boat, that's gonna limit our future opportunities."

"So what you're saying is I should stick to fishing?"

"Might be safer."

We drank in silence until our beers were gone. Then he stood up to leave. "Be seein' ya. And thanks again for the great day."

~ ~ ~

As soon as Bryce Wickstrom left I got on the phone to a man named Billy Nelson, who ran a fine boat repair place in Islamorada. Now that the Monroe County Sheriff's Department had released my burned out Hell's Bay from their custody, I was anxious to get it fixed up and back in the water. Billy was a good guy and he knew what it meant for a guide to be without transportation. I gave him a brief description of my boat and its troubles. He said he was about to close up for the day, but that he'd wait until I got there.

The Matecumbe Boat Yard sat on an oversized lot on the ocean side, about ten miles from my house. The centerpiece of Billy's operation was a blue metal building with big doors on both ends and enough interior space to hold two or three boats and their trailers at the same time. A small office was attached to the north side, and there was a big gravel parking area out behind.

There were two boats in the shop when I got there, and maybe a dozen more outside in the lot. Some had for sale signs on them. I parked in front of the office and got out. Billy must have heard me coming, because he came out of the shop right away. He was wearing dark gray coveralls and wiping his hands on a little red towel.

Billy Nelson looked a bit younger than me, perhaps mid-thirties. He was medium height, lanky but not thin, with a fair complexion and close-cropped reddish-blond hair. He walked right over and looked inside my boat. "Holy cow, Sam. When you said a boat fire, you weren't kidding. How did this happen anyway?"

"Not sure. The Yamaha had been running rough, so I took the cowling off and tinkered around with the wiring and the fuel line. Then I cranked it over, and she just blew up." I decided to leave out the part about Snooks' involvement in the whole episode.

Billy hopped up in back and had a closer look at the charred remains of my outboard. He wiggled a few dangling wires and tubes. "This thing looks totally fried, Sam."

"Yeah, I know, but what about the rest?"

He took his time, inspecting the hull both inside and out, along with the center console. "You're going to need fiberglass repair and likely a bunch of re-wiring. Just how much I can't tell until I get down inside things."

"But you think it can be fixed?"

"I expect so, but it's too early for me to even attempt an estimate. You got insurance?"

I handed him a card with my insurance contact information. "I talked to them yesterday. They knew about your shop, and told me to go ahead. They'll be expecting a call from you when the time comes."

Billy said he'd be in touch as things progressed, and we left it at that. My Hell's Bay was in good hands, and I felt relieved.

CHAPTER 21

I drove back to my house from Billy Nelson's place, washed and stowed the gear still sitting around from the tarpon trip, and hosed-off Snooks' boat. I knew he was going to want it back in about a week, or maybe less. I went upstairs and got on the phone. Snooks and I needed to have a little talk.

He was home and answered on the first ring.

"Hey, it's Sam. How are you feeling?"

"Okay I guess. I'm staying out of the sun like the doctor ordered."

"Good."

"But I'm bored."

"You up for a brew at the Safari? And maybe a bite afterwards at Habanos?"

"Damn straight."

"I'll pick you up."

It took us less than fifteen minutes to get there, still in time for the four-to-six Happy Hour. I chose a booth because I thought Snooks might be self-conscious about his bandages, and the bar was crowded. We had a good view of the Atlantic, which was calm and reflecting silver in the late afternoon sun. A dozen laughing gulls were busy picking up fish scraps from a cleaning station at the marina. A blue-water guide had just finished bagging up a mixed catch of snapper and dolphin for her clients, and the gulls were enjoying the leftovers.

I caught Flo's eye to order our beers, but she waved

125

me over to the bar instead. "What? Are you guys feeling snooty tonight?"

I laughed. "No, just tired. Snooks had a little incident a couple of days ago."

"Yeah, I can see the bandages. What happened?"

"Boat fire."

"His or yours?"

"Mine."

"Is he gonna be okay?"

"Yeah, I think so. We were lucky it wasn't worse."

"What about your boat?"

"Same. I'm probably looking at a new outboard, along with some deck work. The good news is it still floats. Snooks got burned putting out the fire."

"Where were you?"

"Someplace else."

Flo laid two Yuenglings up on the bar and raised an eyebrow. "That's it, just 'someplace else?' I mean it's not like I haven't shared some things with you of late."

I gave her a sheepish look. "Fair enough. Snooks and I went out to Schwimley Key a couple of days ago, looking for that Mabel person you told me about last week. I was off on the island when the fire started. We still don't know exactly what happened."

Flo had been wiping the bar with a towel, but this stopped her. "Did you find Mabel?"

"Nope. But somebody's been living out there. By any chance have you seen her since we last talked?"

Flo shook her head. "You know, I'm starting to get worried about this whole thing, Sam."

I had to agree with her. "Now the Sheriff's Department is involved along with the Park Service, because of the suspicious nature of my boat fire. And I'm gonna need another favor. Two, actually."

"And they are?"

"First, this is just between the two of us. I don't want any wild rumors spreading around, and the Safari is just the sort of place where it could happen."

She placed her right index finger vertically in front of her lips. "Got it. And what else?"

"Please keep your eyes and ears open. If you pick up anything about Schwimley or about Mabel, I'd appreciate a heads-up. There's something odd happening around here, and I have a feeling it's about to suck me in."

"You mean this is getting personal?"

"Could be."

Then Flo did something surprising. She reached across the bar, covered my left hand with her right one, and kept it there. It was soft and moist and warm. "If I hear anything, you'll be the first to know. But in the meantime do me a favor back?"

By now her face had come up close to mine, close enough that I could see golden highlights in her emerald eyes that I hadn't noticed before. "Sure. What's that?"

"Please be careful out there."

Holding hands with a bartender at the Safari Lounge was a new experience. Under different circumstances I might have made a joke about it, but the look in Flo's eyes told me that was a bad idea. Instead I gave her hand a gentle squeeze and then we slowly disengaged.

I carried the two Yuenglings back to the booth,

from which Snooks had been looking expectantly in my direction for the past five minutes.

"What took you so long? I'm thirsty."

"Yeah, sorry about that. Flo had some, ... ah, questions. Because of your bandages."

"What did you tell her?"

"As little as possible, but I had to say something."

Snooks took a big pull on his Yuengling, set the bottle back on the table, and wiped the back of one bandaged hand across his mouth to clean off the foam. "How did it go out there today with Wickstrom?"

"The man knows how to fish. They weren't eating off the Ninemile Bank, but we caught one nice tarpon out on the Yellow Brick Road."

"Good!"

I had brought Snooks to the Dead Animal Bar because I thought he deserved a night out, but also because I wanted to talk to him about Bryce Wickstrom. "How much did you tell him about the day my boat caught fire?"

"You already asked me that while we were driving back from the hospital. And like I said then, I didn't tell him much. Why?"

"Because he asked me today what happened out there at Schwimley Key, and I just wondered why he was so interested."

Snooks took another pull on his Yuengling. "Maybe he just doesn't want another of his guides put out of business."

"Yeah, he pretty much said the same thing. Then he talked about us going fishing again, and that made me a little uncomfortable because I wouldn't want to cut into your business. After all, you made the first contact."

Snooks shrugged and said he wasn't worried.

We worked on our beers for a while longer, not saying anything. The four-to-six happy hour expired and the crowd began to thin out. I thought about ordering another round, but my friend was looking a little saggy around the edges so I suggested instead that we should move on to dinner at Habanos. He liked the idea.

~ ~ ~

Fifteen minutes later we were drinking sweet tea and waiting for our orders of blackened yellowtail snapper to come out of the kitchen. Then I remembered something. When Flo first told me about Mabel, she mentioned that the old lady sold her cut flowers at Habanos as well as at the Safari Lounge. Might they know something here?

Our waitress was a slim dark-haired woman in her mid-thirties called Lupé Sanchez. She was a Habanos veteran, frequently in charge of the place in terms of supervising the busboys and other help. I figured if anybody in the restaurant knew about Mabel, it likely would be Lupé.

I caught her eye and she came right over to our booth.

"More tea? Your fish should be out in just a minute."

"Tea's fine, thanks. But I have a question. Do you know a woman named Mabel who comes around selling flowers?"

Lupé nodded in recognition. "There is a lady who

does that, yes. Or at least she used to. But I did not know her name was Mabel. Why do you ask? Do you need flowers? Because I have a cousin down in Marathon..."

"No, it's nothing like that. I just wondered if you might have seen her lately."

Lupé shook her head. "And I am guessing we might not see her again."

"Why is that?"

"From something she said last time she was in here, maybe three weeks or a month ago. I do not remember exactly, but she said something about coming into some money. That she might no longer need to sell her flowers, which I do not think was a very profitable business in any event."

"Did she say where the money was coming from?"

"No, señor. And of course I did not ask."

CHAPTER 22

I'd only been home a couple of minutes when my phone lit up. It was Mike Nunez calling from his office up in Everglades Park. Evidently he was working late. "We got a likely match between follicles on a hairbrush we got from Stella Reynard and the tissue in those blue shoes."

"Did Stella tell you where the brush came from?"

"Yep. Schwimley Key, right? And there's somebody named Mabel who lives out there?"

"Maybe that's *used* to live out there, given the DNA match."

"Either that or Mabel is wandering around someplace without any feet."

I knew that people in law enforcement sometimes resorted to black humor as a way of relieving tension. This may have been one of those times, but still I didn't much like it.

In light of the new DNA evidence, it seemed like another trip to Schwimley was in order, and it turned out Mike had already set things up. "Stella and I have decided it should be a joint venture involving both the Park Service and the Sheriff's Department. There's a bit of a jurisdiction issue here since the key is private property but inside the Park boundary. I think you know she and I have a good working relationship, so that won't be a problem. Anyway Sam, you wanna go along? We're thinking day after tomorrow."

"You bet. Wouldn't miss it."

"I was hoping you'd say that. You know the way in, which will save us some time."

"And we can use my canoe as a shuttle. It's real shallow around Schwimley."

"I know that Sam. It's my park, remember? Oh, and it's gonna be a good-sized group. Stella is bringing an assistant to help with the crime scene, assuming we have one."

I counted it up in my head. "So that would be a total of four people including me? Sounds like more than one boat's worth."

"Yeah, I know. I'm gonna trail down my Park Service flats boat, and Stella's bringing a skiff that belongs to the Sheriff's Department. Is it okay if we meet at your dock?"

"Of course." Then I had an idea. "And say, do you know Dave Ackerman? He's our local state wildlife officer."

"Yeah, I think I've met him. Why?"

I explained about our encounter with two guys hunting crocodiles out by Long Key, and the fact that Snooks probably had seen their boat the day I was exploring Schwimley. "I did see several crocs on the island. That's why I'm thinking maybe you should invite Dave to come along."

"Do you suppose those same two guys were planning to hunt on Schwimley until they spotted Snooks and took off?"

"Yeah, or maybe they didn't actually need to hunt them personally."

"Why not?"

"Because Mabel could be a supplier? Apparently

she told somebody at Habanos that she had a new source of income besides just selling flowers."

Mike Nunez managed to sound skeptical and a little exasperated at the same time. "Aren't we getting ahead of ourselves here? We really don't know one damned thing about this woman. But sure, I'll give Dave a call. Hell, it's gonna be a zoo anyway. Then we'll have everybody represented out there except the Coast Guard and the Border Patrol. I assume he has a boat."

"Of course. He practically lives in it."

"Okay then, I'll tell him to meet us at your house. And I'll be at your dock no later than 7 AM. You do have a boat ramp don't you?"

I assured Mike I did.

~ ~ ~

It had been a long day and I was ready to turn in. Once again I called Katie before going to bed, and once again both her phones went straight to voicemail. This time I didn't bother leaving messages. I had called the university a couple of days earlier and learned she was in class, so at least I knew she was still alive.

I fixed up the coffee pot for the next morning and tucked myself into bed, but it took some time before my anger subsided enough to even attempt sleep. Something was way wrong on the marriage front. Whatever was going on with Katie, a simple phone call wasn't too much to ask.

I was nearly out when there was a knock on the door. This was unusual at any time, but especially at night. I pushed back the covers, threw on a robe, and went to see who could be coming around so late. I pulled open the door, and there stood Flo Delaney from the Safari Lounge. Her usual bartender outfit included Bermudas and a Dead Animal Bar t-shirt, and I had never seen her in anything else. But tonight she was wearing a low-cut yellow sleeveless blouse, a full-length blue skirt, fancy little silver flip-flops, and a couple of toe rings.

This was an all-new Flo, and somewhere in my head an alarm bell went off.

"Sorry to bother you so late, Sam, but I just got off work. Can I come in?"

I said sure, and then stood aside as she crossed the room and took a seat at my kitchen counter. I suspected from the way things moved that she wasn't wearing anything under the blouse, and the alarm bell got louder.

"Can I get you something? Maybe a cup of coffee?"

"That would be great. Unless you happen to have a little Maker's Mark? You know I never drink at the bar, but afterwards..." She trailed off.

"How do you take it?"

"Straight, with a couple of ice cubes. Will you join me?"

"Uh ... sure."

I poured our drinks and invited her to join me on the couch in the living room. Something was up, but I still wasn't sure what was going on. In spite of our frequent meetings at the Safari Lounge, and the fact that we'd held hands the last time I was in there, I realized I knew absolutely nothing about Flo's personal life.

She took a sip of her bourbon. "Thanks, Sam, and sorry again for the late hour. I expect you're an early riser like all the other swamp guides."

"No problem. We're friends, and I'm always glad to see you. But..." I paused, unable to come up with a subtle way to ask the obvious question.

"But what?"

"Please don't take this the wrong way. But why are you here? Is there a problem?"

She shook her head. "No, not really. It's just that I'm ... a little lonely tonight. All those people at the bar, most of them paired-up and everything, sometimes it gets me down. I guess this is one of those times."

"What about family?"

She took another drink and set the glass down, probably more deliberately and carefully than necessary. "I have a son. He's a great kid, but he's in the Merchant Marine and out of the country most of the time. He usually tries to get down here at Christmas, and maybe for my birthday, but that's about it."

It was time to either drop the subject or dig deeper. I chose to dig.

"What about his father?"

"Long-gone and don't ask."

"And your parents?"

"Both dead. Actually they were my adoptive parents. I never knew the other ones."

"Were they good to you?"

That brought a warm smile. "Oh yeah. They had a little place down on Big Pine Key, where my dad ran a car repair shop in our front yard. But they were old when they got me, already early-sixties, and I've been on my own since I was seventeen."

She drained her glass, turned, and put her hand on

my shoulder. "You got any more bourbon? It makes me feel good just talking. And did anybody ever tell you how sexy you look with those blue eyes and that little dimple on your chin?"

I probably should have asked her to leave right then. Instead, I went out to the kitchen, refilled our glasses, and rejoined her on the couch. We drank and talked, and then we drank some more. After a while she leaned over, took my head in her hands, and kissed me full on the lips. One thing led to another after that. I found out for a fact she wasn't wearing anything under that yellow blouse, and she ended up spending the night.

~ ~ ~

I woke up the next morning alone, with a helluva headache and a guilt trip the size of an elephant. It wasn't the first one-night hook-up in my life, but it was the first since Katie and I had found each other. It would have been easy to blame it all on Flo, but that was too simple. The alcohol probably had weakened my resolve at the same time it fueled my fires, but I knew in my heart that was a long way from a sufficient excuse.

Had I been surprised when Flo showed up at my door? Yes. Had I found her attractive in her off-work attire, and was I a bit intrigued? Yes again. Was I out for revenge, frustrated and angry at Katie? Perhaps a little bit. Should I have kicked Flo's lovely ass out the door as soon as I suspected what might be going on? Probably, but now it was too late.

Details about how things had gone after we went to bed were a little foggy, thanks mainly to the bourbon.

As best I could recall the sex had been good but not great, and the shortcomings (such as they were) had been on me.

I got up, splashed a little water on my face, and went out to the kitchen to make some coffee. She had left a three-word note beside the pot. The first word was 'sorry,' but it was crossed out. The second two were 'Thanks' and 'Flo.'

I checked my phones for messages, hoping I might have slept through a late call, and that hearing Katie's voice would make the whole thing go away. But of course there was no message. It probably wouldn't have made any difference.

CHAPTER 23

As promised, Mike Nunez showed up at 7 a.m. sharp two days later. There was plenty of room at my dock for his boat, now that my Hell's Bay was up in Billy Nelson's repair shop. Billy had called the day before, said things looked "do-able," but it was too early to give me an estimate or even a target date for when the repairs might be finished.

Mike had brought the same little Maverick he'd been driving the day Snooks and I met him back in the glades. He tied it up to my dock and climbed out. He was wearing blue jeans, a short-sleeved khaki shirt, and a dark green ball cap. The shirt and cap had patches sewn on them with the official Park Service emblem – an upside down arrowhead with a tree and a bison in the foreground and a snow-capped mountain in back. Whoever had come up with that logo obviously hadn't given much thought to the everglades.

We shook and I asked Mike if he'd like some coffee.

"Maybe a quick cup. Oh, and what about that red hat you found that might have belonged to Mable?"

I went to my office desk and got him the hat.

He sat and drank and looked at the hat. "You say you found this on Clovis Key?"

"Yep."

"I wonder how it got there."

"Maybe the same way her shoes got to that lake back in the glades?"

Mike laughed. "And we've got no clue about that

either. I'm telling you Sam, so far this case is a real stumper."

About 7:30 Stella and a red-haired assistant named Penny Raintree motored up my canal, followed a few minutes after by Dave in his Fish and Wildlife skiff. The multi-agency amphibious landing on Schwimley Key was ready to begin. It all looked very official. Each of the boats had its own set of lettering and decals, and everybody but me was wearing a uniform.

It took three trips in my canoe before we had the whole crew on shore. As I was walking up the path leading to the interior of the key, a strange thought came from out of nowhere. What if we found some nice lady sitting outside the little cabin, enjoying the sun and birds, and wondering what all the fuss was about? And what if her name wasn't Mabel? I shook my head to get rid of the image, because it was crazy. We had the blue shoes and the red hat, and the DNA. It was Mabel's cabin, and now she was gone and almost certainly dead.

Once we got to the cabin, Stella said she and Penny would start there, doing all the usual things like dusting for prints, checking for blood spatter, and sorting through whatever personal belongings they could find. Dave Ackerman headed for the pond, where I'd told him I'd seen crocodiles on my earlier visit. He was skeptical, because in Florida it was alligators and not crocs that usually inhabited fresh water. I reminded him that I was a zoologist who knew the difference, but he went anyway "just to make sure."

That left Mike Nunez and me to explore the rest of the island. We split up – Mike going north and me south – but we agreed to meet back at the cabin in no more than two hours to compare notes.

I had my binoculars and camera, some evidence bags, and a field guide titled "Birds of the West Indies." It was left over from college days. Still fresh in my mind was the fleeting glimpse of a tiny red and green bird during my previous visit. The field guide was old and tattered, but still one of the best, written by a man named James Bond. Most people didn't know it, but Ian Fleming had known the actual James Bond and had gotten permission to use his name for the fictional character in his 007 spy novels.

I followed the path from the cabin about half way back to where I had tied up my canoe, and then headed off cross-country toward the south end of the island. It was rough going. There were no trails. The undergrowth was thick and so were the bugs. It took me about a half hour to reach an impenetrable growth of mangroves at the southernmost point of the key. There were some birds around, including a half-dozen white-crowned pigeons, a pair of gray catbirds, and one male cardinal. None of these birds was unusual or unexpected.

I anticipated an empty-handed return to the cabin, and had just started back when something red and gold caught my eye at the base of a black mangrove tree. I put on some gloves and picked it up. It was a 16-gauge shotgun shell. It had been fired, probably recently based on the lack of corrosion on the brass. I placed the shell in an evidence bag and searched the surrounding area for more but didn't find any.

That was an interesting discovery, but it paled in

comparison with the next one. A bird started calling from high in the foliage of a gumbo limbo tree just ahead. It was a soft rolling trill, repeated over and over again in monotonous sequence. The call was familiar somehow, but the place was all wrong. I walked around the base of the tree scanning up into the branches with my binoculars, to no avail. The bird kept vocalizing, but it stayed out of sight. I was just about to give up when I remembered where I had heard that call before. It was on Cuba, five years ago, when Katie and I had traveled on one of those pre-arranged tours for our honeymoon. We were on a field trip southeast of Havana when our guide, who was a very good ornithologist, had taken pride in pointing out one of the island's common endemic birds – the Cuban tody.

Had the little red and green bird I'd seen three days earlier on Schwimley Key been a tody? It made sense but then it didn't. The colors and size and call were right, but the location didn't fit. Todies are small distant relatives of kingfishers, known from the West Indies but nowhere else. To my knowledge, not a single tody had ever been seen in North America.

Todies are year-round residents, meaning that they do not migrate and probably don't even wander around very much. But stranger things have happened, or at least equally strange. In 2016 a bird called the Cuban vireo showed up in Key West – another supposedly non-migratory species found only on that particular island. I recalled one of my college profs pointing out the obvious – that most birds had wings and they could fly, so anything was possible. I'd also had bird-watching clients who regaled me with stories about odd birds showing up in unexpected places. Ornithological lore was full of such things. But a tody in Florida? They were bright little birds, and charming in a way. Maybe somebody had smuggled in a pair as pets, and they'd gotten away? I knew Florida was full of exotic escapees, from parrots to pythons.

The calls continued and I kept looking. The deadline to rendezvous back at the cabin was nearly at hand, but I wasn't about to leave. And my motive wasn't just academic. If in fact there were a population of Cuban todies on Schwimley Key, it would cause an uproar. No doubt the National Park Service would rekindle and redouble whatever efforts they had once made to wrest the island out of private hands.

Did the appearance of this little bird on Schwimley Key have anything to do with Mable's disappearance off of it? And if so, who was responsible and what was their motive?

But all of this was premature. Had I actually heard a Cuban tody? There was only one sure way to prove it, besides shooting it out of the tree. I could just imagine the look on Mike Nunez' face if I came back with the splattered remains of a dead tody in an evidence bag. And anyway, I hadn't brought a gun. The obvious thing to do was get a photograph. I backed away from the gumbo limbo about thirty feet, sat down and waited, with my camera at the ready.

It took about twenty minutes before the little tody – and it *was* a tody – emerged from the foliage and flew down into a patch of wild poinsettia where it flitted around catching insects. I got better than a dozen shots before it flew off to the west, out of sight.

Gangbusters!

Contrary to my expectations, Stella and Penny were the only ones around when I got back to the cabin. They were sitting on the ground with their backs to the front door, evidently comparing notes. They stopped talking and looked up as I approached.

"Hey, Sam. How'd it go out there?"

I decided to hold the specifics until the entire group had reassembled. "Not bad. How about you? Find anything interesting here?"

Stella shook her head. " Not much. We dusted for prints and got some, but there was no blood spatter."

"What about any paperwork that might give us a clue as to Mabel's background?"

Again Stella said no. "We looked of course, but we didn't find a thing. If I had to guess, I'd say the place has been scrubbed. Assuming this woman got herself in harm's way, which seems pretty obvious, the perp must have had strong motive to hide her identity from anybody else who might come out here."

Just then Mike and Dave came out of the woods together, walking in our direction. Both were empty-handed, but that didn't necessarily mean anything. I hoped and expected they might have stories to tell, just like me.

Mike took charge once we were all together, suggesting we take seats around an old picnic table down next to the pond, and make our reports. He asked me to go first. Naturally I started with the tody.

Dave Ackerman was skeptical until I showed him the images on my camera. Then he just sat there, obviously dumbfounded.

Penny Raintree got all excited. "Can I look? I've never seen a tody except in a book." I handed her my camera and she started scrolling through the images. "Oh wow, what a cool bird!"

Stella didn't get it. "What's the big deal about some little bird?"

I attempted to explain. "It's just that this little bird has no business being anywhere except Cuba. And evidence of a breeding population on Schwimley Key, assuming there is one, would put this place right at the top of conservation priorities for the National Park Service."

Mike enthusiastically agreed. "We need to find out about this right away, Sam. This may or may not have anything to do with the missing woman, but that's almost beside the point. I want you to survey this whole key for todies, and do it as soon as possible. The Park will pay you for the work." He paused, shaking his head. "And in the mean time we need to keep this strictly among ourselves. Can you imagine what would happen if news of this got out to the birdwatchers? Talk about messing up a crime scene!"

Stella apparently had never encountered the zeal of dedicated birdwatchers. "I thought this place was off limits to the public, so why would that be a problem?"

"Finding a Cuban tody in the Florida Keys would be the coup of a lifetime, Stella. Mike's right. Some of those folks would stop at nothing. But unfortunately, the cat may already be out of the bag." I lifted the evidence bag with the shotgun shell out of my daypack and held it up. "Of course if somebody has been trying to shoot these little birds off the island, he or she may be no more anxious to publicize it than we are."

Mike suggested I could be jumping to conclusions, and he probably was right. "That shell doesn't prove anything. There are all sorts of logical reasons somebody might have been shooting out here. Perhaps Mabel was out hunting something to eat."

I asked Stella if they had found a shotgun in the cabin.

She shook her head. "No, no weapons at all."

Dave Ackerman pointed to my evidence bag. "That's a sixteen-gauge shell, right? Hell, you hit a little bird with that and all you'd have left are little pieces of feathers."

I laughed. "That would be the idea wouldn't it, if somebody wants todies to disappear of Schwimley Key? For sure nobody would think of shooting a crocodile with bird shot. Speaking of which, Dave, did you find any over there by the pond?"

Ackerman cleared his throat. "You were right, they're crocodiles and not alligators. I counted four live ones in the water or lying right next to it. But it was farther on over toward the coast that things got really interesting. That's where I found a couple of rotting carcasses, and they'd been skinned."

Had Mabel been poaching? Was that one of her sources of income? Or had someone else been there? Stella Reynard asked Dave to show Penny Raintree the site, in hopes they might find some forensic evidence. He agreed, and the two of them set off while Stella, Mike, and I stayed at the table to continue our postmortem.

We hadn't yet heard from Mike, so I asked him

whether he'd found anything on the north side of the island.

He shifted his position on the bench, uneasy. "Uh, yeah. There's a shell mound up there, right at the edge of a little sandy beach."

I knew that shell mounds were accumulations of debris left over from hunting, fishing, and food-gathering activities of Indians, often dating back to pre-Columbian times. They were valuable for archaeologists attempting to learn about the lifestyles of earlier societies, in this case of the First Americans. Intact shell mounds varied in size, and might not be obviously different from ordinary topographic features such as small hills. I asked Mike how he was sure.

"Because this one has been excavated. Or I should say partially excavated. About half the thing has been cut away, and a bunch of stuff is exposed along one side."

Stella apparently thought the shell mound was a more interesting find than my tody. "What kind of stuff?"

He shrugged. "Mostly pieces of shell. At least one of them looked like it came from a sea turtle. I didn't want to poke around very much."

It wasn't hard to figure our Mike's reluctance to dig up the shell mound, though he must have been tempted. First, the Park Service had very strict policies about the treatment of prehistoric sites. But second, and probably more important in his case, I knew that Native Americans were particularly loath to disturb anything that had been left by their ancestors.

~ ~ ~

About a half hour later Dave and Penny came back and joined us at the picnic table. They had taken photos of the butchering site and collected one small crocodile carcass as evidence, but they had found no other forensic evidence that might give us a clue about the identity of the poacher or poachers. Based on its state of decay, Penny guessed that the croc had been dead no more than two or three days.

I reminded Dave about Snook's probable sighting of the two guys in a gray Yellowfin the day of my boat fire. "It seems like the same crew we found working out at Long Key may have been hanging around here. By the way, did you get anywhere with the registration on that Yellowfin?"

"Some, but apparently not enough. Fish and Wildlife ran a search on owners of late-models that happened to be gray. Turns out one of them belongs to Hector Morales."

"You mean the guy with the pet shop up in Miami? The one who might be dealing in illegal items, like stuff made from crocodile hide?"

"The very same."

"I assume you got a search warrant?"

Dave shook his head. "We're working on it. The Judge wanted to know how many gray Yellofins were out there before he would consider signing it."

Mike Nunez muttered something I couldn't hear, and rolled his eyes. "But let's assume those two guys are working for Morales and using his Yellowfin to cruise around here hunting crocs. I still have to wonder how they ever expected to make land on Schwimley, given the shallow water that wraps all around this place."

"Maybe they had help," said Stella.

Dave shrugged his broad shoulders in puzzlement. "Help from who?"

"It's whom."

"What?"

She grinned, slapping a mosquito that had landed on her arm. "Never mind. I'm just speculating here, but perhaps this Mabel person was in on it, assuming that was her little wooden boat we saw tied up at the end of the canal when we got here this morning."

I confirmed it almost certainly was her boat, because it matched the description Flo had given me of the one Mabel used when she came ashore to sell her flowers. "Those two guys could have had their own canoe, but Snooks didn't see one and neither did Dave and I when we confronted them the other day out at Long Key. Right, Dave?"

Dave agreed. "Nope. No sign of a canoe."

CHAPTER 24

It was already four o'clock in the afternoon, and a trip back to Islamorada should have been in order, but apparently Mike Nunez had other ideas.

"Before we all go our separate ways, and while all of this stuff is still fresh in our minds, I think Team Mabel should talk a little strategy."

I liked the part about "Team Mabel."

Mike coughed out a mosquito that had found its way into his mouth. The bugs were starting to get bad. He passed around his bottle of repellent, told us to lather up if we wanted to, but made no move to get up. "Let's start with what we know. We have a woman named Mabel who used to live by herself on Schwimley Key and now she's gone missing. Items of her clothing and some body parts have been found scattered across Florida Bay. We know she grew and sold cut flowers for a living. That's what we know for certain." He paused to swat a mosquito that had landed on his right cheek. It spashed blood when he hit it. "She also could have been poaching crocodiles, looting an archaeological site, and maybe even gunning Cuban todies, if that's what the shotgun shell was all about. Or maybe someone else has been doing all those things. Anybody want to suggest where we go from here?"

I seized the opportunity. There was something that had been bothering me about this whole Schwimley Key business, and this seemed like a good time to bring it up. The fact was I had become increasingly uncomfortable, maybe even suspicious, that we weren't getting the full story. It had started on my first visit to the island, and nothing since had diminished my concern. Much as I liked the guy, it was time to confront Mike Nunez.

"You know, Mike, there are some things about this whole set-up that just don't make sense."

He got fidgety. "Like what?"

"Like who actually owns this place, and why the Park Service hasn't managed to get hold of it after all these years. I mean look, anybody can see this little key's an ecological gem. I just can't understand why nobody seems to know anything about it. Or care, apparently."

Mike just sat there looking glum, so I kept going. "It's not as if the Park staff doesn't know what's out here. Even if the owners – whoever they are – wouldn't let you on, there's always Google Earth. I had no trouble spotting the pond that way before Snooks and I came out here the other day. And that's not all. These woods are mature and diverse and there's all kinds of wildlife, including crocodiles and white-crowned pigeons. And now with Cuban tody..."

Mike put up a hand to cut me off. "Yeah, okay Sam, okay. I get it. And you're right, I guess it's time I filled you all in on a couple of things."

There was a lengthy pause. When he finally spoke, it was slow and measured.

"When you first made the possible connection between those blue shoes and a woman named Mabel living on Schwimley Key, I naturally wanted to find out more about this place. So I started poking around up at

Park headquarters. And right away I ran into roadblocks."

"What roadblocks?"

"I'll try not to exaggerate. 'Stonewalled' probably is too strong a term. Let's just say I got the distinct impression that the Park Service brass really didn't want to talk about Schwimley, or let me into their archives. It was only after I started throwing around words like 'murder' and 'crime scene' that they finally opened up."

"We don't actually know it was murder, do we?"

Mike shrugged. "Maybe, maybe not. But I wanted to get their attention."

"And it worked, right?" The suspense was killing me, and Mike's reluctance to talk wasn't like him. "Can't you just tell us what you found out, for god's sake?"

Mike wiped a hand across his forehead, and swatted at another mosquito. "I'm not totally clear on all the details, okay? But here's the bottom line: this Mabel person we're looking for? Turns out her last name is Schwimley."

There was a stunned silence, finally broken by Dave Ackerman. "So this is her island?"

Mike nodded. "As far as anybody can tell, she is – or was – the last surviving member of a family that has owned this place since the 1930s, long before Everglades National Park was officially dedicated in 1947."

I was curious about the particulars. "Why hasn't the Park Service tried to get hold of it after all these years? From what we're learning, Mabel was living hand-to-mouth. Wouldn't she have been willing to sell?"

Mike shook his head. "Apparently Mabel was a true recluse. She liked living out here all by herself, and she had no interest in selling. But there's another thing, and this is where it gets tricky."

Mike paused, maybe for effect. "The other reason that Schwimley Key hasn't sold is the Park Service didn't want to buy."

I was starting to get pissed off. "And why the hell not? I know it isn't your job to negotiate Park real estate, but still..."

"Sam, it's not as bad as you think. As I'm sure you know, Washington has been strangling our budget for years. The million or so it might take to buy this place, even with a willing seller, would come at the expense of other urgent needs, mostly for maintenance. Our whole system is falling apart."

"Yeah, I get that Mike, but acquisition of something as extraordinary as Schwimley might never come again. Surely an appeal for additional funds could be made, perhaps from private sources."

"Except in the long run it might not be necessary. The original deal made with the Schwimley family included two key provisions. First, the contract would expire in the year 2025, after which there could be a re-negotiation. But second, the land could never be sold to another party, and it would revert to the Park when the last surviving Schwimley heir finally died."

"And that would be Mabel?"

"As far as anybody knows, yes."

Stella Reynard had been sitting there like a

spectator at a tennis match, watching Mike and me go back and forth. "Well holy crap Mike, did the whole damned Park Service just become a suspect?"

That actually got a laugh from Dave Ackerman, and Mike took the opportunity to change the subject. "Anyway, people, let's agree on some assignments in terms of where we go from here. First, I think we need a regular presence on the island until this case is resolved. Stella, can your department handle that?"

"We're stretched pretty thin as it is, Mike. I'll ask, but I don't know who we could spare."

"Same with the Park Service. With all the deferred maintenance, my boss says every extra dollar goes there and not into more personnel. But I have an idea. Sam, you're going to be working out here on the tody search. Maybe you could step it up a little and get out here at least once a day for the next couple of weeks?"

"I'm supposed to be a fishing guide, Mike, not a cop."

"I'd say yes and no on that. After all, there was a reason we paid for you to take all that law enforcement training. Maybe now it's time for us to collect on our investment. And anyway, for the moment you're a guide without a boat or an income, right?"

He had a point, but the best I could manage was an unenthusiastic shrug. "Sure, I suppose so."

"Here's what I'm suggesting. I'll leave my Park Service skiff here for you to use until you're ready to get back into the guiding business. Hopefully by then we'll have this whole thing wrapped up. In the mean time, do your visits to Schwimley and keep us informed."

It sounded like a reasonable plan. Mike agreed to

pay my usual per diem, which would help a lot. I did have one condition. "If you want me to do this, I'd like my law-enforcement status a bit more official."

"Official as in how? You're already a paid consultant for the Park Service."

"I'd like to be deputized by Stella, so it would apply to the whole county and not just Park land."

Stella said she'd look into it. "But what about a weapon? Do you want to be *that* kind of a deputy?"

"No, that won't be necessary, Stella. The Park Service already has issued me a Glock."

"And you might want to bring it along on your trips out here," said Mike. "Just in case."

I wanted some clarification. "All right, but just what am I supposed to do if I run into somebody making mischief?"

Mike and Stella looked at each other, as if they weren't exactly sure who was in charge. Mike broke the silence. "Just keep an eye on things and let me or Stella know right away if you find anybody – and I mean *anybody* – nosing around. But don't get in anybody's face. I don't want my birdwatcher-in-chief getting shot up before you have a chance to find out if we have a breeding population of Cuban todies on our hands. Maybe that bird you just saw was just a loner. That would make this whole situation a lot less interesting from a biodiversity standpoint."

"That individual might be more of a loner than it used to be, if somebody's been out here shooting at 'em. But in any event, I'd be happy and interested in doing a tody count." I was less interested in the cop part, and 'happy' didn't come to mind at all, but I agreed to the plan.

Once we had that settled, Mike suggested we get back to the Schwimley case. "I'd like to start by making a list of all the possible motives and suspects, assuming for the moment that she was the victim of foul play. Anybody want to begin?"

Dave Ackerman raised his hand. "All right, how about this? Mabel caught some crocodile poachers out here and got in harm's way. And like I said, Fish and Wildlife already has its eye on Hector Morales as a possible trafficker up in Miami. We know he owns a Yellowfin. Neither of the two guys we saw in it the other day fits the description of Morales, but they could be working for him. That's the angle my department would like to pursue if it's all right with you. Stella? Mike?"

They both agreed. Then Mike offered another possible scenario. "Maybe her mishap had nothing to do with crocodiles, but instead with that looted shell mound I found this morning. And Sam, didn't you hear a rumor that Mabel might have been expecting some extra income?"

Stella frowned, putting some vertical wrinkles across her otherwise flawless forehead. "And the motive for murder, assuming there was one?"

"Maybe it's like with the crocodiles. Either she caught somebody out there digging in the mound, or she was the culprit herself and her fence got greedy once he figured out what was here."

"Fencing what? I mean what's so valuable about a shell mound?"

"Can't be sure," said Mike. "But I did see pieces of

sea turtle shell sticking out of the exposed part. There's a market for jewelry made from that material, all strictly illegal if it came from the U.S. And there could be Indian artifacts buried in with all the other debris. Maybe there's some unscrupulous jeweler out there. In any case, I'd like to handle that line of inquiry, unless anybody has objections."

Nobody did, but Stella had a question about the identity of a possible fence.

Dave Ackerman and I looked at each other, apparently because we both had the same idea. I let him do the talking. "You know Pete Donovan, right? He owns that tourist trap called Pelican Pete's Emporium."

Stella nodded. "Sure, but what's the deal there?"

"We suspect him of trafficking in illegal contraband behind the counter. In fact we caught him once, with Sam's help. It was just one piece, a pendant made from turtle shell. But there are rumors about more sea turtle items, Indian stuff, maybe even crocodile products as far as that goes."

Stella thought it was a stretch, but we all agreed that Mike should pursue the shell mound angle just in case.

As for Stella herself, she volunteered two things. First, she would work up what little forensic evidence they had found in the cabin. "And then, no matter where that gets us, I'll take the lead in digging further into the background of this Mabel Schwimley. Where did she come from? Who were her parents? Where did she go to school? Was she ever married? How did she end up out here all by herself? My department has access to all sorts of national databases that might hold some clues."

I was curious about those things myself. "Care to speculate on any angles related to her disappearance or death?"

"Speculation is all it would be at this point, Sam. But suppose for the sake of argument there are other people out there who could profit from her death."

"You mean like a long-lost relative, or maybe the whole National Park Service?"

That last part was supposed to be a joke, but it must have hit a little too close to home, because Mike shot me a look.

"Just kidding of course."

CHAPTER 25

So now I was a fishing guide without a boat who had just been hired as a birdwatcher by the National Park Service. It was an almost comical change of plans, but at least there was a plan. The same could not be said for my personal life.

The one-nighter with Flo hovered in the background like an interrupted dream. There was regret mixed with fear. At first I tried to convince myself it was just the reasonable fear that Katie would find out, but that wasn't all of it. Introspection has never been my long suit, which may explain why it took a while to get around to the rest. I was afraid of what was going to happen the next time – and there surely would be a next time – when Flo and I ran into each other. Would she give me the big wink and maybe flirt a little? Or would she act like it had never happened and then go about pouring my drinks as if I were just another customer? Either way, or any way in between, I realized I had no damned clue how the whole thing was going to play out.

There was one obvious truth to be faced. Part of me wished the whole thing had never happened. But when I replayed the night we spent together, another part of me wanted to do it all over again.

I finally made contact with Katie the evening the law enforcement team and I got back from Schwimley Key. It had not been satisfactory.

Her phone rang four times and I thought it was

going to voice mail again when she finally answered. "Sorry I missed your calls. I've been busy with work."

"Boy I guess you have. Must be something important."

"Not really. Just busy. What about you?"

I started filling her in on the doings out at Schwimley Key, but stalled out short of the details when I couldn't detect any real interest on her part. "Any chance you can come down this weekend?"

"Sam I'd love to, but the local DA has dumped a couple of forensic cases in my lap and he's pressing for results."

"Does any of it involve animals?"

"No, just plant stuff. One is stomach contents. The other is identifying some seeds they got off tire treads. Of course you're welcome to come up anyway."

"Really?"

"What do you mean, 'really?' Of course, really. What's wrong, Sam?"

"Nothing, sorry. I guess this whole business has me on edge." I explained why I wouldn't be able to get up to Lauderdale until next week at the earliest, because of my duties out on Schwimley Key. "You're sure you can't get away? I won't be staying overnight out there, at least not all the time."

There was a moment's hesitation. "Sorry."

"I love you, Katie."

"Love you too. Bye."

Something wasn't right. Or was it just my imagination coupled with a good dose of guilt? There was no way that Katie could have learned about Flo and me, unless it came from Flo herself, and that was something I could not imagine.

These musings were interrupted by two phone calls in quick succession. The first was from Billy Nelson from the Lower Matecumbe Boat Yard. He'd found a used Yamaha that looked good, at a price my insurance was willing to pay. I told him to go for it. He'd already stripped out all the bad wiring and was about half finished with the fiberglass repairs. It would be about a week before he was done, but I decided it could have been a lot worse.

I had just hung up with Billy when the phone rang again and this time it was Snooks. He'd been up to see the docs in Tavernier, and they said he could go back to work.

"So, uh, I guess I need my boat back. How long before yours is ready?"

I told him it would still be another few days, but it wasn't important because I was about to go to work for the Park Service counting todies, and I had a ride. "Let me pull your Dolphin out of the canal and I'll trail it right over."

"Good, thanks. And afterwards, wanna go for a beer? I'm thirsty. And what the hell is a tody?"

I gave him the short version and asked where he wanted to go.

Snooks snorted. "What, is there some place other than the Safari Lounge where we like to drink, besides your deck?"

"No, I suppose not. See you in about a half hour."

So here came another meeting with Flo, ready or not, assuming she was working that night.

~ ~ ~

Flo was there as usual, and she came right over as soon as we found a place at the bar. She didn't wink or flirt, but neither did she give me the cold shoulder. Her green eyes caught mine as she took our order.

Things had changed, of course, and I could see it right there in her eyes. Exactly how had they changed? I couldn't tell for sure, but it seemed there was a warmth. And right behind that was a question. She held my gaze for no more than three seconds. Then she turned away and got busy pouring our beers and rustling up some chicken wings from the kitchen.

The rest of the evening was just the usual chitchat, and it wasn't until later that night when it came to me what actually had happened back at the Dead Animal Bar. Flo was leaving it all up to me. The decision should have been an easy one. I was a married man, in love with a beautiful intelligent woman, right? Then why was I stewing instead of sleeping? And besides, who said Flo wasn't beautiful and intelligent in her own way?

CHAPTER 26

Counting birds is a complicated business because they keep moving around. Suppose you find a bird in a particular place, and then find another one of the same species a day later in some other place. How would you know if they were different individuals or if you had counted the same bird twice? One way would be to mark each bird in some distinctive way, such as with colored plastic bands attached to their legs. The trick is you have to catch them first. That rarely is easy and sometimes it hurts the birds. It certainly didn't seem like a good idea when I was dealing with something as small – and almost certainly rare – as the todies on Schwimley Key.

I envied botanists like Katie. Plants just sit there patiently, waiting to be marked and counted and mapped. Piece of cake.

How was I going to figure out how many Cuban todies were living on Schwimley? Ornithologists often resort to measures of relative abundance without necessarily knowing exactly how many individuals are out there. This works if all you need to discover is that one place is lots better for the birds than another. For example, I could stand in the center of Schwimley Key and count all the todies I saw or heard in fifteen minutes. Then I could move to another key, or even to Cuba if they would let me in, and do the same thing. If I counted ten todies on Schwimley and only five on the other island, then I could conclude that Schwimley was twice as good for them as the other place. But I was about to undertake a one-key survey, so that approach wasn't going to be helpful.

The technique I settled on is called spot-mapping. The plan was to walk systematically over the whole island searching for todies, and then to mark their locations on a map using a hand-held global positioning device. Assuming individual todies tended to stick to relatively small territories, as the literature suggested, then I likely would find the same bird repeatedly in the same general area day after day. If it worked like it was supposed to, the result of several days worth of surveys would be clusters of points on my map. The total number of clusters – not the individual points – would equate to the number of todies on the island, or pairs of todies if they were living that way.

That night I drew a rough map of Schwimley Key and made several copies on the little printer I kept attached to my computer. I set out the next morning with one of the maps attached to a clipboard, along with a GPS, binoculars, a camera, and a handful of evidence bags just in case. The plan was to complete one survey of the whole island, finding and marking the locations of as many todies as possible, and then repeat the process over the next several days, creating one map per day. It was unclear at the outset just how many surveys would be needed, because it depended on the results. The more sightings the better, but equally important would be the tightness of the clusters of those sightings.

I drove Mike Nunez's Park Service skiff as far in toward the edge of the island as I could without running aground, then offloaded myself and my gear into the canoe for the rest of the trip. Normally I would have been concerned about leaving a boat alone out there all day, where anybody could come along and steal it. But the Park Service logo and big lettering on the side made that unlikely.

Several things got in my way that first day, and they combined to make the survey less than perfect, although I eventually got the job done. The first was Mabel Schwimley's green wooden boat, which sat up on shore just where it had been the first time I had been out there. Because it apparently had not been moved, I wondered if Stella and her crime scene crew might have forgotten to include it in their forensic survey. I decided to check it out just in case.

Leaves and other plant debris covered the slatted floorboards, suggesting the boat had not been used for some time. Other than that it looked empty. I tipped the craft up on its side and looked underneath. There was nothing except damp soil and rotting debris. I dropped the old rowboat back down on its keel with a thud, and that was when something rolled out from under the front seat.

It was the shell of a young sea turtle, about four by six inches. I picked it up for a closer look and found two neat round holes drilled into the anterior end. The shell was faded and worn but I could tell it was from a hawksbill – the local species most valued for its colorful scales. In light of the holes, which clearly looked to be of human origin, I wondered if it had been used as some sort of ornament or decoration. Had it come from the shell mound Mike had discovered on the north end

167

of the island? If so, how had it ended up in the bottom of Mabel Schwimley's boat? Had I just screwed things up by touching it with my bare hands? Better late than never, I secured the shell in a paper evidence bag and stored it in the canoe before proceeding to the interior of the island.

Mike would want to see this.

I began the tody count on the south side of the island, working my way systematically back and forth along an east-west line, moving about twenty yards north at the end of each sweep. The wind had started to blow, and I regretted the time lost examining Mabel's boat, because wind speeds often increased as a day progressed. Wind can be a birdwatcher's nemesis, especially in wooded landscapes. The noise drowns out songs and calls, and all that foliage flapping around makes it harder to pick up any movements. My mistake was not having the patience to poke around in the rowboat at the end of the day rather than at the beginning.

Nothing happened for the first hour and a half of my survey, either because there weren't any birds or because I couldn't see or hear them over the wind. I was just about to give it up and come back the next day, when the wind briefly abated and I heard a familiar call about fifty yards ahead. It was faint but clear, and not far from the place where I had seen that first tody two days earlier.

This time there were two of them, sticking close to an area where local runoff had carved a small vertical bank into the rolling terrain. There was a small hole in the bank, and my hopes rose. Like their kingfisher relatives, todies nest in holes in the ground. I sat down where there was a good view, with my back to a big gumbo-limbo tree, got out my camera, and waited.

It seemed like forever, but it couldn't have been more than twenty minutes before one of the two birds flew in with a good-sized beetle in its bill. It disappeared into the hole and then came right back out minus the beetle. I had found a nest with young. It was not possible to determine whether the male or female had fed the young, because in todies the sexes look pretty much alike. But I had seen enough. There was at least one pair of Cuban todies breeding on Schwimley Key.

Now it was time to go looking for more.

I had gone no more than a hundred yards when something happened that made me forget all about birds. I was walking along, scanning up into the trees, when suddenly there was a strange rubbery sort of feeling underfoot. It was like nothing I had experienced before. I looked down into the black lidless eyes of a monster.

The eastern diamondback is the largest rattlesnake in the world, and I had just stepped on one. Six-footers are not uncommon, and this one was close to it. Even mere four-footers are capable of swallowing cottontail rabbits whole. The snake began trashing about, trapped under my right boot. By pure luck I had come down just behind the snake's head. As a result it was unable to twist around far enough to bury its fangs in my leg, which otherwise clearly would have happened.

There was nothing rational, not even conscious, about my next action. All the appropriate muscles fired, boosted by a big shot of adrenalin. The result might have qualified as the world record standing high jump, if there had been any such Olympic event. There also was backwards trajectory to it. I landed hard on my butt about six feet from the takeoff point. My backside would be sore the next day, but at least I was safely out of harm's way.

The creepiest part was that the snake never rattled. It coiled and stayed right where it was, while I stood up, brushed the dirt off the back of my pants, and waited for my pulse to return to something like normal. Then we went our separate ways.

A man named Sandy Sprunt, who was a seasoned Florida naturalist, once told me that diamondbacks in the Keys largely have gone quiet over the years. Rattlesnakes don't rattle to frighten their prey, they do it to warn potential predators not to come any closer. The strategy doubtless works for animals other than people, and even for some of us, and it probably has saved the lives of innumerable rattlesnakes. But just enough of us over the years have used those rattling rattles to find the snakes and then dispatch them. There aren't nearly as many rattlesnakes in the Florida Keys as there used to be, and it is the naturally quiet ones that have survived. Call it evolution in action.

I completed my first survey of Schwimley Key over the next four hours. There weren't any more snakes, but neither were there any more todies. The wind was blowing hard by the time I left, and it was all I could do to paddle back out to Mike's boat. Then it was a choppy ride all the way home. Some big waves broke over the bow of his little Maverick, and I was thoroughly soaked by the time I reached the shelter of my own neighborhood.

Wind is a dirty little secret about the Florida Keys, especially if you are a fisherman or a birdwatcher or a boater, and I was all three. The wind and the tides control our lives. There are days, sometimes whole weeks, when the biggest job for a guide is to keep a client safe and dry on the way to someplace sheltered and calm enough to fish.

Snooks must have gotten blown out that day, because he was waiting at the dock when I got back, and it wasn't even four o'clock. He knew about a hidden door key, and he must have heard me coming, because he was waiting with two beers when I pulled up beside my dock.

I tied up the Maverick, took my gear into the house, and checked for messages. There were none, so I went back outside and sat down beside Snooks.

He took a sip. "So how did it go out there?"

"Windy. How about you?"

"Same, but that's not what I'm talking about."

"You mean the todies? Found a couple." Then I told him about the snake.

"Jesus Christ. You okay?"

"Sure. It missed. You get any fishing done?"

"Yeah, if you could call it that. Had a semi-googan today who insisted he wanted to catch yellow-tailed snappers out on the ocean side. I never should have let him talk me into it."

"He get seasick?"

Snooks chuckled and swallowed some beer. "No, I'll give him that much credit. We pitched around for a couple of hours out on a patch that has been hot lately, before we gave it up."

"Did he get dinner?"

"Oh sure. I almost always can do that."

For anybody else that would have been a brag. For Snooks, it was just a statement of fact.

We both looked up as a squadron of brown pelicans flew over, no doubt on the prowl for anybody in the neighborhood cleaning fish. It must have been a slow day all around, because the last we saw of the birds they were flying off to the northeast, still in tight formation.

Snooks fidgeted with his ponytail and then took another pull on his Yuengling. "You okay otherwise?"

I assumed he was talking about my Hell's Bay. "Yeah, Bill says it's coming along fine. Should be ready by the time this tody gig is over."

He shook his head and looked down the canal where a lobster fishing boat had just come home for the day. Laughing gulls were circling in, expecting scraps when the crew washed down the deck. "Wasn't asking about that."

"What, then?"

"Yesterday, at the Dead Animal, something didn't feel right."

"What was it?"

He shrugged. "Just something about Flo is all. Didn't seem herself. I thought maybe you knew what was going on."

"Nothing's going on that I know of. Maybe she was tired, or had a headache or something."

That stood him up. "Okay then, I'll be seeing you. Thanks for the beer."

Snooks had to know I'd just fed him some bullshit. We'd been friends for a long time, and so it made for a very bad end to an otherwise interesting day. It didn't get any better when I went inside to call Katie, because she didn't answer, as usual.

Two hours later the phone rang and my hopes rose. But it was only Mike Nunez, wanting to know how it had gone out at Schwimley. He was happy about the todies, alarmed about the snake, and anxious to see the turtle shell.

I didn't sleep worth a damn that night. It could have been the wind, which kept rattling my windows until nearly dawn. I tried to tell myself that was all there was to it, but I knew better. Maybe some guys could cheat on their wives, lie to their best friends about it, and then sleep like a baby. But I wasn't one of them.

CHAPTER 27

I tried to drag myself out of bed the next morning about six, but it didn't happen. The day before had been too long, and the night too short. During a brief moment of consciousness I made a plan for the day, but then I flopped back over in bed and didn't wake up again until nearly eleven. I couldn't remember having slept in that late since high school days, when it had been a regular occurrence on weekends.

Three cups of coffee and a shower finally got me going. By noon the wind mostly had died away, and it was time to put the plan into action. Afternoon bird counts weren't usually as productive as those in the morning, because adult birds usually got full of food by lunch time. The only exception was during breeding season, when finding adequate food for a nest full of youngsters could take all the daylight hours. If there were other todies breeding on Schwimley Key, I ought to be able to find them before the sun went down. Either way I needed to get out there before dark in order to set up camp, because my plan included an overnight stay on the island. That way I could start the next survey at first light.

A fateful decision, as it turned out.

I loaded up my pack with enough food and water for forty-eight hours, along with the bird survey equipment, a change of clothes, and my Glock. Then I rummaged around in the storeroom and unearthed an old sleeping bag left over from Boy Scout days. It had seen no use in years, and it smelled like everything else in Florida that had stayed indoors for too long in a damp dark place.

The only tasks remaining before departure for the island were three phone calls. Katie didn't answer, as usual, but Stella and Mike both did and I told them my plan. Stella said to be careful. Mike said to let him know if anything came up.

The trip out to Schwimley was uneventful, and everything looked just as it had the day before. I went first to the cabin, deposited my gear and supplies, and opened things up to let in some fresh air. Then I walked to the north side of the island and began my second survey. If I only made it to the center of the island by evening, the rest could be finished the following morning.

The winds were calm and the skies were clear. Conditions were perfect for an efficient and potentially productive bird count, except for one thing. Unlike the first half of yesterday, I spent at least a third of the time watching the ground instead looking up into the trees. Snake encounters will do that to you.

I started at the shell mound about one-thirty, tracing a zigzag path southward across the interior of the island. The first interesting discovery came about an hour later, but it wasn't a tody. There were two more shotgun shells on the ground, lying right next to each other. Both had been fired and both were 16-gauge, just like before. The tody hunter, if that's who it was, clearly had gotten around. He or she evidently hadn't bothered picking up the used ammo. But after all, who was there to notice?

I put on gloves this time, picked up the shells and put them in evidence bags, and then looked around for dead birds. There were none, but that didn't mean much. Even if a dead tody were lying out there someplace not yet been eaten by a scavenger, the odds of my coming on that tiny speck of feathers were as good as zero.

Flying and singing todies were another matter, and by dark I had found two more pairs of the little birds, at least one of which was feeding young in a nest. It was exhilarating, tempered only by the possibility, even the likelihood, that there had been a lot more of them before the gunner had set to work. But still, three pairs were more than enough to put Schwimley on the map.

Something occurred to me as I made my way back toward Mabel's cabin for the night. If the hunter had been paying attention, he or she must have known the job of exterminating those little birds off the island wasn't over.

The cabin and its supplies proved adequate for an overnight stay. The Coleman lanterns still worked, and there were enough charcoal briquettes to heat up two cans of beans and one of creamed corn on the barbecue. A nip of Maker's Mark preceded the dinner, and another one followed. After all, it had been a satisfactory day of discovery. It deserved a little celebration. I had intended to roll my sleeping bag out under the stars, but the mosquitoes quickly changed my mind. Instead, I carried the bag and the lantern back inside, shut the door, and hoped the cabin didn't leak too much air.

Mabel must have learned how to caulk things up,

because only one or two of the little buggers came whining around as I was falling asleep. One thing for sure, there wasn't any noise from traffic or neighbors to keep me awake. In no time I was dead to the world.

I probably had been asleep no more than two or three hours when something loud woke me up. At first I just lay there, trying to figure out what I had heard. Then it came again, and this time there was no doubt. It was a gunshot. I shook myself more fully awake, got out of the sleeping bag, and pulled on my boots. Then came voices. They were male and there were at least two of them. At first I could not make out the words, but then they started getting louder, and I realized the speakers were coming my way.

"Dammit, Luther, quit draggin' your end!"

"Big sonofabitch, ain't he?"

This was not good. I tried to remember if any of my gear remained outside the cabin that could give away my presence. Encountering armed strangers in the dark seemed like a really bad idea, and a part of me wanted to lie low and let them move on. Of course another part of me wanted to go outside and find out who the hell was shooting at things on Schwimley Key in the middle of the night.

I had just about decided to let the intruders pass on by, and then go out and confront them from behind, when the voices stopped. There weren't any footsteps either. I stood there in silence for a half-minute or so, listening in vain for any clue as to the whereabouts of my visitors. I groped my way in the dark toward the little table in the middle of the room where I had left my backpack, trying not to crash into something on the way. I made it as far as the table, then stopped again and listened. Still there was nothing.

It was time to act, so I extracted a flashlight and my Glock from the backpack, opened the door, and stepped out into the night.

What happened next is a little blurry, but the first thing I remember was waking up with my face in the dirt. I rolled over and struggled up to a sitting position. Then I felt for the cause of a headache that was building fast at the base of my skull. It was an egg-sized lump, and my fingers came back wet and tasting of blood.

Then there was the sound of an outboard someplace off to the east, faint and fading but unmistakable. The odds of anybody else being all the way out here in the dark were diminishingly small. The individuals responsible for my headache, and who knew what other sort of mischief, had just escaped Schwimley Key.

There were two options, both of which made sense up to a point. One was to pack up and get myself to the emergency room pronto. But it was pitch-dark and finding my way back to Mike's boat would be tricky, assuming it was still there. The other option was to tuck in for the night, hope the head stayed intact, and then beat it back to Islamorada in the morning after doing a brief look-see around the island. I decided to go for plan B, probably because I was curious to learn who had been out there and what they had been up to.

Cell service was medium-good on Schwimley, so I indulged in a call to Mike Nunez before settling back down to attempt sleep. He was groggy because of the hour, and he sounded both angry and worried when I told him what had happened.

"You sure you don't need help? I probably could get the Coast Guard to do a rescue. They're still mad about the last time you stiffed them."

"No, that's okay Mike. I'm feeling a little better. I'll call you first thing when I get back in the morning."

"Yeah, you be sure and do that. But as long as you called, what about the todies?"

I had forgotten all about those little birds that had no business being in the Florida Keys. I filled him in and he got pretty excited.

"Good! You say *three* pairs? That's great, Sam!" There was a short pause, but he went on before I could interrupt. "Now you're probably wanting out, so you can go back to something safe, like fishing. And I don't blame you, in light of what just happened."

"You got that wrong, Mike. I don't want out, I want in."

"You're already in, Sam."

"No, I mean *really* in." I paused for effect, or maybe just to collect my thoughts because things were still a little fuzzy. "Look, in the last couple of weeks somebody tried to blow up my boat, then I nearly got bit by a huge rattlesnake, and now I just got conked on the head. This is personal. There are some bad guys messing around on Schwimley Key with who knows what all in mind in addition to shooting little birds, and I want to help catch them. If you don't let me in I'm likely to go chasing after them myself."

"Did you say rattlesnake?"

"Did I forget to mention that?"

"Yeah, Sam, you forgot to mention that. You sure

you're okay?"

He had a right to wonder. "Yeah, I'm okay Mike, really. Just pissed. Like I said, I want in."

"Okay, I hear you. You just take it easy, and we'll talk tomorrow."

CHAPTER 28

I woke up the next morning to the sounds of a cardinal singing outside and a bell ringing in my head. Getting out of the sleeping bag was a struggle, but at least everything still worked. The lump was still there on the back of my head, but the blood had dried and it didn't seem to be getting any bigger.

Coffee was an essential next step, and I had come prepared with a little jar of instant. Foul-tasting, especially because I didn't take time to heat the water before stirring in the magic crystals. But at least it was real caffeine. Breakfast was two energy bars, and then I was ready for the day, more or less.

The long-term plan was to get back to Islamorada and have a doctor take a look at my head. But first a little stroll around the key was in order. What had my assailants been up to last night, and what evidence might they have left to give me a clue?

It didn't take long, because right outside the cabin door there was a trail of blood. It led from the north edge of the pond, past the cabin, and then on down the trail to the head of the canal. The grass between the pond and the cabin was matted down under the blood trail, as if something heavy had been dragged along as it bled out. Whatever those guys had shot, it was way the hell bigger than a tody, and they had taken it with them. I could think of only two possibilities. One was a crocodile. The other was a human.

There were some footprints in the soft earth along

the blood trail, and I regretted not having anything to make casts. I took some photos with my phone, and hoped it might be enough.

Before packing up I followed the blood trail in the opposite direction from the cabin, back toward the lake. The blood stopped at the water's edge, at a point where the vegetation showed signs of recent and heavy disturbance. I searched the area carefully for any sort of evidence that might give a clue as to who had been out here and what they were doing, but found nothing.

I did collect some of the blood in a glass evidence vial I'd somehow had the foresight to bring along. Then I walked back to the cabin, collected up my stuff, and walked out to the head of the canal. It was a relief to see the canoe just where I'd left it the day before, tied up right next to Mabel's rowboat. I loaded my gear on board and pushed off. I was still a bit dizzy, and plenty angry, but at least I was headed home.

The sense of relief didn't last long. I hadn't paddled more than a half dozen strokes when the canoe started filling with water. There was time to reverse course back to the head of the canal before the thing swamped, but only just. I threw my pack up on the bank, got out, and pulled the canoe up out of the water. Then I flipped it over and found four holes in the hull, evenly spaced between the bow and the stern. I must have been unconscious the night before when those clowns had shot up my canoe.

I thought about calling Mike or Stella Reynard for help, but decided to try Snooks first. It would be less embarrassing that way, and besides he had his own canoe. He came on after two rings, and I filled him in.

"Good grief, Sam, what next huh? Listen, I'm with a client but I'll ditch her and come right out."

"You sure? I can call somebody else."

"Nope. It was only a half-day, which is mostly over, and besides we're not catching anything. I'll waive my fee and I expect she'll consider herself lucky."

"Thanks, Snooks. I owe you one. And bring some duct tape. I'm thinking maybe we can patch up my canoe enough to get it out to your skiff."

I was preparing to sit down and wait for Snooks, when something occurred to me. I got up and walked over to the spot where my canoe had been sitting overnight, and there, right in the grass, was a rifle shell. My assailants may have cleaned up after themselves at the spot where they had shot the crocodile, assuming that was their target, but they had gotten sloppy down here.

~ ~ ~

Two hours later I was back home with no boat and no canoe, and with a nasty egg on the back of my head. At least I was still vertical.

Snooks volunteered to drive me up to emergency in Tavernier, and I took him up on it. He hadn't taken the time to change out of his fishing clothes, and his client must have been into bait because he still smelled like shrimp. But beggars cannot be choosers, and I was grateful for the ride. On the way we dropped off my canoe at Billy Nelson's repair place. I said 'don't ask' and Bill didn't, but I saw him shaking his head as we drove away.

Snooks started to laugh as soon as we were back out on the highway.

"What?"

"Must be my day for hospitals. First one for boats, then one for people." Snooks must have noticed my look. "Sorry. Feeble attempt at humor."

"That's all right. But my head still hurts. Just drive, okay?"

The wait in the emergency room was brief, but the visit to the doctor took a while because they wanted to do an x-ray. Fortunately it was negative. After making sure both my pupils were the same size, and that my reflexes were more or less normal, they let me go with a prescription for some sort of pain killer. I recognized the name of the drug. Because it was one of those opioid things that could be addictive, I asked Snooks to skip the pharmacy and take me straight home. The drugs could wait until and unless things got worse. And besides, I needed to be clear-headed. In light of all that had just happened, it was time for Team Mabel to have another meeting.

There was some fresh blood for Stella to get analyzed if we were going to figure out what or possibly who had bled out on Schwimley Key. For Mike Nunez I had a sea turtle shell he could add to his collection of things taken from the mound on the island. But mostly I was anxious to get together with Dave Ackerman from Florida Fish and Wildlife. If my suspicions were right, a couple of poachers had whacked me on the head the night before. If those two bozos in the Yellowfin were the same ones collecting crocodiles on Schwimley, that was bad enough. But now it was personal.

Given my weakened condition, I hoped the crime-fighting trio of Mike, Stella, and Dave would agree to meet that afternoon at my place in Islamorada. As soon as I got home I called Stella and asked her to set up a conference call for the four of us. She quickly got everybody on the line, and I even threw in the offer of free beer. But it didn't work out because none of them could make it. I should have realized that, unlike me, they each led full-time complicated cop lives involving more things besides Mabel Schwimley and her little island home out in Florida Bay.

As an alternative to meeting at my house, everybody suggested I come to each of them separately the next morning, assuming I felt better. I assured them I was doing fine, which was close enough to the truth, so we set things up.

Stella asked if I could start with her and come early, because there was somebody I needed to meet and it had to be no later than eight-thirty. I said no problem and asked who it was.

"My boss."

"The District Commander?"

"Yep. He wants to ask you some questions about this deputy position you requested."

I had not met Captain Danny Pasquale, head of the Islamorada substation, but I'd heard some good things about him.

"Can you give me a hint?"

"Nothing for sure. I described the circumstances best I could, and they seemed sympathetic. But apparently he and the Sheriff are having trouble figuring out what sort of a category you would fit into."

Putting Stella in a jam was the last thing I wanted to do. "Didn't mean to cause trouble. Maybe I should just drop off the evidence."

"No, no, Sam, that's all right. Come on back to my office as soon as you get here, and we'll see what happens. The front desk will be expecting you."

The Sheriff's Department would be step one in the morning. Mike Nunez would be step two. But he said he was stuck in a day-long staff meeting at Park headquarters and could only get away as far as Florida City for a coffee break. We agree to meet at MacDonald's about ten-thirty. It really wasn't an inconvenience once I found out what Dave Ackerman had in mind for step three. It turned out he wanted to send me undercover to a particular pet store up in Miami that specialized in reptiles. I asked him if the owner happened to have a big Yellowfin registered in his name.

"Yep, the very guy."

"I thought you told me the judge wouldn't issue a warrant for that place."

"He changed his mind."

Something told me not to ask how that had happened. Instead, I reminded Dave that I already had met Hector Morales the night he and Pelican Pete Donovan were having drinks together at the Safari Lounge.

"Does he know you're a cop, or a semi-cop, or whatever they call it between you and the Park Service?"

"Not that I know of."

"Well then, it should be all right. And we really do need to get an expert into that pet store. Figure out what the guy's been up to, if anything."

"How do I find this place?"

"You don't. We'll take you there. You're having coffee with Mike at MacDonald's, so that's where we'll meet up. Around noon okay?"

I said it was, and we ended the conference call.

As long as I was going to be spending a bunch of the next day sleuthing in Miami, it seemed like a good time to head on up to Lauderdale afterwards. Katie and I were overdue for some face time. I called both her cell and the land line, but as usual got no answer. I hesitated about what to do, but decided to leave a simple message. She should expect me for dinner, and we could go out someplace if cooking was inconvenient.

I felt better for having taken the plunge, and slept well that night despite a lingering headache.

CHAPTER 29

The next morning Stella Reynard and I were seated on opposite sides of a standard issue metal desk in her cubicle at the Monroe County Sheriff's Department substation in Islamorada. The little office was cramped but tidy, with just barely enough room for her desk, two chairs, a couple of filing cabinets, and a floor-to-ceiling bookshelf crammed to overflowing with piles of paper, some law books, and various magazines. She and I had already met with Captain Pasquale, and I had come away with a piece of paper identifying me as a forensics consultant for the department. It fell short of the deputization I had requested, but it was better than nothing.

Stella was in full uniform, unlike some of the other detectives we passed at their desks on our way back to her office. She wore regulation dark green pants, a short-sleeved white shirt with a star over the left breast pocket, and sergeant stripes on each arm. Her only jewelry was a pair of quarter-sized gold loop earrings. The crisp white shirt did a spectacular job of showing off her bronzed complexion, and the uniform did nothing to hide her trim figure.

Stella had gotten us both a cup of coffee on the way from Captain Pasquale's expansive office back to her little space. We each took a couple of swallows before getting down to business. Even though it was not yet nine-thirty, the coffee already tasted stale and bitter.

"Sorry about that, Sam."

I thought she was talking about the coffee. "I guess that pot must have been left over from the night shift."

She laughed, took another sip, and made a face. Then she looked around for a place to set her half-empty cup that wasn't already occupied by one of the many stacks of paper covering her desktop. The piles were neatly organized, but there were lots of them.

"I don't mean about the coffee. It turns out we don't normally deputize anybody outside the department unless they have a full-time job elsewhere in law enforcement. The Sheriff decided your association with the Park Service fell short of that standard."

"That's okay, Stella. Thanks for trying. I'm sure we can make this work."

"What's in that old briefcase you've been carrying around all morning?"

"It's a gift from your newly-appointed forensics consultant. Three gifts, actually."

The briefcase was a leftover from my days in academia, one of those old-fashioned leather jobs with a flap that buckled over the top. I opened it up, reached inside, and extracted the blood sample along with the rifle and shotgun shells I'd brought back from Schwimley Key. "Thought you might be able to get some prints of those shells, and maybe other sorts of forensics evidence that could link them to a specific weapon. And I'm really curious about the blood."

Stella held up the vial of red fluid and turned it in the light slanting across the room from the small window on the east wall of her office. "Sure it's not your blood from that head wound? And since my new forensics consultant apparently also was a crime victim a couple of nights ago, would he now like to file a report?"

I poked at the lump that was still tender, and summarized what had happened, or at least the parts I remembered.

Stella had been taking notes. "Let me get this straight. You heard one of your guys call the other one 'Luther.' But other than that, you have no idea who they were or what they were doing on the key?"

"Nothing for sure. But my guess is those guys were poaching crocodiles, and that vial of blood you're holding leaked out of one as they were dragging it across the island. Could be human blood, of course, but it should be easy for your lab people to figure that out."

"Why easy?"

"Because reptilian red blood cells have nuclei, whereas human blood cells usually don't. I could do the job in five minutes if I had a microscope. I assume your people have microscopes?"

She didn't like the jab. "All right, Mr. Smart Guy. Wanna do that right now? We only have one tech up here in Islamorada, but I can check to see if she's around."

"That's Dr. Smart Guy to you lady. But sure, let's do it."

Stella made a brief call, then turned her attention back to me. "She can see us in about fifteen minutes. Meanwhile, I have some news I think you'll find interesting."

She tipped back in her chair, laced her fingers behind her head, and didn't say anything.

Finally I couldn't stand it any more, which probably was the idea. "What news?"

"About Mabel Schwimley."

"Did you find something from her cabin?"

Stella shook her head, and her big dark eyes twinkled. "Better than that. Or probably better than that. We did a background check."

"Pay dirt?"

"Pretty much." She picked up one of the manila folders on her desk and flipped it open. "My report's not ready for distribution, but I can summarize." She paused to shuffle through some papers that looked like handwritten notes. "Mabel Schwimley was born on May 17, 1950, in Allenstown, Pennsylvania, the only child of Harold and Doris Schwimley. He in turn was the son of Gustav Schwimley, who apparently made a bundle in banking and railroads back in the twenties and early thirties. One of the things he did with all that money was to buy property and start naming pieces of it after himself."

Stella looked up from her notes. "Times must have changed, because I cannot imagine a real estate mogul doing something like that today."

I caught the look in Stella's eye, and there was no humor in it.

"And one of those places was Schwimley Key?"

"You got it. I guess a part of his ego trip was refusing to sell it to the feds when they started putting together Everglades National Park."

"When was that?"

"The initial authorization was in 1934, but the Park wasn't officially dedicated until 1947. So it was along in there."

"I am impressed, Deputy Reynard. You've really done your homework."

She cocked her head a little to the left and favored me with a smile, revealing prominent white teeth that were perfect except for a little gap between her upper incisors. "Thanks, but it's really not all that hard these days, given all the search tools we have available."

"Did you figure out how Mabel herself ended up on Schwimley?"

Stella shrugged her shapely shoulders. "That's where it gets a little murky, but let's not get ahead of ourselves."

"Sorry." Not that I was interested or anxious or anything.

She went back to shuffling papers. "Mabel graduated from a local Catholic high school in 1967 and then attended Villanova for a couple of years. But there's no record that she ever graduated."

"What about marriage or children?"

Stella shook her head. "No record of that either, nor is it clear how or even when she ended up on Schwimley Key. After the years at Villanova, her trail pretty much goes cold."

"The Park Service might be able to help there."

"Yeah, I'm gonna call Mike Nunez about that once I have this report organized enough to send it to him. But there is one other thing you need to know, and it helps explain her marginal existence."

"How's that?"

"As best we can determine, Mabel's father was a very rich man, but he left it all to charity."

195

"You mean he disowned her?"

"We couldn't find any paper on that, but it seems likely."

"And then somehow she ends up out on that key, living all by herself. You gotta wonder what happened along the way."

Stella nodded. "And it must have been a helluva life once she got there. I wonder how she stayed alive, just selling those cut flowers."

"Don't forget the possibility she also was trafficking in crocodile hides and Indian artifacts."

"Good point. And maybe that's what got her killed."

I thought of one other thing that could be important. "Did you get any photos of Mabel Schwimley? It would help the search effort if we knew what she looked like."

"We had some luck there, but maybe not enough because there's nothing recent. I did get copies of her photo from an old Pennsylvania driver's license, and another one from her high school yearbook."

She opened one of the folders on her desk and shoved across two images. They showed a stern-faced young woman with straight brown hair and a wide face. I couldn't shake the feeling that Mabel Schwimley looked familiar, but Stella was right. The photos had been taken way too long ago to be much help.

I had more questions for Stella before we headed downstairs to have a look at my blood sample, but she squeezed one in ahead of me.

"Say, I just thought of something. Didn't you and Dave Ackerman run into a couple of guys poaching crocodiles out by Long Key a while back? And then maybe your friend Snooks saw them out near Schwimley the day your boat caught fire?"

"You're putting two and two together, and figuring these were the same guys that conked me on the head the other night? Sure, it make's sense, Stella. It's just that we can't make the connection. Not yet, anyway."

"It would help if we learned that a man named Luther works in the reptile pet shop you're going to visit today up in Miami."

No fleas on Stella Reynard.

CHAPTER 30

It turned out the blood probably was reptilian, or at least it definitely wasn't human. The lab tech from the Sheriff's Department said she might be able to nail it down specifically to a crocodile with a little more research and analysis. I suggested somebody with Florida Fish and Wildlife also might be helpful with that, so we agreed to split the sample. After completing the necessary chain of custody forms, I left half the blood with Stella and her tech and headed north to Homestead with the other half.

People who spend much time in the Florida Keys have learned the hard way that getting somewhere on time can be problematic. There's only one road connecting the Keys to the mainland. If anything unusual happens on that road it can make for a real logjam. Some of the logjams around Islamorada are predictable. Traffic can back up for miles when the drawbridge at Snake Creek goes up to let a sailboat pass underneath, or when concert-goers at Founders' Park clog things up trying to find someplace to park.

I'd already passed these particular barriers by the time I reached Stella Reynard's office, and I had every reason to expect smooth sailing from there on up to Homestead. It probably would have worked out that way, except for some googan who jack-knifed his boat and trailer on the Tavernier Creek Bridge. I barely had gotten back out on the highway when everything stopped. We're all used to slow traffic down here, but a dead stop usually meant something bad had occurred.

It was nearly ten o'clock, and my planned ten-thirty rendezvous with Mike Nunez at MacDonald's was in serious jeopardy. Still, I waited twenty minutes before making the call, in hopes things would start moving again. Mike answered after four rings. There were voices in the background, and it was obvious I had interrupted something.

"Hi Mike, it's Sam. And listen, I'm gonna be late. There's some sort of a tie-up on the highway down here. We're not even moving, so who knows when I'll get up there. Guess you're still in that staff meeting?"

"That's all right. Looks like I might not be able to make it myself. Something has come up."

"Anything I should know about?"

"Actually, yes. The boys from NPS Investigative Services are back. Our recent findings out at Schwimley Key have rekindled their interest in the case of the blue shoes."

"Not surprising."

"No, it isn't. And they want a meeting of Team Mabel asap. Everybody around here is all stirred-up, from the Park Superintendent on down."

"Because of the history of the key, the Schwimley family, and all that?"

"You got it. I'm trying to set something up for tomorrow afternoon, here at Park headquarters. You could bring me that turtle shell at the same time. I just got off the phone with Stella, and she's on board. Can you talk to Mike Ackerman when you see him? I couldn't get through."

"Sure, but I was planning on heading on up to

Lauderdale this afternoon to visit Katie. Maybe spend the night, and then we've got some business." That last part was made up, but I wasn't about to drag Mike into my personal life. "Any chance the meeting could be moved back a day?"

"Can't do it, Sam. Like I said, this thing has gotten way up on everybody's radar. But we probably could go ahead without you."

No chance in hell I was going to let that happen. Whatever Katie and I were going to accomplish in the next twenty-four hours, it was going to end by tomorrow morning.

CHAPTER 31

By the time traffic broke loose and I made it to the MacDonald's parking lot in Florida City, Dave Ackerman and a woman I did not recognize already had their coffee and were seated by a window, looking out in my direction. Neither was in uniform, and they must have driven an unmarked car because there was no sign of a Fish and Wildlife vehicle in the parking lot.

I walked inside, got my own cup, and joined them at their table. Dave introduced me to Agent Vera Rutledge. She was slim, with a narrow face to match, and young, probably mid-twenties. Dave explained that Vera was there to wire me up for my adventure inside Hector Morales' pet store.

"I'm also giving you my cell phone, in case you get a chance to get some photos when the guy isn't looking." He handed me a fat envelope. "And here's some cash."

I drank some of my coffee, which was strong and good. "I think I know the answer to this, but just for the record – what exactly am I trying to purchase?"

"Anything you think he shouldn't be selling. The most obvious examples would be sea turtles, crocodiles, and any items made from them. Based on our suspicions and observations, some of which you know about, crocs and croc products would be most likely."

"And if I'm successful, what happens next?"

"Then we raid the place."

"You mean us?"

Dave shook his head. "Oh hell no. Armed agents will be nearby, out of sight, and waiting for my signal. It will include both state people and some folks from the U.S. Fish and Wildlife Service, since both sea turtles and crocs are federally listed."

Dave drained the last of his coffee and stood up. "Ready to go? We'll ride together from here, and I'll bring you back to your jeep after it's over."

I explained that I planned to drive on up to Lauderdale afterwards to see Katie, and that I would rather not have to come back down to MacDonald's before heading north. We agreed to stop next at one of those gas and fast food islands on the Florida Turnpike near the point where we would make our exit toward Miami.

Traffic was relatively light at mid-day, and the drive took only about twenty minutes. We pulled in together in a remote section of the parking lot. I got out and took off my shirt, so Vera could tape a little recorder just above my left hip. I put the shirt back on but left it un-tucked so the device would be inconspicuous. Then we all got in Dave's car and headed out.

Casa de los Reptiles occupied the corner spot in an L-shaped strip mall off Flagler Street in the Little Havana section of downtown Miami. Adjacent establishments included a hair and nail salon, a Radio Shack, a Subway, and a place that loaned money against your car title. We parked in front of the Subway. Dave and Agent Rutledge made a conspicuous show of walking inside the restaurant, just in case Hector

Morales happened to be looking in our direction. After a couple of minutes I got out, all wired-up, with Dave's cell phone in my pocket along with the wad of hundreds and twenties he'd given me in case the man had something to sell.

Morales was talking to a woman and a boy as I walked in. They were speaking animated Spanish, and the vestigial remains of my high school classes in that subject were insufficient for me to follow. However, the word 'tortuga' came up a lot, and I gathered they were having trouble deciding among a variety of pond turtles the man had for sale. I was glad for the distraction, because it gave me a chance to view the store's contents before dealing with Morales himself.

A glass countertop ran the full length of the back wall, and underneath it were accessories for keeping your critters at home, like heaters, fake rocks and plants, food, and aquaria. A door behind the counter probably led to a back room, but it was closed and there were no windows. Wooden shelving along the other walls supported dozens of glass terraria, aquaria, and wire cages, each holding one or more specimens. The variety and abundance of both reptiles and amphibians was impressive, but I saw no crocodilians. No surprise there really, but naturally I wondered what might be in the back room. Among the creatures out in front were banded geckos, green anole lizards, a Chinese water dragon, several chameleons, a pair of corn snakes, several cages of fire-belly toads, at least a dozen ball pythons, and several species of tropical frogs and lizards that I did not recognize. I was startled to find a lone water moccasin glaring out from a partially filled aquarium in a back corner. Who would want a venomous snake for a pet?

One whole section was devoted to turtles, but I could not get close enough to determine the species because that was where the woman and boy were attempting to make their choice. I had the impression it was a mother and son, and the son had his eye on something bigger and more expensive than the mother was willing to spend.

It took another ten minutes before the sale was completed, and the couple left with their selection. They must already have had housing and food at home, because a lone turtle was all they bought.

Hector Morales waddled out from behind the counter, and we met in the middle of his store. I reached down to press a button activating the recorder hidden under my shirt.

"Good afternoon, sir, and thank you for your patience. As you may have noticed, that young man and his mother were having difficulties deciding which of our many fine turtles he would take home. And how may I help you?"

"Well, my wife is particularly fond of..."

"Have we not met, señor? You look familiar."

It hadn't taken him long to recognize me, and there was no point in pretending otherwise. "Yes, actually we have. It was down at the Safari Lounge in Islamorada."

A look of suspicion might have flashed across Hector Morales' pale round face, but it was gone before I could be sure. "Of course, now I remember. But I confess to not remembering your name. You are...?"

"Sam Sawyer."

We shook.

"And you are interested in purchasing one of my specimens?"

"I am."

"Anything in particular?"

"As I started to say, my wife has a fondness for crocodilians of all sorts, including products made from their hides. I know this is an unusual request, but we have been having some marital difficulties of late, and I was hoping you might be able to help. It is very important – urgent even, if you understand my point."

Morales shook his head and smiled. "I am sorry to hear of your troubles, señor, but as you can see there are none of those creatures here." He waved around the room, as if to emphasize the point.

Since there was nothing to lose, I pulled the roll of bills out of my pocket, and made sure he had a look. "Perhaps in your back room there might be something? As you can see, I came prepared to pay top dollar. For the right item, that is."

The reptile dealer hesitated but I could see he was eying the cash. "Please wait here."

Morales went in the back room, closing the door behind him, and returned in about five minutes carrying a cardboard box. He set the box on the counter and invited me to look inside. There were two baby alligators and a purse made from alligator hide. Close, but no cigar.

"Those are very nice, but what I had in mind was something less ... common."

"I do not know what you are talking about."

It was make or break time. "I think perhaps you do

know what I'm talking about. But if you cannot help me, I am sure there are others who can." With that I turned and walked toward the door.

It would have been a disappointment and an embarrassment to walk out empty-handed, and it almost happened.

"Uh, no wait, señor. Please come back."

Once again Hector Morales disappeared into the back room, and this time he came back out with two boxes, one much larger than the other.

"Perhaps these are what you are looking for?"

The larger box held a live American crocodile, about three feet long, with its mouth taped shut. In the smaller box was an attaché case, almost certainly made from crocodile hide. It was essential that the man say the words, and that money change hands. Getting a photograph would be the ultimate bonus.

"And these are what, exactly?"

"That, my friend, is a young American crocodile, as I think you know. And you have my word the case is made from one of their skins. Beautiful, are they not?"

"Beautiful they are. But what about cost? Much as I would like both items, together they might be out of my price range."

I could almost hear the wheels spinning in Hector Morales' head, probably as he tried to estimate the size of the bankroll I had flashed earlier in front of his face. "The live animal is by far the most valuable. For him, it would be four thousand. For the case, another fifteen hundred."

"You must be joking."

"About such things I do not joke, señor."

"Perhaps not, Mr. Morales, but you have seriously overestimated what I can pay."

"And just how much is that?"

We had entered the negotiation stage, which was good. "Two thousand. For both."

"Three."

I took the plunge and decided to push my luck. "Done, but on one condition."

"What is that?"

"That I might see what else you have in your back room? In case my wife might require more – how can I put this – persuasion?"

He shook his head emphatically. "No, I am sorry, but that is impossible. There is some important business to which I must attend that requires me to close the shop. So now it is time for you to pay what we agreed, and then leave."

I pulled out the roll and peeled off thirty hundred dollar bills. There would be no look at whatever else Hector Morales had for sale on the black market, but it was likely the raid team would get in there. In any event, the recording and the evidence I was about to carry out of the shop should be enough to put the man out of business.

I was nearly out the front door when two men came out from the back room and joined Morales behind the counter. One was bigger than the other. They both wore bib overalls, faded ball caps, and ragged colorless t-shirts. The reptile dealer quickly hustled them back out of sight, but not before we exchanged glances. I was pretty sure there was mutual recognition.

I took a chance and called out "Hey, Luther!"

But they were gone.

~ ~ ~

Naturally enough, Dave Ackerman and Vera Rutledge were thrilled with my report, and with the crocodile and attaché case they now had secured in the trunk of their car.

"There was one little problem, though."

"What's that?"

"I think they made me."

Ackerman was puzzled. "We already talked about that. Morales knows you as a fishing guide from Islamorada, not as somebody involved with law enforcement. So why is that a problem?"

"Not him. It was two other guys in the back room. I think we'd seen each other before. You remember that pair we encountered on the gray Yellowfin?"

"You saw *them* in there?"

"Seems likely. And maybe the last time we met, they were doing all the seeing."

"Why is that?"

"Because they had just hit me over the head from behind."

Dave got it of course. "Holy shit, Sam."

"Yeah. And now this raid of yours better happen fast, before everybody in that little shop takes off, maybe with all the rest of the evidence tucked underneath their arms."

Dave got on the radio, and made the call. The combination state and federal team would be there in less than five minutes.

I wondered what we were supposed to do next, but Dave cleared that up.

"Now let's get the hell out of here. Didn't you say you had a date in Lauderdale?"

CHAPTER 32

It was late afternoon by the time they got me back to the Florida Turnpike. Traffic already had turned awful. It was another two hours before I made it to the Griffin Road exit, and it probably would be another thirty minutes from there to the condo I shared with Katie in south Fort Lauderdale.

Dave Ackerman called just after I got off the turnpike, with a promised report about the combined state and federal raid on La Casa de los Reptiles. It had gone well. Morales was there along with two other guys named Luther and Orville Perkins, who turned out to be cousins from Florida City. The agents had discovered so much stuff in the back room that they had decided to take everybody into custody.

I was curious about that back room and asked Dave what they had found.

"In addition to four young crocodiles about the size of the one you brought out, there were two more of those attaché cases and some purses, all made from either croc or alligator hide – we're not sure which at this point."

"Anything else?"

"You bet. They also found a half-dozen young sea turtles living in a big saltwater aquarium, along with several adult shells. Oh, and there were a whole bunch of baby alligators, which may or may not have been legal depending on whether the guy had the right permits. We're checking into that."

"That's great, Dave. Looks like you've got these guys nailed for possession and sale."

We both knew there was more.

"Yep, now if we can just tie 'em to Mabel."

I was skeptical. "Like maybe they killed her for the crocodiles? Seems a stretch."

"Yeah, but who knows what actually happened out there, Sam. And I'd sure like to make these Orville and Luther cousins as the two guys who conked you over the head the other night."

"Maybe that's too much to hope for. And anyway, wouldn't that fall under county jurisdiction rather than Fish and Wildlife?"

"Sure, and we're ahead of you on that one. The Miami Dade Sheriff has agreed to let Stella Reynard sit in when we interview the prisoners – separately, of course. Who knows, they might turn on each other as part of a plea bargain."

It sounded like a plan, and my hopes rose that possibly – just possibly – the whole Mabel Schwimley case might get wrapped up in the next couple of days. Then I could get back to fishing. That and untangling my personal life, the first step of which was uncertain but imminent.

~ ~ ~

It was nearly dark when I pulled into the parking lot next to our three-story condo building. I knew which windows were ours, and the lights were on. If Katie was home, which seemed likely, we were about to have our first face-to-face conversation in over three weeks. I had been mulling over how to start things off, and had rehearsed two very different possibilities, depending on my mood. Either I confessed the one-night stand with Flo right off, or first I self-righteously demanded that Katie explain why she wouldn't return my calls.

The actual confrontation with Katie didn't start out either way, because it was Tuesday. I didn't now anything about it of course, but this was the evening she hosted a weekly graduate seminar in 'Recent Advances in Forensic Science.' They met at our condo, listened to a guest speaker, and then had drinks and snacks afterwards. Apparently I had arrived just in time for the drink and snack part, and the place was full of chattering people when I walked in the front door carrying my overnight bag.

Katie didn't even see me at first, because she was standing outside on our little veranda, deep in conversation with a dark-haired man in a blue suit. He didn't look anything like the other six people in the room, whom I took to be the students based on their relatively scruffy appearance – three men and three women.

I just stood there, not knowing quite what to do. Eventually the chattering ebbed, as the students realized a man they didn't know had just walked into the room. The ensuing quiet must have gotten Katie's attention, because she caught me eye and came inside, saying something over her shoulder to her companion out on the deck. She was wearing dark blue slacks, a simple pink blouse, and heels that rattled on the tile floor as she crossed the room. I just had time to wonder about her unexpectedly formal attire, before she gave me a quick peck on the cheek and then turned back to introduce me to her students. The man in the blue suit stayed outside, but he was looking right at me.

After Katie had gone around the room introducing her students, none of whose names I would remember, she called to the man on the porch. "Stu, please come and meet my husband, Sam Sawyer. And Sam, this is Stuart Brodsky. He's an Assistant District Attorney for Broward County."

"Stu" came inside and crossed the room. The man was medium height, with a square jaw, broad face, and black-framed glasses. He looked like Clark Kent except for the hair, which he'd teased up into one of those popular spiky cuts. It was sort of like Superman had stuck his finger in an empty light socket. When we got close enough to exchange a desultory handshake, I could smell the pomade that must have kept his hairdo from collapsing.

Katie was quick to explain the man's presence. Maybe too quick?

"Stu was tonight's guest speaker. I try to get my students in contact with people who actually are on the ground using the forensic methods we teach. His talk was very informative."

I said 'nice to meet you' and thought Katie didn't sound much like herself.

It got quiet in the room, and the students must have decided it was time to leave. Assistant DA Brodsky went with them, but not before he confirmed a meeting with Katie. "I'll expect you in my office tomorrow, about two-thirty?" Then – perhaps more for my benefit than hers – "You know, to talk about the Sanderson case?"

Katie said "Right, see you then," and closed the door behind him.

So we had come down to it. The appearance of Superman in my old living room tipped the scales toward a confrontation rather than a confession. That, and the fact that our bathroom smelled like his hair goo.

We sat together in the living room, facing each other across a low coffee table. "How have you been, Katie?"

She crossed one leg over the other and adjusted her blouse. "Fine."

"I keep leaving messages, but you never call back. Is there something I should know about?"

"No, it's just that I've been ... busy."

"Come on, Kat, you can't have been *that* busy."

She glanced out the big bay window that looked north toward the airport and the lights of downtown Fort Lauderdale. I followed her eyes, and we both watched a big jetliner come in for a landing.

"I have been busy thinking, Sam. About us."

I waited expectantly for more, but it didn't come. Instead she brushed away a strand of dark hair that had fallen in front of her left eye, and looked again out the window.

"Look, I know this is complicated, my living down in Islamorada and you up here. But I thought we had this thing worked out. And didn't we have a good time when you came down to visit a couple of weeks ago?"

She turned back from the window, and met my eyes. "It was closer to four weeks ago, not two. Yes I had a good time, but that's not really the point, is it?"

"Then what *is* the point?"

Katie sighed, pressed her hands together between her knees, and stared down at the floor. "The point is that I have a life up here – a complicated, professional, life. And it's really beginning to take off. Right now I have more forensic cases than I can handle. I can't just drop everything and scamper down to your little hideaway in the Keys whenever I feel like it."

"And that's all that's keeping you up here, this professional life of yours? Well you may not have noticed, but I've got one too. And my busiest time is on the weekends, because those are the only days a lot of my clients can get away."

"How come you can't be a fishing guide in Lauderdale? We've got lots of water around here, in case you haven't noticed. "

"I'm not a blue water fisherman, Kat. We've talked about this before. And speaking of noticing things, what's with Stu in the suit? He was practically drooling when I first saw you two out on the deck. And that hair grease he was wearing is stinking up our whole condo."

Katie flared at that, and she had a right even if she didn't know it. Who was I to talk about extramarital relationships, even assuming she was having one?

There comes a time in any argument marital when it can go one of two directions. It can go in the door-slamming, tires screeching in the driveway direction, but maybe with some good sex afterwards when the fleeing party slinks back home. Or it can go like one of those songs on the radio that doesn't actually end but just gets fainter and fainter until you can't hear it anymore. It de-escalates, which might be good, but it doesn't necessarily accomplish anything.

I opted for de-escalation. "Sorry, Katie. It's been a long day."

She nodded and shrugged. "Me too. I guess."

"What happens now?"

This got another shrug. "I suppose we go back to business as usual."

"Usual meaning you won't answer my calls?"

"I'll answer your calls, Sam. Just don't come after me about my personal life, okay? You lost that privilege when you moved out."

It stung, but she was right. Even more right than she likely understood.

I sighed and held out my hands, palms up. She reached across the table and took mine in hers. I thought we might be getting somewhere, but it wasn't what I expected.

"I need time to think, Sam, about what our future is going to look like. You should be thinking about that too."

"Fair enough. I will, I promise."

"In the mean time, I think you should go."

So I did. Two hours and one hundred fifteen miles later I was back home in my 'little hideaway' in Islamorada, as Katie had called it.

There were two messages waiting for me on the landline. Neither was from Katie. The first was from Dave Ackerman, who said there was news about Hector Morales and the pair he referred to as "those two bubbas from Florida City." I should call him in the morning for details. The second call was from Billy Nelson. My Hell's Bay and the canoe were ready to be picked up.

It was late, nearly midnight, but I didn't feel like sleeping. Instead I got a beer out of the refrigerator and went out on the deck. The night was cool but calm. A tarpon splashed somewhere down the canal, and then a whip-poor-will called from the wooded lot across from my house. I knew they only wintered here, literal snowbirds. Soon all the Florida whip-poor-wills would be heading north.

Should *I* be heading north? Was I really just hiding out down here in Islamorada, like Katie suggested?

My thoughts turned toward the Hell's Bay, and how good it would be to have that fine little boat back at the dock. It was time to go back to work, to get back on the water where I belonged. Fishing was an escape, perhaps, but it also was a passion and I was pretty damned good at it.

I decided Katie was wrong. This wasn't about hiding or running away from anything. It was about a choice between a lifestyle and a life companion, and that was trouble enough. I needed advice, but who could give it? Snooks was my best friend, but he'd never married. He talked about ex-girlfriends sometimes, but never explained why they were all in the past.

Then there was Flo. It made my head hurt to think about her, so I went to bed instead.

CHAPTER 33

First thing the next morning I drove up to Billy Nelson's shop, paid deductibles that the insurance wouldn't cover, and retrieved my boat and canoe. He'd done a superb job as usual. I left the Hell's Bay on its trailer in my side yard, with the canoe up on blocks sitting beside it. Both craft would stay there until the next client came along. Some of my regulars had made other plans when they learned I was unavailable, and I expected it could be a while before Sawyer's Backcountry Charters got fully back up to speed.

A critical step toward that goal was to put messages out on email and Facebook, letting everybody know I was available once again for fishing and birding trips. Social media had little personal appeal, and it seemed only remotely connected with the business of guiding clients out into the actual rather than the virtual world. But most of the other guides were doing it, Snooks being a conspicuous exception, and it was perhaps doubly critical as a way of getting bookings back to something like normal. Tarpon season was about to begin in earnest, so there was little time to waste.

Half the day was gone by the time I had finished with electronic messaging and dealing with several inquiries that showed up right afterwards. By then it was time to leave for the meeting Mike Nunez had set up at Everglades National Park headquarters between the members of Team Mabel and the brass from Investigative Services. I called Mike to give him the good news that I would be returning his Maverick that afternoon.

I loaded Mike's boat back on its trailer, and headed for the mainland. Nothing happened along the way, except the usual crazy spring traffic, and by three o'clock we were all assembled in a meeting room down the hall from the Superintendent's office. The meeting got off to a late start, because Dave Ackerman and Stella Reynard had been tied up with interviews involving Hector Morales, the Perkins cousins, and their respective lawyers.

The room where we met was a bright airy place, with windows that looked out onto a good-sized freshwater pond. I could see alligators, turtles, anhingas, and egrets in and near the water. These could have proven a distraction, committee meetings being far from my favorite activity. However, once things got started, I forgot all about the pond and its denizens. It turned out the people from Investigative Services had some serious business in mind.

Mike Nunez started things off by introducing Special Agent Rhonda Wilcox, who he explained would be running not only this meeting but apparently the whole Mabel Schwimley investigation from now on. Dave Ackerman and Stella Reynard both squirmed in their seats when they heard that, not without reason in my opinion, but they didn't say anything.

Rhonda walked up from the back of the room and took a seat at the head of the table. She was medium height, hefty but not overweight, with dark hair pulled back in a tight bun that only heightened her aura of humorless severity. She was out of uniform, dressed in a white short-sleeved shirt, black slacks, and low heels. She had been carrying a stack of fat manila folders, and she spread them out on the table in front of her before starting the meeting. She began by introducing her partner, a thirty-something man named Joe Rossini, who came up and sat to her right. He also had a sturdy no-nonsense look about him. He had a big head, shaved clean into a shiny round dome, and a broad face with close-set pale blue eyes. Joe may have been formidable in his own right, but Rhonda made it clear who was in charge without explicitly saying so.

Once we had all introduced ourselves, Rhonda got right down to business.

"Thank you all for coming. We are here to talk about the disappearance and likely death of one Mabel Schwimley." Then, with a nod in my direction, "I want first to thank Mr. Sam Sawyer, who I understand was the person who tracked her down as the likely occupant of a pair of shoes found in a remote area of this Park about a month ago. Prior to his discovery, I confess we – that is NPS Investigative Services – were prepared to let the whole thing go as another case of a deceased Cuban immigrant, most likely unauthorized and unidentifiable. Now all that has changed."

Agent Wilcox opened one of the folders and shuffled some of the papers inside. "I suggest we divide this meeting into two parts. The first will be to identify possible suspects in her disappearance, and to discuss any and all relevant evidence." She paused long enough to look around the table, and then continued. "Second, we need to plan for the next steps in this investigation. Are we all agreed?"

Some heads nodded, but nobody said anything.

"Good. Then let's get started. I understand that Dave and Stella are just back from interviewing one set of suspects. So why don't we begin with that." It wasn't a question the way she said it.

Dave began by describing the raid on Hector Morales' reptile shop, including the evidence recovered at the scene as well as the contents of my clandestine tape recording. This was familiar territory, but I had not yet heard anything about the results of their interviews, and that was next on Dave's agenda.

"Everybody lawyered up as soon as we had them booked into the county jail, and I thought at first we weren't likely to get much of anywhere. Morales was represented by a fancy Miami attorney, while the Perkins cousins – that's Luther and Orville – needed public defenders."

Rhonda Wilcox had a question for Dave. "You had them in separate rooms?"

He nodded. "Sure. I stayed with Morales, while Stella divided her time between Luther and Orville. Higher-ups from Florida Fish and Wildlife and the U.S. Fish and Wildlife Service did the actual questioning.

"Morales stonewalled us at first, refused to say anything at all, until we played Sam's recording and went through the list of contraband we found in his store. After huddling with his attorney he came back with the defense that he hadn't known any of the stuff was illegal, that Luther and Orville were his sole suppliers, and that they had assured him it all had come from trips overseas. He said he thought the crocodiles were from Africa."

The vision of the Perkins cousins as international travelers didn't work at all, and everybody laughed except Rhonda Wilcox.

"Of course he must have known we could check the DNA on his crocodiles and probably figure out whether or not they were the American species. But it didn't come to that, because of what was happening in the other rooms. Stella, you want to fill us in on that?"

Stella Reynard cleared her throat, took a drink from a water bottle she had brought with her, and consulted some notes. "Sure. The feds and the people in Dave's shop made a decision right off to try turning the Perkins cousins in a plea deal, and it worked. Orville and Luther both jumped at the chance of reduced fines and no jail time, and then they did a very thorough job of ratting out their boss. I won't bore you with any of the details except one. That Yellowfin Sam and Dave saw them driving? Not only is it registered to Morales, but it is at this very moment parked in the Perkins' back yard in Florida City."

Dave Ackerman laughed. "Or make that 'was' parked in their back yard. I think by now the feds may have confiscated that boat. And they're searching the whole property, with the Perkins' permission. That was part of the plea deal. We can't predict the final outcome of the Morales prosecution at this point, but I don't think there's any doubt he'll end up permanently out of business."

This was all good, but it left an obvious big question unanswered, and I didn't give anybody else the chance to ask it. "What about Mabel and Schwimley Key? That's why we're all here today, right?"

Stella Reynard was sitting next to me, and put her hand on my shoulder and gave it a little squeeze. "Of course we asked about that, Sam. But here's the deal. Orville and Luther admitted poaching crocodiles off Schwimley, and they readily admitted knowing Mabel. They said they gave her a hundred dollars every time they went out there, but then one day she just wasn't around anymore. Or at least that's what they claimed."

"And what about my getting hit over the head? Or the fire on my boat?"

I could tell that Stella was getting uneasy about something, because she wouldn't make eye contact. "Maybe you want to handle this one, Dave?"

Stella wasn't one to pass the buck, so I knew something was fishy.

"We decided not to get into that, Sam. Not at this point."

"And just why the hell not?"

"Because we thought then they might clam up and not to give us Morales."

"You're telling me a case of poaching takes priority over arson and assault, maybe even murder?" I knew it didn't make sense, but I was upset and probably not thinking straight.

Dave emphatically shook his head. "Of course not, Sam. But one doesn't rule out the others. We made sure of that. While our people are going after the Yellowfin in the Perkins' back yard, they'll also search the house. Actually it's an old doublewide with a tin shed attached. Maybe they'll find something we can use to connect them to you, like maybe a rifle that matches the shell casing you picked up?"

Rhonda apparently didn't know all the details. "I heard about your fire, but what's this about an assault? And what sort of evidence do we have that might connect it with these two guys?"

I filled her in on the details: that I had heard one of them call the other one Luther, and that I had collected an empty shell casing next to the spot where my canoe had been shot up.

"Were there any prints?"

I looked at Stella, because I hadn't yet heard about their examination of either the shotgun or rifle shells I had brought back from Schwimley.

She shook her head. "Sorry, there was nothing usable."

I wanted more, or at least more talk, but apparently Rhonda Wilcox was ready to move on. "If I'm reading this right, we can't rule out these two guys as being responsible for Mabel Schwimley's disappearance, and they might even have had a motive if she got in the way of their poaching operation. But it's obvious we aren't close to probable cause. Even if we could get them for assaulting Sam, that wouldn't connect them directly to Mabel. And I must say that murder seems unlikely here, since all they had to do was go somewhere else to shoot their crocodiles." She stopped, and glanced around the table. "Who else have we got?"

Mike Nunez put his hand up. "Pete Donovan. He's the guy I was telling you about that runs Pelican Pete's Emporium down in Islamorada."

Joe Rossi wiped a hand across his forehead as if he was brushing aside a strand of hair that wasn't there anymore. "And remind me again, just what is his connection to Schwimley Key or this Mabel woman?"

Mike repeated what the rest of us had heard before. Pelican Pete was suspected of dealing in Native American artifacts and in contraband made from items such as sea turtle shells. A shell mound on Schwimley had been looted. Maybe it was Pete and he'd run afoul of Mabel in the process. Or maybe they'd had a business relationship that had gone sour. Or maybe he'd gotten greedy and decided to stop sharing his illegal gains with her.

It was a lot of maybes, and I think we all knew it. Certainly Rhonda Wilcox wasn't going to let Mike off the hook. "But what about hard evidence? If I understand correctly, you haven't even been able to prove the man deals in this stuff, let alone that any of it came from Schwimley Key."

I did my best to come to Mike's defense, because he was a friend and because I sympathized with his feelings about looting prehistoric sites. "We know that Pete Donovan has some sort of a relationship with Hector Morales, and I can't imagine they have very much in common – unless Morales has been supplying Donovan with products to sell on the black market. I think we need to get inside the Emporium and find out what he has."

Rhonda still wasn't having any of it. "I can try to get a court order for that, but without having at least one piece of solid evidence linking the man and his shop to the contents of that shell mound, I'm guessing it won't work."

"I may be able to help with that." I reached down

under the table and brought up a cardboard box. Inside it was the little hawksbill shell I'd found inside Mabel Schwimley's rowboat. I had intended to give it to Mike after the meeting, but this seemed like the right time.

I reminded everybody that we previously had found a piece of hawksbill jewelry at Pelican Pete's Emporium. Then I opened the box and held up its contents. "Unless I am mistaken" – (and I knew I wasn't) – "this is the shell of a young hawksbill with holes drilled in the anterior edge, just like the one Pete sold me last year only a little bigger. And it looks really old, like it could have come from that shell mound. For sure it came from Schwimley Key. I'm wondering if this might be enough to get another court order to search Pete's back room?"

This time Rhonda guessed that it might be. "Meanwhile, what else do we have?"

Nobody said anything, and when the silence finally broke it was Rhonda herself. "There is one other thing I should mention before we go on to the second half of our agenda. We've been hearing rumors – and so far that's all they are – that some powerful real estate interests in this state may have their eyes on Schwimley Key for future development. We're talking *very* powerful interests, though I'm not prepared at this time to be any more specific."

I immediately saw two problems, the first of which was environmental. "But why would anybody even be thinking about that? The water around Schwimley is so shallow, the place is virtually inaccessible."

"Again, there's nothing specific at this point, but there are rumors about a heliport, or even maybe digging a deep-water canal."

"Inside the *Park*?"

Rhonda condescended to explain, and believe me that's what it felt like. "Remember what I just said about those real estate interests being powerful?"

Mike Nunez just sat there, which made it seem like he'd known about this ahead of time. I decided to put it to him with my second problem. "But Mike, didn't you tell me that when the last Schwimley heir finally dies, the key goes to you guys? Why would these powerful interests want to kill her off? Seems like that would queer the whole deal."

Rhonda Wilcox put up her hand to stop Mike from responding. "We've thought of that, of course. And it is problematic. Maybe there was some sort of an accident. Maybe they were just trying to scare her into signing an agreement."

I was getting tired of all these maybes, but then I thought of one myself. "Or maybe there's another Schwimley heir out there someplace? One who might be more cooperative?"

The Special Agent from Investigative Services gave me a knowing look, but she kept quiet. It was Stella Reynard who spoke next. Her black eyes flashed, and I could tell she was hot. "Excuse me, but I thought this was supposed to be a meeting where we shared information. How come we can't have a name? My boss isn't going to like this. We've probably had a murder in his county – and remember that Schwimley Key is on private land, not in your Park – and you won't even tell us the identity of a possible suspect?"

"I'm well aware of who owns Schwimley, Deputy

Reynard." Rhonda took the time to flip through the contents of another manila folder. "All right, I can give you one name, on the condition that you hold this absolutely confidential. It's Grimes."

I was stunned. Ed was some sort of a developer, so it fit. But I had no idea he was interested in Schwimley. "You mean *Ed* Grimes?"

Rhonda nodded. "You know him?"

"He's a client, mostly into birds."

"How well do you know him?"

"Reasonably well, I suppose. You tend to learn things about a person after spending a whole day with them out on the water, and we've done that maybe a half dozen times over the last couple of years. Why?"

"No reason in particular for now. But yours could be a useful point of contact depending on how things unfold."

I was prepared to leave it at that, but Stella wasn't. "I'm guessing this Grimes person might be the front man on the deal, and not one of those 'powerful interests' you mentioned?"

This time Rhonda Wilcox absolutely stonewalled us. "That would be a safe assumption. I'm sorry, but that's all I can say at this point. And now I suggest we take a fifteen minute break, maybe cool off a bit?"

One way to cool off would be to go jump in the lake. Instead Dave Ackerman and I just walked around it, checking out the wildlife. He asked me about a chunky bird perched low on a shrub at the water's edge.

"That's a green heron."

"Never seen one of those before. I don't like that woman, Sam."

"I don't think we're supposed to. But she is organized."

"Yeah, that's fair enough. And if there's one thing this whole mess needs, it's organization."

We both watched as a big alligator surfaced out in the middle of the lake, and quickly sank again out of sight. Then we went back inside for the second half of the meeting. It didn't take nearly as long as the first half because it mostly involved Rhonda Wilcox handing out assignments.

First up was Pelican Pete Donovan. With the hawksbill shells as evidence, she would attempt to get a court order. If that succeeded then Mike would coordinate some sort of a raid on the Emporium, maybe along the lines of what Dave and I had just done at the Morales reptile store.

Rhonda herself, evidently with Joe Rossi in tow, would continue looking into the real estate angle. She would keep us posted on their progress, and maybe get the rest of the team involved depending on what they learned. I asked if she wanted me to talk with Ed Grimes, but she said not yet. It all seemed a bit mysterious, but apparently that was that.

This left the Perkins cousins. We had no evidence linking them to the death or disappearance of Mabel, or to the fire on my boat, but there was a chance we could make them for hitting me over the head that night out on Schwimley Key. For sure one of them had called the other one Luther, but that probably wouldn't be enough by itself. The rifle and shotgun shell casings had no usable prints, but if the Fish and Wildlife search of their property turned up one or more weapons that matched in terms of gauge or caliber, that could add another piece. So a lot was riding on that search. Who knew, maybe they'd even find something that linked Orville and Luther to Mabel. Like a footless body buried in their backyard? It was too much to hope for.

Stella seemed anxious to keep after it. "Those boys are going to have to find a new way to make a living, now that their sugar daddy is going out of business. And I don't imagine they're about to go straight. I'll talk to the Sheriff, maybe coordinate with Miami-Dade. And Dave, be sure and let me know if your people find anything useful out at the Perkins' trailer. These boys need to go down for what they did to Sam, if nothing else."

Rhonda Wilcox assured Stella that nobody was going to drop the case against the Perkins cousins. "But there's one more thing, and this is top priority. We need to find out what actually happened to Mabel Schwimley, and we need a body."

Rhonda had made copies for everybody of the old head shots of Mabel Schwimley that Stella had dug up. She passed these around, and I was reminded again that there was something familiar about Mabel in her younger days. I stared at my copies while Rhonda continued with her instructions to the group, but it didn't come to me.

"Mike, I'm asking you to coordinate another Park-wide search. I've talked to the Superintendant, and she agrees with me on this. I realize you've already spent a lot of time looking, and you may have decided by now that it's a dead end. But we need to redouble our efforts out there. And Stella, the same goes for the rest of

Monroe County. The corpse must be out there someplace."

"I'll bet it's inside the belly of a big crocodile out in the glades. Then what are we gonna do?"

Everybody laughed at Mike's joke, even Joe Rossi. Everybody except Rhonda Wilcox, that is.

It was only later, on the drive home, that it came to me why Special Agent Wilcox had made such a big deal about finding Mabel's remains. As far as I was concerned she almost certainly was dead, and the more pressing issue was who had been responsible. But without a death certificate the Schwimley estate technically still survived, and so did the family's hold on the key itself. Only after that last surviving family member was officially deceased could the Superintendant hope to expand the real estate of Everglades National Park.

Rhonda Wilcox began collecting up the contents of her manila folders, and at first I thought the meeting had come to an end. But it turned out she still wasn't finished.

"One last thing before I let you go." She gestured around the room. "You've done a good job so far keeping a lid on this case, and I congratulate you on that. But we probably can't expect it to last much longer, especially now that the arrests of Morales and the Perkins cousins are a matter of public record. I have decided it would be best if we took the proactive approach. Therefore I have scheduled a press conference for tomorrow morning, 9 AM, in this room. Both print and television media are invited, so we are expecting a big crowd and lots of coverage."

Stella raised her hand. "Have you spoken with my boss about this?"

"Of course, Deputy Reynard. It turns out the Sheriff himself plans to be here. Mike, Joe and I will represent the Park Service. And Mr. Ackerman, while Florida Fish and Wildlife are not as directly involved, I suggest you plan to attend as well."

Rhonda had not mentioned my name in the context of the press conference, and that was fine by me. I did have one concern. "Ms. Wilcox, you may or may not have heard about a little bird called the Cuban tody that we have found on Schwimley Key?"

"Yes, I think Mike mentioned something about that. Why?"

"Because I hope it doesn't come for discussion tomorrow. If word got out through the press, we could be facing a real traffic problem out there."

"How's that?"

I explained about birders and life lists, and I think she got it.

"Actually there are several things we need to keep off limits at the press conference," said Rhonda. "And I'll be sure to add the tody business to my list. We also can't talk about the possible real estate connection I mentioned, or about this Pete Donovan person, since we don't yet have any solid evidence there."

It made me wonder why she wanted to have the press conference at all. But I supposed she knew what she was doing, and as long as I didn't have to be involved it wasn't really any of my business.

CHAPTER 34

"She's gone."

"You mean gone, as in quit?"

"No. Just gone."

Snooks and I were at the Safari Lounge, catching up over a beer and some chicken wings. It was one of their newer features. A guy named Burt was tending bar, and there was no sign of Flo. Naturally, I was curious.

"Where did she go?"

"Michigan, I think."

"Why?"

"To see a friend, I think."

"What sort of a friend?"

"How should I know?" That was when Burt's patience ran out. "And listen mister – Sam, is it? – as you can see we're pretty busy tonight, so did you want to order something, because otherwise..."

"Bring my friend and me another round of Yuenglings. And make it real glass mugs this time, okay?"

Snooks had been fidgeting with his ponytail, like he always did when something was bugging him. He spun on his bar stool. "Showed that guy, didn't ya?"

"Sorry."

"What's the matter?"

"Nothing."

"Then why the third degree about Flo? So she's on a little vacation. Why is that important?"

Burt delivered our beers, and Snooks stopped talking long enough to take a swallow. Then he set the mug back on the bar, and wiped foam off his upper lip with the back of his hand. "But now that I think about it, Flo was acting a little funny the last time we were in here together. Is there something going on I should know about?"

"Maybe." Snooks was a good friend, maybe the best one I'd ever had. "I think Katie and I might be in trouble."

"You mean like in marriage trouble?"

"Yes."

"I sure am sorry to hear that. She seems like a great gal to me. But what does it have to do with ... oh hell, and this has something to do with Flo?"

"Something. That and a dickhead up in Lauderdale named Stu."

"Who's he?"

"Katie's new boyfriend. Maybe."

We drank and chewed on our chicken wings for a while, without either of us saying anything. Snooks finished first, and then he used one of those little paper napkins they hand out at bars to start wiping the hot sauce off his fingers. It took three of them before he was satisfied with the cleanup, which actually may have been a stalling tactic.

"I probably shouldn't stick my nose in where it doesn't belong. So I'm just gonna say one thing. Well maybe two things. From what I have seen of Katie and Flo, they're both great gals. And I could see you going in either direction here. But one thing's for sure, you can't do both." He shook his head. "No, that's not it.

What I mean is, you *shouldn't* do both."

Snooks had nailed it, of course. "And the second thing?"

"The second thing is I'll bet Flo didn't just run off to Michigan by accident."

"You think she got out of the way on purpose?"

"Bet my boat on it, Sam. And while she's gone you better figure things out with Katie, so that when Flo gets back they both know the score."

Snooks drained the last of his Yuengling. "And now I need some bourbon. This advice to the lovelorn business can be stressful."

We each got Maker's Mark on the rocks with a splash of water, and moved over to one of the tables by the window to watch the sunset. A mild northeasterly breeze rippled the Atlantic, so that each line of broken waves reflected gold against a darkening purple sea. A line of black cormorants flew southwest, low to the water, probably heading for a power line that paralleled the Channel Five Bridge where they would spend the night perched on the wires.

Things had gotten a little tense back at the bar, so it seemed like a good time to change the subject. "Did you fish today?"

"Yep, but just in the morning. Had a client who really knew how to throw the fly. We went looking for permit."

"Any luck?"

"Yeah, he got one nice fish, maybe twenty, twenty-five pounds. Took us all over the flats before we got him to the boat. But then the tide went slack and that was the end of it."

"Still, even a one-permit day is a good one, right?"

Snooks grinned. "You bet. And say, it sure looked busy out by Schwimley Key today as we were coming back in. I guess they're still investigating that woman's disappearance?"

Since everybody I could think of had been up at Park headquarters all afternoon, I wondered what he was talking about. "Busy how?"

"Must have been five or six flats boats anchored up, and all sorts of little craft running back an forth to the island. A couple of canoes, some rubber rafts, personal watercraft, that sort of thing."

What the hell?

"Did you recognize anybody, or any of the boats?"

"No. It just looked like the usual assortment of private craft. I did notice lots of people had binoculars around their necks, and a couple had cameras with big telephoto lenses. Like maybe they were bird watchers or wildlife photographers or something. Why?"

The Cuban todies. It looked like somebody from Team Mabel had blabbed. If that was the case, it no longer mattered if the subject had come up at Rhonda Wilcox' press conference. But who had leaked the information, and when?

CHAPTER 35

When I first became interested as a teenager, bird watching was a relatively quaint activity involving a decent pair of binoculars and a pocket-sized field guide to aid with identification. Today the hobby has flown into the electronic age. If you have the right "apps" your phone can do almost anything ornithological. I even heard of one recently where your device records a bird song, analyses it, and then tells you the species. Of particular relevance to the poor little Cuban todies on Schwimley Key, assuming any had managed to stick it out, there now were electronic message boards for posting 'rare bird alerts' when and (critically) where something unusual turned up. Finding a Cuban tody in Florida was the next step beyond unusual, and I was not surprised to find the vicinity of Schwimley Key already full of birders when I arrived the next morning at seven-thirty. Obviously the word was out.

I called Dave Ackerman and Mike Nunez as soon as I recognized the size of the problem, but they both were stuck in Rhonda Wilcox' press conference up at headquarters, so it would be a while before they could get down. In the mean time, it was up to me to fight off the tody armada as best I could. I regretted not having kept Mike's boat for a couple more days. Having a Park Service logo on the hull would have added some gravitas when we pulled up along side a boatload of bird watchers and politely asked them to leave.

The waters around the key were plainly marked as off limits, and most of the folks we confronted did the right thing. However, a few of them got belligerent about it, questioning my authority and assuring me they had no plans other than to briefly go ashore and find one of the little birds. What, they asked, could be the harm in that? One of the parties was particularly troubling, because it included a reporter for the *Miami Herald* who was carrying a camera attached to a huge telephoto lens. I could see the headlines already.

Much to my relief, Dave arrived in his Fish and Wildlife bay boat about two hours later, having skipped out on the tail end of the press conference. Technically he was out of his jurisdiction, but I didn't think that was going to be important under the circumstances. I was just glad for the help. Mike showed up an hour after that in his Park Service skiff. That pretty much scattered all the birders, including several who had paddled back out to their respective mother ships during the roundup. By late morning all that remained was one empty boat, a center console Mako with a light blue hull. It was anchored straight out from the opening in the mangroves that led to the interior of the island.

I volunteered to take my canoe and go ashore in pursuit of what we all assumed was one last party of tody-seekers. Dave and Mike stayed around to keep a watch out for any late arrivals.

A small rubber raft was sitting beside Mabel's rowboat when I arrived at the head of the canal. I got out and walked toward the interior of the island. When I reached the cabin and still hadn't seen or heard anyone, I stopped and yelled 'hello on the key' as loudly as I could. There was almost no wind, and my call broke across such a profound stillness as to be almost embarrassing. The only sounds prior to mine had been a few distant bird songs, and they stopped as soon as my call had echoed across the island.

Then came a reply, not loud and not close, from someplace off to the north.

"I'm here. Have you found one? I'm coming!"

The voice sounded familiar, and ten minutes later out of the woods walked Ed Grimes. It shouldn't have been a surprise, given what I knew about Ed's passion for enlarging his avian life list. But I was surprised nonetheless.

Ed waved as soon as he recognized me, and I waved back.

"You do know this island is private property, and you're not supposed to be here?"

He kept walking and didn't say anything. When he got close, he put out his hand and we shook. He was wearing a khaki vest with lots of pockets, and a floppy canvas hat. The requisite binoculars and camera hung around his neck.

"Well good morning to you, Sam. Thought you were a guide, not a cop. Are you going to arrest me now, or can you take me into custody after I've had a chance to find one of those Cuban todies that are all the talk?" He tried to laugh and make it sound like a joke, but it didn't come out right. Instead it was more of a harsh humorless guffaw. "But seriously, I'm not supposed to be here?"

"Seriously, you're not supposed to be here. Among

other things, this whole place is a crime scene. Remember a couple of weeks ago, on the day we found the flamingo, we talked about the case of the blue shoes?"

"Yeah, what about it? What does it have to do with this place?"

"We think those shoes belonged to a woman who used to live here."

"Huh." Apparently Ed Grimes was undeterred by this news. "As long as I'm all the way out here, would there be any chance we could look around for one of those todies? There's a whole day's guide fee in it for you – once we find the bird, of course. And the more the better."

"So that's $600 per tody?"

"Yep."

"For as many as we can find?"

"Yep."

It was tempting. "No, sorry. There's a couple of guys from Fish and Wildlife and the Park Service waiting for me out on the water, and I'm under orders to get everybody off the island."

"Not even time for a quick look?"

"Okay. We'll watch and listen on the walk back to our boats. Maybe we'll get lucky."

My encounter with Ed Grimes was disquieting, and not just because he attempted a bribe. There was something else, something all wrong about the whole episode. But at the time I just couldn't put my finger on it.

I got on the phone to Mike and told him I had Ed Grimes in tow. "I'm gonna take one more look around the island, and then we'll be out."

Ed and I spend the next half hour walking around the interior of Schwimley Key, during which two things happened. One was good, and the other was even better. First, there didn't seem to be anybody left on the island but the two of us. Second, I heard at least two todies singing, and they were on opposite ends of the island. Ed was delighted, even though I wouldn't let him go looking for the birds, because he'd already decided that hearing one was enough for him to officially expand his life list by one new species.

We passed by Mabel Schwimley's little cabin on the way back, and I decided, more or less on a whim, to take another look inside. There was no reason to expect any changes over the last week, or that Stella had missed something during her initial search of the place. But I was right there, and Snooks could wait a while longer for my return, so why not?

Things looked much as they had on my first visit. The only obvious difference was that some animal – probably a rodent – had torn into the boxes of dry cereal and crackers on the food shelf. I was on my way across the room when I caught my toe on something and ended up sprawled face down onto the floor. Ed Grimes had followed me inside, and he rushed right over and offered to help.

"You all right, Sam?"

"Yeah, just tripped is all." I rolled over and got back up into a sitting position, then let Ed give me a hand up.

Once I was back on my feet, I looked back across the room to see if there was anything obvious that had caused my fall. It was then that I saw a single nail sticking up out of the floor. I walked over, gave it a pull, and a whole section of wooden planking came up with it.

The resulting hole in the floor was about two feet long, six inches wide, and maybe a foot deep, and there was something down inside. My first thought was that a dark and dank place like this would be the perfect location for my second encounter with an everglades diamondback. But the object in the hole was rectangular and immobile, and that pretty much ruled out snakes. When I pulled it up out of the hole, I realized that it was an old-fashioned child's lunchbox. It brought back some good memories, because it was much like the kind I remember my mother packing on school days with a peanut butter and jelly sandwich, an apple, a cookie, and a little thermos of milk. But this one was old and dirty, with a faded painting of a big steamship on the front that could have been the *Titanic*. It also was heavy.

Law enforcement protocol doubtless dictated that I immediately secure the unopened lunchbox in an evidence bag, especially with Ed Grimes standing right there. But I hadn't brought any evidence bags with me, which was all the excuse I needed. I carried the box over to the little table in the center of the cabin, opened it up, and extracted the contents, with Ed looking over my shoulder.

Mabel Schwimley's lunchbox, assuming it was hers, included these items:

– A gold-framed locket with a faded picture of a man and woman inside.

– A silver Hamilton pocket watch, with the letter 'S' engraved on the back in ornate gothic script.

– An old rusted fly reel still spooled with the tattered remains of a line that looked like it once might have been dark green.

– A Parker fountain pen, silver with gold trim.

The pen had engraving on the cap, but I couldn't read the small print in the half-light of the cabin. I carried it outside for a better look and read the words: "For Mabel, with love from Mom and Dad. June, 1959."

I went back inside the cabin and used my phone to take a series of photographs of the box and its contents. Then I put everything back inside and wrapped the box in a cotton pillowcase I found folded up with some blankets on a shelf in the back of the room. I was going to have to confess to Mike and Stella that the lunchbox and its contents would have my fingerprints on them, but they could take it or leave it. This was a major discovery. I just hoped that one or more of the items might lead us to Mabel's killer.

Ed must have read my mind. "Do you think that stuff belonged to the woman who ended up over in the everglades? What did you say her name was?"

"I didn't say. But we think it was Mabel and if this was her cabin it stands to reason this stuff is hers. Or was."

CHAPTER 36

By the time Ed and I got back on the water nobody else was around except Dave and Mike. Each was in his own boat but they had clustered together at the spot where I'd anchored mine. Apparently they'd succeeded in chasing off any late-arriving birders. I paddled out to join the group, and then we all watched as Ed pulled his raft up onto the Mako and left.

I couldn't wait to share the news about what had been hidden under the floorboards in Mabel's cabin, but Dave Ackerman didn't even let me get started. "Now that the situation here is under control, we need to go get a sample of your blood, and the sooner the better."

"Why?"

"Because of something the Fish and Wildlife people found in that mobile home belonging to the Perkins cousins up in Florida City. It was a hatchet, and it was covered with blood stains."

"Like something they might have used to dispatch a crocodile?"

Dave shook his head. "Maybe, but there was hair mixed with the blood, especially on the blunt edge of the blade. You're the reptile expert here, Sam, but crocs never did look all that hairy to me."

I could see where he was going with this. "You're thinking the hatchet might be what Orville or Luther used to hit me over the head that night?"

"One sure way to find out, assuming you're willing

to get clipped and bled."

"More than willing, under the circumstances." I held up my collection from Schwimley Key. "But first, isn't anybody going to ask me what's in this pillow case?"

~ ~ ~

An hour later we were all assembled at my place back in Islamorada. The group included Stella Reynard, who had driven down from headquarters. I put on the coffee and laid out a plate of fig newtons in case anybody was hungry. We all had a cup, but the newtons remained largely uneaten, probably because they were so stale they rattled like stones when I emptied the package onto the plate.

I spread the evidence from the pillowcase out on my dining room table and we each took a seat. Stella apologized for missing the stuff in the first place, but I quickly put that to rest.

"Stumbling over that nail was a fluke, Stella, just one of those lucky breaks. Don't beat yourself up over it. There is one other thing I wanted to ask you about, though."

"What's that?"

"It's about your forensics assistant that came along that day we first explored Schwimley Key. What was her name? Penny something?"

"Penny Raintree."

"Is she a birder?"

"I have no idea. Why?"

"Because somebody must have leaked the story about Cuban todies being on Schwimley Key. I can't imagine that any of us in this room would have done it.

But the birding community is pretty tight, and there is a certain prestige to being the first one to report a new sighting, especially for something this rare."

Stella nodded. "I'll check into it. If she was responsible, she'll get a lecture about her professional obligation not to mess up a crime scene. But I don't suppose she did anything illegal."

We all put on latex gloves Stella had brought along, and began passing around the items I had found in Mabel's cabin. After about fifteen minutes Mike asked us to summarize what we thought, each in turn. We all agreed that the various objects, while interesting, unfortunately didn't lead much of anywhere. Apparently my initial optimism had been premature.

The watch with the engraved 'S' probably was a family heirloom. The pen obviously had been a gift from Mabel's parents, and we all supposed the photo inside the locket was of the same couple. None of us had any ideas about the possible significance of the old fly reel. Stella said she would do a computer search for possible photographs of the older Schwimleys to compare with the one in the locket. But even if she found a match, nobody could figure out how it might get us any closer to finding Mabel's killer or killers.

At this point Mike Nunez turned our conversation toward matters not necessarily related to the contents of Mabel's cabin. "Dave, you need to fill us in on what your Fish and Wildlife people turned up on that property belonging to the Perkins cousins. But first, I'd like some advice on ways we might be able to link Pelican Pete Donovan to the shell mound on Schwimley Key. Sam, did you get by that place today while you were on the island?"

"No, sorry, I was more on the lookout for birdwatchers."

Mike looked a little peeved. "In any event, we need to get somebody into Pete's shop with a wire. If we can make a connection between the shell mound and what he might be offering behind the counter, then we might be getting somewhere. Sam, you did a helluva job in Hector Morales' place. Are you up for another round?"

I started to explain that it probably wasn't a good idea, because Pete knew who I was, but Stella didn't give me the chance.

"A sting operation may not be necessary, or even possible, because it appears our friend Peter Donovan has gone missing."

A stunned silence followed, eventually broken by Mike Nunez.

"When?"

"Don't know for sure. We only heard about it at roll call this morning. Apparently the guy's girlfriend called in late yesterday afternoon, said he hadn't come home from work the night before. Apparently he wasn't answering his phone, and none of the help in the store knew anything."

Stella stopped long enough to drain the last of her coffee. "We'll probably wait the customary forty-eight hours before we start a formal search. But if he hasn't showed up by then, that would be all the excuse we'd need to search his store for any sort of evidence about what might have happened to him."

Mike asked if he could come along when they conducted the search, and Stella said sure.

Since that seemed to be that regarding Pelican Pete, at least for now, we next turned our attention to the crocodile hunting Perkins boys, and the contents of their old doublewide up in Florida City. I threw away the fig newtons, which weren't doing anything but taking up space on the table, and everybody poured themselves another cup of coffee.

Dave Ackerman pulled a sheet of paper out of his shirt pocket, unfolded it and consulted a typewritten list.

"We have good news and bad news. First, we found a 30.06 lever action rifle that matches the caliber of the shell casing Sam found next to his canoe. That's consistent with the theory that those were the guys who shot it full of holes. The bad news is we did a forensic comparison between their 30.06 and the shell casing Sam found by his canoe, and the results were inconclusive. What we really need is a bullet so we can do a striation comparison. Sam, did you look around for any slugs?"

"Sure, but no luck. We could go back with a metal detector I suppose."

"Good idea." Dave went back to his list. "We also found two twelve gauge shotguns, but the shells Sam picked up on Schwimley were sixteen gauge, so that looks like a dead end. That leaves the blood-stained hatchet with hairs attached."

Stella hadn't yet heard about that so Dave explained what they'd found. "Next we need to compare the blood and hair with Sam's. And if there's a match, then I think we've got these guys for assault along with poaching. Since that's something the

Sheriff's Department is more prepared to do than Fish and Wildlife, I'm hoping you can help out? I can get you our evidence by tomorrow afternoon at the latest."

Stella readily agreed, but then pointed out the obvious. "Even if we can make them for poaching and for the assault on Sam, that still doesn't get us anywhere with who killed Mabel. Where do we go next on that?"

She had us stumped. Despite a multi-agency and nearly month-long effort, we still hadn't gotten any farther than learning that she had been the wearer of those blue shoes and red hat, and that she was gone to parts unknown. Unless, perhaps, there was a clue in the items Mabel had stashed under the floorboards of her little cabin. As Stella collected them up for safe keeping in their evidence locker, I could not shake the feeling that one of them contained an important clue, if only I could figure out what it was.

CHAPTER 37

After the meeting I followed Stella Reynard up to the Sheriff's Department, in order to donate my hair and blood for comparison with the Perkins' hatchet. That took only about fifteen minutes down in their forensics lab, but then Stella invited me up to her office, saying she wanted to talk. I assumed it was going to be about the case.

She got us bottles of water from a refrigerator out in the hall, and we settled on opposite sides of her desk. I was anxious to get home, since I'd promised myself to give Katie a call that evening and knew it would take time to build up the courage. But Stella took an inordinate amount of time unscrewing the cap to her water bottle, and I got the feeling she was having trouble making up her mind about something.

I decided small talk might get things rolling. "You should have seen all those bird watchers out at Schwimley Key today. What a zoo."

Stella fiddled around with one of her gold loop earrings. "But you really like birds, don't you Sam? And you seem to know an awful lot about them. How often do you take clients bird-watching instead of fishing?"

"About one in ten of my trips is for birds and other wildlife. Why? Are you interested?"

"Actually, I don't know much about birds or fish, but I'm sort of interested in both. I was wondering if, uh, we might go out some time." She paused for a drink of water, and then gave a nervous laugh. "Out in your boat, that is."

I had never seen Stella this uneasy. "Sure, we could do that. We could fish and look for birds. When would you like to go?"

"How about Sunday? That's my next day off."

I had flirted with the idea of sneaking up to Lauderdale that day, if Katie would have it. But I could tell this was something important to Stella. "Sure, Sunday works. Can you be at my dock by eight?"

"Of course. And thanks. What should I bring?"

"Bring a pair of binoculars if you have one. I'll take care of the rest, including food and drinks along with fishing gear." I made a move to stand up. "And now, I've..."

"You know that isn't really it, Sam."

I sat back down. "What?"

"This isn't about fishing or bird-watching."

I could have played dumb, but Stella deserved better than that. "I guess I sort of figured that out. What is it about, if you don't mind my asking?"

Stella looked out her window, where the top of a coconut palm was waving in the breeze. "It's about my life outside of the job. Down here in the Keys it seems like everybody is either fishing, or taking a client fishing, or worrying about somebody doing the wrong kind of fishing. It makes me feel like I'm on the outside of something, looking in. I thought if I got involved, maybe there could be something to my life besides chasing bad guys."

She paused for a sip of water. "Don't get me wrong, Sam. I like my job and I think I'm pretty good at it. And for the most part the other people in the department treat me with courtesy and respect. And for sure you guys on Team Mabel are great. It's just that at the end of the day..." She stopped and shrugged, and her eyes flicked away.

"You grew up in New Orleans, right?"

"Right."

"And what was that like?"

"I was a city kid. We didn't live in the best neighborhood and my brother died in a gang fight. Everything was indoors or on the street, except softball. I was really good at softball." She laughed, but it had an edge. "Hell, Sam, growing up my idea of a wilderness experience was playing left field. And now here I am stuck in the middle of the great outdoors."

It occurred to me that Stella Reynard also was a black woman stuck in the middle of a mostly white place, and maybe that had something to do with it. But I didn't know her well enough to go there, at least not yet.

"It would be an honor and pleasure to introduce you to that great outdoors, Stella. See you on Sunday."

~ ~ ~

Despite her assurances, Katie didn't answer the phone that night. But she did return my call about an hour later.

"Sorry I missed you."

"Working late?"

"Oh, the usual."

I wondered if "the usual" meant good old Stu, her friend the Assistant District Attorney. I also wondered if there was any chance of getting our conversation beyond platitudes.

"I was hoping to get up to Lauderdale this weekend, but things have gotten busy. Any chance you could get down here instead?"

"No, sorry." There was a long silence and at first I thought maybe she'd just hung up on me. "But if I did come down, I'm not sure you'd like the direction things might take."

That sounded ominous. "What direction is that?"

"A trial separation."

"Trial separation? Hell, Kat, we're already separated. What are you talking about?"

"Don't patronize me. You know damned well what I'm talking about."

This time she really did hang up. So much for progress on the marriage front.

I made myself a Makers Mark on the rocks and took it out onto the deck. It was one of those beautiful quiet nights in the Keys, under the sliver of a new moon, with just enough breeze to sway the palms. But I scarcely noticed. Just over three weeks ago, Katie had come down and we'd had a wonderful time together, one of the best I could remember. How could things have gone downhill so fast? Was it only about Stu the wonder boy, or was there something else?

Of course then there was Sam the wonder boy and his one night fling with Flo. And Stella Reynard. Had she also just come into the picture, or was I reading too much into our conversation earlier that afternoon? One thing seemed obvious. Sam Sawyer might be a helluva fisherman, a good birder, and maybe even a pretty fair cop. But right now I was just a klutz flailing around in the dark when it came to women. Maybe it was time for another talk with Snooks. He wasn't any kind of authority on marital relations, but he was a friend.

CHAPTER 38

I spent the next two days on the water with Marshall White, who had flown down from Boston for some tarpon fishing. It was good to get back in the guiding business and we did all right. Three fish ate his fly, two hooked-up long enough to make it exciting, and we got one to the boat, a nice 120 pounder. But Katie and Mabel never totally left my mind, and Flo and Stella kept coming and going.

And then it was Sunday.

Stella Reynard showed up fifteen minutes early, but I already had the Hell's Bay loaded up with binoculars, a bird guide, fishing gear, and enough drinks and food in the cooler for a full day's outing if that was her wish.

I had never seen Stella out of uniform, but it was worth the wait. She was wearing shorts and a sleeveless yellow t-shirt that showed off her bronzed and well-muscled arms and legs to great effect. It would make for a lot of sun exposure, but that was her business. At least she'd brought along a pair of high-quality wrap-around sunglasses. Because we weren't going back into the everglades, the bugs should be tolerable. I had plenty of repellent just in case.

We walked together down to my dock, and I asked her to step into the boat and take the seat in front of the center console. Then I got in behind her at the wheel, and we made ready to cast off.

Stella was carrying a good-sized canvas tote bag,

and I inquired as to its contents.

"I've got a camera, a pair of binoculars I checked out of our store room, and some other sheriff stuff. Oh, and a hat." She paused long enough to pull a baseball cap out of the bag and put it on. It was black and gold, and emblazoned with the logo of the New Orleans Saints.

"Be sure and turn that thing around backwards before we get started."

"Why?"

"So the wind doesn't get caught up under the bill and blow it off your head. My friend Snooks tells all his clients he'll only go back once to pick up a lost hat. After that, it's gone."

Stella laughed but took my advice about the hat. "You think he means it?"

"Probably not, but it's part of his routine."

Then she turned serious. "Before we go, I have a confession to make. I checked with my assistant, Penny Raintree, the woman who went with us to Schwimley Key the other day? Turns out she is a bird watcher, and she was the one who leaked the news about the Cuban todies. Sorry it caused you all that trouble."

"What are you going to do about it?"

"I put a letter of reprimand in her file. But my recommendation to Danny – uh, that's my boss, Captain Pasquale – was not to do anything else. She's young and she's sorry, and I don't expect she'll make that sort of mistake again."

"Sure. And besides, if it hadn't happened I might never have gotten back inside Mabel's cabin and found all that stuff under her floorboards. It could have been a blessing in disguise, depending on whether any of those treasures help lead us to her killer."

I started up the Yamaha, then asked Stella to go forward and untie the bow line while I did the same for the stern. A gentle breeze blew at our backs as we made our way down the canal and out toward open water. We came on two good birds before we even got to the end of the canal, both perched low on mangrove prop roots. One was a yellow-crowned night heron and the other was a snowy egret – two of my favorite species. I slowed to a stop and suggested that Stella glass the birds while I described something about their characteristics and habits. Then we had a look in my field guide as a way of confirming what we'd just seen.

Stella noticed that the night heron had much bigger eyes than the egret, and she asked about that. I was impressed with her powers of observation, because it wasn't something a beginning birder normally would catch.

"Night herons are just that, mostly active under low light. That's what those big red eyes are all about."

She began thumbing through the field guide. "Wow. I had no idea there were so many different kinds."

"Yeah, and especially for wading birds like herons and egrets, there's no place better than the Florida Keys for seeing them. You've come to the right place."

She closed the book and looked up at me. "And apparently with the right guy."

Once out into Florida Bay, my plan was to drive north and west as far as Cape Sable without any side-trips. Then we would poke around inside Lake

Ingraham using the trolling motor, mostly looking for birds. After that we'd make our way back, checking out a variety of keys and shoals for both fish and birds. I had decided the best thing for a novice fisherman like Stella was to go for mangrove snapper in the moats around some of those keys. An added bonus was the possibility of bringing home dinner, and the idea of sharing a meal with her at the end of the day had its appeal.

Unfortunately, we never got that far.

Our route from Islamorada to Cape Sable took us north of Schwimley Key, but not far enough north to miss the pod of turkey vultures circling over the west side of the island. I cut the engine, got out my binoculars, and counted at least thirty individuals. Most of the flock stayed high, but as I watched several of the black birds dropped down and perched in the mangroves along the shore.

Stella had seen it of course, and she was using her own binoculars. "What do you think's going on over there, Sam? That's Schwimley Key, right?"

"Right. Vultures eat only carrion, and they hunt mostly by smell. With that many birds, it must be a pretty big stink."

"Do you suppose we oughta go take a look?"

"Afraid so. Sorry to screw up your day off. Maybe it'll just be a raccoon or crocodile or something, and we can still get in some fishing afterwards. But we're gonna have to go back and get my canoe, 'cause there's no other good way to get on the island."

~ ~ ~

Forty-five minutes later we were anchored up in

the usual spot out from the canal leading to the island's interior, and I was in the process of untying the canoe and dropping it into the water. Vultures still circled over the island, but there weren't as many as before. This probably meant one of two things. Either they'd given up because there wasn't anything down there to eat, or they were already down there eating it.

At least there weren't any other boats around. The Park Service had put up some extra large "No Trespassing" signs since I'd last been out here, and it must have been working.

My choice would have been for Stella to stay behind to guard the boat. She wasn't dressed for crashing through the underbrush on Schwimley Key, and I hated the thought of those beautiful bronze legs getting all scratched up. But there was room in the canoe for two people, and there was no way I was going to tell a Deputy Sheriff what she could or could not do in her own county.

"You in on this? It might be a false alarm, and I can call you if I find anything."

Stella went to the trouble of pulling down her sunglasses, so I'd be sure to catch the full effect of a hard stare. "No way I'm not coming, Sam."

"The bugs could be awful in there, to say nothing of snakes and crocodiles."

"So I'll put in for hardship pay. I've been there before, you may remember. Now let's get started."

~ ~ ~

Finding a carcass somewhere on Schwimley Key could have been difficult, but the vultures made it easy. As soon as we broke out into the clearing around

Mabel's cabin, we spotted at least a dozen of the big black birds perched in some poisonwood trees just beyond the western edge of the pond. I could see movement beneath the trees, suggesting some of them already were down on the ground enjoying the breakfast buffet, whatever it was.

One piece of "sheriff stuff" Stella had brought in her tote bag turned out to be a department issue Glock. When we were about half way around the pond she fired off three rounds. All the birds that had been in the trees immediately took off, but when we got close enough we could see that a few had stayed behind on the ground. Stella shot again and the stragglers flapped noisily up into the air, joining the others already circling over our heads.

Turkey vultures are so-named because they have red heads devoid of any feathers, which makes them look superficially like actual turkeys. But the similarity ends with the head. Nobody should even think about carving up a vulture for Thanksgiving, especially in light of what the birds themselves actually eat.

In this particular case it wasn't a raccoon or a crocodile, it was a human. My first thought was that we might finally have discovered the remains of Mabel Schwimley. But if so, where had she been all this time?

The body was on its back, in a position where it would have been staring up into the sky, had the vultures not already had plucked out the eyeballs. My first clue it wasn't Mabel was that the corpse was wearing a tattered and blood-stained Hawaiian shirt. The second clue was a heavy gold wristwatch attached to the left arm. The third was a gold chain around the neck.

We hadn't found all of Pelican Pete Donovan, but we had found most of him. Only the left leg was missing. I looked back over my shoulder, half expecting to find a pair of mud-yellow eyes staring up at me out of the pond, followed by a row of gray scales. But there wasn't anything out there.

Stella quickly pulled two other pieces of sheriff stuff out of her tote bag – a camera and a hand-held radio. She handed me the camera and asked me to start taking pictures, while she got on the radio to headquarters to report that Peter Donovan was no longer a missing person. She also asked for a crime scene team.

Getting the team in and the body out was going to present a challenge, given the shallow waters around Schwimley Key, but I had an idea.

"This pond probably is just big enough for an amphibious helicopter with a skilled pilot. I'm guessing the Coast Guard has both."

"Good idea, Sam. I'll give them a call and find out."

"Oh, and while you're at it, remind your crime scene people to bring a metal detector. I want to check for bullets at the spot where the Perkins cousins shot up my canoe."

Stella got back on the radio and set things up, including the necessary coordination between the Coast Guard and the Sheriff's Department. They estimated an ETA of about forty-five minutes. Our job in the mean time was to guard the body, which probably would mean just keeping away the vultures and crocodiles, since it was unlikely any other people would be coming around. Still, we couldn't rule out the lone scofflaw birder, even though we hadn't yet seen any.

Technically we should have backed off and left things alone until forensics arrived, but I couldn't resist nosing around a bit, and neither could Stella. Given the missing leg, one logical conclusion would have been that Donovan had been killed and partially eaten by a crocodile. But I knew the American species wasn't known for attacking humans. A more likely scenario was that something or somebody else had killed the man, after which the crocs had started eating the corpse, starting with its left leg.

This was pure speculation of course, until I noticed something that gave weight to my working hypothesis. "What do you see about the man's arms?"

Stella bent in for a closer look. "The right one is a lot bigger around than the left?"

"Yep. This corpse has started to bloat, but can you think of any reason one of the arms would swell up more than the other?"

"Not offhand. Oh wait ... could it be from a snakebite?"

"If so, there ought to be fang marks. I don't see any. Do you suppose we could lift up the arm and look under it?"

"That comes pretty close to disturbing a crime scene, Sam. I think we should wait. We'll know soon enough."

I didn't like it, but she was right. In the mean time, there was something else I wanted to check out. "Can you keep an eye on things here, while I take a walk up to the north end of the island? I shouldn't be long."

"What?"

"I want to go take a look at that shell mound. I promise not to disturb anything."

It took me about fifteen minutes to get there, and things were way different than the first time I had visited the spot. Not only were there signs of recent disturbance to the mound itself, but lying next to it were a rake, a trowel, and a bucket. Looking past the mound, I spotted a green canoe tied up to a mangrove back by the shore. It was the type of canoe with a squared-off stern, and there was an electric trolling motor attached to the transom. It seemed obvious someone had taken a trip to the island with the goal of excavating the shell mound, and then something must have happened before they had a chance to pack up and leave in the canoe. Could it have been Pelican Pete? And if so, how did his body get all the way over by the pond?

I knelt down to take a look inside the bucket, and came eye-to-eye with an everglades diamondback rattlesnake coiled up right next to it. A small shrub and some accumulated litter had provided all the cover the snake had needed to escape my attention sooner. I immediately jumped back, doubtless propelled by a big shot of adrenalin. The snake never moved or rattled, just like the other time.

Once I had calmed down sufficiently, I used the rake to pull the bucket far enough away from the snake to get a look inside. It contained two things. One was a piece of coral that had been carved into something that resembled a bird. The other was a piece of tortoise shell.

Some parts of a Pelican Pete puzzle were coming together, or at least they seemed plausible. But others made no sense. We likely had him as the individual who had been pilfering Native American artifacts off the island, using a canoe for transportation. I expected that Mike Nunez would find a treasure trove of the stuff when he finally got into Pete's back room, assuming the man hadn't already sold most of it on the black market.

As to the Pete's fatal accident, or whatever it was, snakebite followed by crocodile scavenging made sense up to a point. I could see one of the bigger crocs dragging his remains back to the pond, perhaps chewing off one of his legs along the way. But if Pete had been bitten by the diamondback while he was digging around in the shell mound, why hadn't he simply gotten back in his canoe and made a run for home? This was where the whole scenario started to fall apart. A croc could have come along and killed the man just after he'd been bitten, but the odds of that seemed impossibly slim. Something else must have happened, but at this point I couldn't think what it might be.

One thing was for sure. If Pelican Pete had anything to do with the death or disappearance of Mabel Schwimley, he was no longer in a position to confess to the crime.

Before heading back to rejoin Stella, I took a look inside the canoe in hopes of finding something that might link Pete to Mabel. If he had taken her off the island in his canoe, dead or alive, there might still be some evidence. But nothing seemed out of the ordinary. In fact, the little boat was empty except for a small cooler. I lifted up the lid, using my bandana in order not to leave fingerprints, but there was nothing inside except two water bottles and an energy bar. Still, it would be important for the crime scene crew to make a more thorough inspection of the canoe, as they would doubtless do for the whole area around the shell mound.

About then I heard a familiar 'whup-whup-whup,' and looked up to see a red-and-white Coast Guard helicopter circling down for a landing on the pond in the middle of Schwimley Key.

~ ~ ~

Stella and I pretty much stayed out of the way over the next three hours, as a four-person crime scene crew from her department completed its work around the corpse and then loaded up the remains of Pelican Pete Donovan for transport back to the county morgue. They confirmed my suspicions about a snakebite, as indeed there were telltale fang marks on the inside of the man's right forearm. They found no other marks on the body, such as bullet or stab wounds, to suggest any other possible cause of death. However, the crew chief, a heavyset man named Charlie Griscom, cautioned against reaching any firm conclusions pending an autopsy.

We never did find Pete's missing leg, even though we spent time searching around the pond and then all the way back out to the shell mound. We also expected to find evidence, such as matted vegetation or a bloody trail, where something or somebody had dragged the body from the mound back to spot where we had found the it. But there was no such evidence, which seemed odd.

There was room in the helicopter for all the items I had found near the shell mound, except for the canoe. Charlie Griscom asked Stella and me to drive it back to Islamorada once they had finished removing the contents and dusting everything for prints. This left us responsible for three vessels – two canoes and my Hell's Bay.

We stood at the edge of the pond and watched as the chopper lifted off and spun around for the flight back to the Coast Guard station next to the Snake Creek drawbridge. As soon as it disappeared off to the northeast, Stella started getting us organized about our own departure from the island.

"You want me to take your canoe, while you take Pete's? And we'll meet at your boat?"

"Sounds like a plan. But there's something I want to do first. Did your crew bring that metal detector I requested?"

Stella snapped her fingers. "Right, I forgot all about that. I think they left it back where we found the body."

We picked up the detector and walked down the trail past the cabin, to the spot where Mabel's rowboat and my canoe sat beside each other at the head of the canal leading away from the island. I pointed to a patch of flattened vegetation.

"See this indentation? That's where my canoe sat the night somebody shot it full of holes."

Stella switched on the detector and began sweeping it back and forth across the area. She had a hit right away, so I put on my gloves, knelt down, and began digging. The soil was loose and damp and after a bit of probing around my fingers hit something solid about four inches down. I pulled it out of the ground and held it up for Stella to see.

"That's definitely a bullet, Sam. Didn't Dave Ackerman say the Fish and Wildlife folks found a lever-action 30.06 in the Perkins doublewide over in Florida City? I can't say for sure, but that slug you're holding looks about the right caliber, don't you think?"

"Yeah, I think so. Why don't you make some more passes with the detector? As I recall there were four holes in my canoe."

We eventually unearthed a total of three slugs from the site, which Stella carefully packaged up in an evidence bag one of her crime scene people had shared before they had left in the helicopter.

I stood back up and brushed off the dirt and bits of dead vegetation stuck to my clothes and gloves. "If those slugs match the Perkins rifle, maybe the net is closing on Luther and Orville as the two guys who gave me that headache the night of my camp-out on Schwimley last week."

Stella agreed. "Looks good. Now let's get out of here."

I helped Stella push off in my canoe, and then walked back to the shell mound. Fortunately, there was plenty of charge left in Pete's trolling motor battery. I drove his canoe out and around to where my Hell's Bay was anchored. Stella had already beaten me there. We tied both canoes off the stern, and headed for home. It was late afternoon by the time we got the whole fleet back to my dock.

CHAPTER 39

I gave Stella Reynard a raincheck on our fishing and birding trip, as we unloaded our gear and pulled the canoes out of the water, using my boat ramp. Our 'cook your own catch' dinner was off the table, so to speak, but I decided to invite her to join me for a drink at the Safari Lounge with maybe some bar food to go along.

"You're on. That sounds like a great idea. Okay if I use your bathroom to wash up first? I'm feeling a little grubby."

"Absolutely. Not that patrons of the Dead Animal Bar are all that picky about such things."

She laughed and headed upstairs. I followed but stayed on the deck while she went inside, because I wanted to call Mike Nunez with the news of what we'd found on Schwimley Key, in case he hadn't heard. He hadn't, so I filled him in.

"I'll be damned. I guess that's the end of Pelican Pete Donovan. And you think it was a snake that got him?"

"Oh it got him all right, but whether that was the actual cause of death remains to be seen."

"And you say he'd been digging at the shell mound?"

"Well somebody had been, and we didn't find anybody else on the island. It sure seems likely."

"I can't wait to get into the back of his Emporium. I'll bet it's crammed with stuff the man has collected, maybe from more places than just Schwimley. Goddam looters. First thing tomorrow I'm gonna talk to the

Sheriff's Department about getting a search warrant. Shouldn't be hard under the circumstances."

"I may be able to help you with that."

Stella had just joined me out on the deck, drying her hands on a towel. I handed her my phone. "Guess who's hot to get inside Pete Donovan's place. Not that I blame him."

~ ~ ~

Once Stella had agreed to help Mike with a search warrant, she and I got in my Cherokee for the short drive over to the Safari Lounge. We were half way up the outside stairs leading to the front door, when a familiar voice called out from the parking lot below us.

I turned at the sound of my name. It was Flo, dressed for work in Bermudas and her standard gray Dead Animal Bar t-shirt.

"So you're back?" Making it sound like a question was world-class stupid, of course, and she didn't let it pass.

"No, Sam. I'm still up in Michigan."

"I mean, uh, are you already back at work?"

"Just about to start. This will be my first shift since I got home."

Flo joined Stella on the stairs below me. The last rays of the evening sun caught Stella's glossy curls and Flo's green eyes as I tried to figure out how to introduce them to each other. It would be easy explaining Stella to Flo. Not so much the other way around. What was I supposed to say – "Stella Reynard, I'd like you to meet Flo Delaney, my favorite bartender."

Before I could get things figured out, they solved the problem by simply shaking hands and introducing themselves.

The guy named Burt was tending bar as we walked in. He waved at Flo and pointed to a clock on the wall. "You're on in ten. Why don't you go out back and get some ice, while I see to your friends here?"

The Safari was jammed. There were only two stools left, and taking them put Stella and me with our backs to the Atlantic. I had hoped to watch the last of the sunset, but she said it was okay because we already had seen plenty of outdoors that day.

We both ordered margaritas, on the rocks with salt, and a double serving of chicken wings from the kitchen. Burt asked us to pay up front, because he was about to go off duty and tabs were supposed to be settled at a shift change. We sipped our drinks and watched as Burt left with my money while Flo came out carrying a big tub of ice that she dumped in a cooler up near the cash register. She got busy with some other customers right away, but I knew an awkward moment was coming when it came time for her to deliver our wings. That took another ten minutes, during which Stella and I reviewed the day's happenings and talked about next steps.

From a personal perspective, I was particularly anxious to get a comparison between the bullets I had found and the rifle belonging to the Perkins cousins. Stella assured me that would be expedited.

"Comparing your hair and blood with that from their hatchet could take longer, because it involves DNA testing. But if the weapon analysis turns up a match, we probably can proceed with an arrest anyway. I'd like to get those boys off the street as soon as possible."

That left Pelican Pete, and I kept coming back to the

big hole in our scenario about what actually had happened out on Schwimley. "If a snake bit me in the arm, Stella, I'd jump in my canoe and get back to the mainland asap. Instead he winds up dead all the way over by the pond. How could that happen?"

She shrugged her bare bronze shoulders. "I agree it doesn't make sense, unless a crocodile got him right after the bite." She put her hand up to stop me. "I know, I know. It's a long shot. Maybe somebody else killed him before he had a chance to get into his canoe?"

"But who? And how? There weren't any obvious marks on the body, unless you count his missing leg. And that's one helluva an unorthodox way to go about murdering somebody."

Stella laughed, revealing once again her full set of white teeth, perfect except for that one little gap, and it was growing on me. "Maybe the autopsy will turn up something. Meanwhile, here comes our chicken wings and I'm starved."

Flo made her delivery. There were two plates, one with full-on spicy, the other less so. The spicy wings were for Stella, she being Cajun and all. The latter were for me, the wimpy Midwesterner. Flo watched as we both dug in, and then asked if we needed refills on the margaritas. I said yes, not so much because my glass had gotten low but because I wanted time to think about what to say when she came back. We needed to have a conversation of some sort, out of fairness to her if for no other reason.

Five minutes later Flo returned with my drink, and the time had come. Other customers beckoned, but I didn't give her a chance.

"How was Michigan?" It wasn't a bold start, but it was better than nothing.

Flo kept staring at the spot where she'd set down my margarita. "Fine. Saw some old friends, you know, and just sort of relaxed. But it's good to be back."

"And it's good having you back."

With that Flo looked up, catching first Stella's eye and then mine. After that she shook her head, just once and just barely, but the signal was obvious. Not now, and not here. Then a man across the bar in a raggedy sleeveless undershirt got loud about where the hell was his Bud Light, and Flo left. Stella chewed on two more chicken wings and took a big swallow of margarita. She used a paper napkin to wipe the hot sauce of her lips, and then turned on her barstool in my direction.

"Flo seems like a nice person. Have you known each other very long?"

"Sort of. As you can see, she's a bartender at my favorite watering hole. Why?"

"Because she looks familiar."

"You think you've met her before?"

"No, it's not that. It's like I've seen her picture or something."

"Huh."

"So it's just here at the bar that you know each other?"

The feeling of being painted into a corner wasn't new, and it wasn't pleasant either. "More or less. Why the particular interest?"

Stella took another swallow before she replied. "Because I'm a detective, and a pretty good one. And I'm a woman and I have eyes that work."

Things were headed into murky territory, and I was trying to figure out what to say when a tap on my shoulder let me off the hook. I spun on my barstool, and there stood Bryce Wickstrom holding a glass filled with ice and an amber liquid that looked and smelled like bourbon. He stuck out the hand not holding the glass, and we shook.

"How's it going, Sam?"

"Good. How's fishing? Oh, and Stella Reynard, I'd like you to meet Bryce Wickstrom."

The Oklahoma oilman smiled and said hello and they shook hands. "Fishing's been okay, but I was wondering if you were available this week. Snooks is busy with other clients, and there's a shark-fly contest I'd like to enter. Would you be available?"

I knew about a local tournament centered on catching sharks with a fly rod, but I'd never been a participant. Sharks have notoriously poor eyesight, relying mostly on smell to find their prey. The whole thing involved chumming them in with something stinky, and then throwing big colorful flies right in front of their noses. In my opinion it did not compare favorably with fly-fishing for species like tarpon and permit. Still, my guiding (as opposed to crime fighting) business had been spotty lately. I knew the man paid well, he definitely had the right skill set, and I was beginning to like the guy. On top of that, proceeds from the tournament went to a local charity, so I said sure.

As it happened, not directly but eventually, my involvement in that particular shark-fly contest ended up turning the whole Schwimley Key business right on its head.

CHAPTER 40

The shark-fly tournament didn't start for a couple of days, which gave me time to come up with a good supply of chum. It was common knowledge that sharks had a particular affinity for barracuda or, more specifically, bloody pieces of barracuda. This meant I needed to catch and kill at least a couple before the tournament actually started. Bryce had said he wasn't available, so I took a chance and asked Stella. I knew she had a day off coming, since our planned birding and fishing day had turned into work. She checked with her boss, who said it was okay as long as she took along her badge and gun and kept her radio and phone on while we were out on the water.

We met again at my dock early the next morning. Cloud cover hinted at the possibility of a rain shower or two, but it was warm and calm and we both had rain gear just in case.

My destination was the vicinity of the Alligator Reef Lighthouse. It was one of a string of such structures marking the edge of the continental shelf along the Atlantic side of the Keys, about five miles offshore. The lighthouses once had played a critical role in keeping seagoing ships from sailing into shallow water, but modern navigation devices had long since rendered them obsolete. Now they served mainly as underwater structures providing fish habitat. I knew from experience that the waters around Alligator Reef Lighthouse were full of big barracuda. A marine sanctuary enclosed the immediate vicinity of the lighthouse, and kill fishing there was not permitted. But I also knew the boundaries of the sanctuary leaked enough fish out into adjacent reef waters to make the trip worthwhile.

Our fishing would be in two phases, as I explained to Stella as we crossed under the Channel Two Bridge from the Gulf to the Atlantic Side and headed northeast toward Alligator Reef. The lighthouse stood out clearly above a calm sea, looking closer than it actually was.

"We'll start out trolling big Rapala lures behind the boat, keeping outside the sanctuary. Once we have enough fish for chum, then we'll switch to fly gear and have some fun with catch and release inside the protected area."

Stella turned to look at the two big spin-casting outfits I had stuck in rod holders at the stern of my Hell's Bay, one on each side of the outboard. "That looks like serious stuff. Are barracuda that strong?"

"You bet they are. The big ones really pack a punch, especially when they first get hooked. I was out here one time with Katie, and she actually lost one of my rods overboard. The fish pulled it right out of her hands."

"Katie?"

"Uh, yeah. She's my wife."

"I guess you forgot to mention you were married."

"Sorry about that. Thought I had."

"How come I haven't seen her around your place?"

I explained about our situation, all except for the part about our supposed "trial separation" that I'd only just learned about myself. No point in cluttering up

Stella's mind with too many details.

Evidently she didn't buy it.

"And this thing between you and Flo..."

"What about Flo? I told you last night..."

"You didn't tell me anything last night, Sam."

"All right, all right. Fair enough. But look Stella, it's complicated. And it's something I've got to work out for myself. Just back off, okay?"

By this time the lighthouse was only about two hundred yards away, standing tall and white against a cloudy sky. "We're almost there and it's time to go fishing. That's what we came for, right?"

I could see the hurt in Stella's eyes, and I immediately regretted my outburst. She might have pushed things too far, but I had no reason to believe it was with evil intent. If anything, just the opposite.

"Sorry."

She sighed and shook her head. "No, you're right. I'm the one that should be sorry. It's none of my business. I just thought that since we were getting to be friends, and friends can share things, that maybe I could help."

An awkward silence followed, probably because neither Stella nor I knew just what to say next. The truth was I had started to value her friendship, and apparently it was mutual. "You *can* help, Stella. What say we start by trying to catch some barracuda? We'll be like a pair of sorry friends trying to help each other."

That brought a laugh, and maybe a tear to one eye.

I got busy rigging up the spinning rods, handing one to Stella and keeping the other in the rod holder on my side of the boat. We each let out about fifty yards of line, and I began a slow clockwise troll around the perimeter of the sanctuary.

Nothing happened for the first fifteen minutes. Then suddenly Stella shouted "Look!" I turned from the wheel to see a big gray torpedo that had come to the surface, following about a yard behind her Rapala lure. I slowed the boat just a bit, and apparently that triggered the fish to strike. Her rod bent in a heavy arc, but she held on as the fish turned and made the first of what turned out to be three good runs.

Ten minutes later we had a fine four-foot barracuda flopping around in my landing net. I took a billy club out of the starboard rear hold and gave the fish three good hard raps on top of its head. Then I laid it out dead up in the bow.

"Sorry about the blood. I think I mentioned we were going to have to kill a couple."

Stella shrugged and said she didn't mind.

We were in between our second and third keeper fish, when her phone rang, and I couldn't help listening to her half of a short conversation.

"Hello?"

A short silence.

"Oh, hi."

A longer silence.

"That's great news, thanks."

Another short silence.

"Yeah, he's here with me now. I'll be sure to tell him. Talk to you tomorrow. Bye."

"Good news?"

Stella grinned. "You bet. They got a match between the Perkins' 30.06 and those bullets we dug up on

Schwimley. Looks like we've got those boys for sure as the pair who shot holes in your canoe. And the blood and hair comparisons should seal their fate on an assault charge."

We celebrated by catching one more keeper barracuda. Then we celebrated again by going inside the sanctuary and tickling three more on the fly. Stella was a novice when it came to fly-casting, so I just peeled off a bunch of line and we trolled a big red and yellow Clouser behind the boat. It worked, and she got the thrill of feeling some really big fish on a fly rod.

Clouds had continued to build throughout the day, and about two in the afternoon a big rainstorm rolled in off the Atlantic, accompanied by strong gusty winds out of the northeast. We both pulled on rain slickers, and kept fishing. But after a half hour it was still raining hard, and I thought Stella was starting to look a bit wilted.

"Wanna call it a day? We've got plenty of chum, we've caught more than our share of good fish, and it looks like this storm is not letting up any time soon."

She sniffed. "Sure, I guess so. If you're sure we've got enough." She paused long enough to shake some of the water off the hood of her blue raincoat. "But this was fun." Then she laughed and looked up into the dark cloudy sky. "Really."

"Wait 'til you try it when the sun's out."

It was a wet boat ride home, but nevertheless I came away with the feeling that Stella might have just gotten herself hooked on my favorite outdoor sport.

CHAPTER 41

B ryce Wickstrom showed up right on time the next morning, ready to go shark fishing. I'd chopped up the barracudas and packed them on ice in my live well the evening before. We got in my boat and headed out the canal toward Florida Bay. I suggested we start out by anchoring at one of the cuts in the Arsenicker Bank, because these were the sorts of places with a tidal flow sufficient to set up a good chum stream. But my client had other ideas. He'd heard a rumor that some tiger sharks were hanging around the Tennessee Reef Lighthouse, the next one down the Atlantic coast from Alligator Reef.

Tournament rules gave different numbers of points for different species, and the tiger shark was at the top of the list, so that made sense as far as it went. However, there were two problems. First, I expected it would be harder to create a good chum line in the open and relatively deep waters out along the continental shelf than it would be in the mosaic of cuts and shoals back on the bay side. Second, tiger sharks were pretty rare and moved around a lot, so there was no guarantee they'd still be there when we got out to Tennessee Reef. Nevertheless Bryce insisted, and he was the client so that was that.

Once outside the canal, I turned left and drove down to the Channel Five Bridge, and then turned left again and headed out into the Atlantic. It was a clear day, but there was some chop on the water, and it was going to be a bouncy ride. The winds were predicted to top out at 25 knots by that evening and I just hoped we were back home by then. Official tournament hours were 8AM to 4PM, so it seemed likely unless we hooked up right at the last minute.

The boat ride took about a half-hour, which put us at the reef by 8:15. Two other boats already were anchored up next to the lighthouse, but they were spin fishermen jigging bait on the bottom, probably hoping to pick up some snapper for dinner. I dropped my anchor about two hundred yards north of the lighthouse, and started filling a chum bag with barracuda parts. By tournament rules we were not supposed to start chumming ahead of fishing, so I waited while Bryce assembled what looked like a brand new ten-weight Sage fly rod. I might have preferred a twelve-weight considering the potential size of our prey, but a ten-weight probably would work. His choice of reels was another matter. Just like when we'd been out for tarpon, Bryce pulled his ancient Hardy Brothers reel out of his gear bag, attached it to the Sage, and began feeding the line up through the guides.

I shook my head in disbelief. "If we tie into any big shark, let alone a tiger, you know that thing's not going to hold up."

"Yeah, that's what you said about my tarpon, and we landed that one, didn't we?"

I never have liked rhetorical questions. "Look, I know it's supposed to be your lucky reel and everything. But maybe just having it with you in the boat would be enough? I've got a like-new Hardy 8000 in my box that would be more than up to the task. That would be sort of like keeping it in the family, right?"

But he was having none of it, and instead he just finished stringing up his rod. "Now hand me a leader, and then let's take a look at your fly selection. Something big and red?"

I helped him tie on an orange and red fly called a megalodon, and dropped a bag full of barracuda chunks over the side. Then we sat down to wait.

We waited and waited, and while we waited we talked.

Bryce Wickstrom poured himself a cup of coffee from a thermos he'd brought along, and took a swallow. "Saw a thing on television the other night about that woman who left her shoes back in the glades. Apparently she used to live on Schwimley Key. A woman named Mavis?"

The Rhonda Wilcox press conference must have made the local news, but somehow I'd missed it. "Actually, it was Mabel."

"Right, whatever. Your name didn't come up, but you've been out there, right? The day your boat caught fire?"

"Yeah, and a couple more times. Why?"

"I understand you know a lot about birds, and I guess there's some sort of an odd variety that's been discovered on Schwimley. I thought maybe you were the one that found it."

"It was me. And it was a Cuban tody, more than one in fact. You know about them?"

Wickstrom laughed. "Hell, Sam, I wouldn't know a tody from a toadstool."

"I mean how did you hear about it?"

He drained the last of his coffee and screwed the cup back on the thermos. "I thought they talked about it at that press conference I saw on T.V."

I wanted to push Bryce about it because I had asked Rhonda Wilcox specifically not to mention the todies in her news conference, but at that point we got interrupted by a gray fin cutting through the water about two hundred feet behind the boat. I tapped Wickstrom on the shoulder, pointed, and told him to get ready. Then I climbed up on the polling platform for a better look.

It was a shark all right, and a big one. It moved in a zigzag pattern back and forth across our chum trail, getting closer with each pass. The fish was nearly within casting range when I spotted the vertical stripes along the flanks that told me it was a tiger.

"Be ready to cast, and then be ready for a fight. It's a tiger, at least seven feet, and it's closing fast."

Bryce nodded and stripped off some line. "Tell me when."

"Not yet ... not yet ... NOW!"

I had to hand it to the man. The big red fly sank right in front of the shark's nose, and it ate. Bryce stuck hard, and the shark turned and bolted as soon as it felt some resistance. I jumped down off the polling platform, unhooked the anchor rope and started the Yamaha. We were going to have to chase this fish if we were to have any chance of getting it to the boat.

The line screamed as the shark took off in earnest, but it hadn't run more than fifty feet before Bryce's old Hardy Brothers reel just blew apart. Pieces of it scattered all over the deck. The line tangled around the butt of the rod, the leader broke, and the shark was long gone before I could even get the boat moving.

If there ever was an occasion when a client deserved an "I told you so," this was it. But somehow I managed to hold my tongue.

Bryce threw down his rod in disgust. "Shit."

"I know, and I'm sorry. That was a great fish."

But that wasn't it. "Huh? Oh, yeah, I suppose so. But look at my reel for god's sake! There's no way in hell I gonna be able to put it back together. It's a goner for sure."

I managed to persuade Wickstrom to go back to fishing, using my newer and much bigger reel, and I loaded up the chum bag with fresh meat. But it was to no avail. Four o'clock came and went, and we didn't see another fish. As predicted, the wind had come up strong by then, and our ride home was both bumpy and grumpy.

CHAPTER 42

I spotted a silver Prius parked next to my boat trailer as soon as Bryce Wickstrom and I returned from our ill-fated encounter with the tiger shark. It was Katie's. Apparently she'd come for another surprise visit, just like the day nearly a month ago when Snooks and I got back from visiting those blue shoes back in the glades.

Bryce helped me tie up the boat, while we talked about our plans for the next day. I insisted this time we'd be going someplace out on the bay side. Katie came out on the deck just as Bryce was leaving and I had started to unpack and clean things up. She was wearing blue shorts, a nondescript gray and white t-shirt, and running shoes. Her hair was wet and she had a towel draped around her neck, like she'd just gotten out of the shower.

"Hi Sam."

"Hi. This is a surprise, but a nice one. Were you out for a run?"

"Just back."

I introduced Bryce, but she didn't seem particularly interested. "Nice to meet you, Mr. Wickstrom."

He said "nice to meet you" back and then headed for his car, a bright yellow Mustang convertible with Florida plates.

Katie watched the Mustang drive off, and then turned back to me. "So I'll see you inside as soon as you're finished down there?"

"Be right up."

Katie went back inside, I finished washing down the fishing gear, and ten minutes later we were together in the living room. I went up and gave her a hug, but she just stood there with her arms at her sides. Then I tried a kiss, which she deflected with a peck on my cheek. Something definitely was up, and I had a very bad feeling.

"Want something to drink?"

"Just some ice water. I've got to get back to Lauderdale tonight."

The bad feeling got worse, as I filled us two glasses and we carried them outside and sat on opposite sides of a round glass-topped table I used for outdoor meals.

"I really am glad to see you, Katie, but this is a bit unexpected, especially after our last phone call."

"Something has come up."

I just sat there in silence, figuring she would get around to it – whatever *it* was – in her own time.

"You remember Stuart Brodsky, the assistant DA I've been working with?"

How could I forget about good old Stu? "Sure."

"He's taken a position with the City of Atlanta, in the DA's office. It's a big promotion, and a real opportunity."

This sounded like good news, but it wasn't.

"He'll be heading up their forensics unit. And he's offered me a job as a member of his staff."

It was a real punch in the gut. I managed to take a big swallow of water, but it stuck in my throat, inducing a coughing fit.

Katie looked alarmed. "You all right?"

I nodded but continued to cough. It took another minute or so before I got my voice back.

"You gonna take it?"

"Probably. I didn't want to tell you over the phone. That's why I'm here."

I was desperate and coughed twice more just to stall for time.

"But what about your teaching? I thought you loved teaching."

"I do. And it looks like maybe they're going to arrange for a courtesy appointment at Emory University. It's a really good school, right in Atlanta. I'll probably be teaching graduate seminars in forensic botany."

The sonofabitch had covered all the bases. "So you're taking this trial separation of ours to the next level, just like that?"

Katie's big dark eyes flashed, her cheeks flushed, and mottled red patches began to grow on her throat. "You make it sound like this is something new. Have you forgotten that you were the one who moved out and not the other way around?"

I just sat there in silence, and eventually she started up again.

"You just goddam punted on your academic career, and then you came running down here to hide out in the Keys. And now you act all surprised that I've decided to move on with my life? Jesus, Sam, come *on!*"

She had me for sure, but I couldn't let it go. "I thought we were good together, Kat. I thought the last time you were down here, you know, it was especially good."

She softened at that, and actually reached across the table to put her hand on mine. "It was always good, Sam. But sometimes things just ... move along, you know?"

If I didn't know it before, I sure knew it now. "Can't we talk about this? You just got here."

She cleared her throat and pulled back her hand. "No, *you* just got here. I've been sitting around for three hours waiting for you to come home."

"I had my phone."

"I tried that. You didn't answer."

"Sorry. We must have been in a dead spot."

"I left a message. Guess you never checked."

This was going nowhere. "That's it then?"

She rose to leave. "There will be some paperwork. I assume we can both deal with this like adults. I'll be in touch."

And with that Katie, the love of my life, walked out of it.

~ ~ ~

I needed a Maker's Mark bad, but drinking alone sounded awful so I called Snooks and invited him over. He must have sensed something was wrong, because he didn't ask any questions about the last-minute invitation. It took him only five minutes, and five minutes after that we were out on my deck, each with our bourbon over ice.

It was nearly dark, and the afternoon winds had started to slacken. Telltale growls and gurgles filled the night air, interrupted by periodic quiet. Somebody on the next canal over must have been working on a diesel inboard, and apparently all was not well. Most likely it was a lobsterman getting ready for the next day's run. I knew it was a hard life pulling lobster pots from dawn 'til dark – harder than a guide's – but at the moment I wasn't in a mood to feel sorry for anybody but myself.

Snooks had the good sense to be patient and let me drink in silence. He must have known I'd get around to whatever it was eventually. It took me another ten minutes to screw up the courage.

"Katie left."

"You mean she was here and now she's gone?"

"She was and she did, but that's not what I mean. I mean we've broken up. She's moving to Atlanta, starting a new career."

Even in the last of the light I could tell that Snooks was fiddling with the rubber band holding up his ponytail, like he always did when he was thinking hard about something.

"Are you okay with this?"

"Okay? Hell no, I'm not okay. But maybe I don't exactly blame her either."

"Because?"

"Because I was the one who started all this by moving to the Keys in the first place. She made that crystal clear this afternoon."

"Are you sorry you ever came down here?"

That was one hell of a good question, and it was the one I'd been avoiding asking myself. Even now, 'yes and no' was the best I could do.

We drank a while, and then I went inside a got us both a refill. When I got back he had a question.

"You gonna tell Flo?"

"No, at least not for now. And neither are you."

He didn't like that. "Don't you think you owe it to her?"

"Maybe, but let me decide when, okay?"

"Got it. And I think we should go fishing."

"What do you mean? We always go fishing. That's what we do except when I'm tangled up in crime stuff. Like now."

"That's part of my point, Sam. But I'm not talking about business fishing. I'm talking about *fishing* fishing. Just the two of us. It think it's what you need right now, to get away from all this personal mess you've been living lately. It's like a damned soap opera. And besides, I've been hearing stories about all kinds of baby tarpon rolling around in the backcountry. I think we need to get in your canoe and go check it out. Could be some good fly action."

It took a while to clear our schedules, but eventually what we did just that.

CHAPTER 43

When Bryce Wickstrom showed up the next morning he was almost perky. I was feeling anything but. Among other things I was hung-over, and the symptoms included a dull pain somewhere behind my eyes that made it hard to focus. Evidently he'd had an easier time getting over the loss of his favorite fly reel than I'd had getting over the loss of my wife.

The last thing I wanted was to go out shark fishing with the man, but a deal was a deal so we loaded up my Hell's Bay and got ready for another day on the water. My plan was to start fishing up-current from some cuts around the perimeter of Rabbit Key Basin, where I knew we could get a good chum line flowing out behind the boat.

The ride out took us past Schwimley Key, as usual. He pointed and asked "That's todyland over there?"

At least he remembered the name. "Yep, sure is."

"I looked up todies on my computer last night. Pretty little birds, I suppose, if you're into that sort of thing."

"That they are."

"And I suppose it's a big deal, them showing up here?"

"A big deal for birdwatchers anyway."

"No, I mean couldn't they turn out to be an endangered species or something? When my company was drilling for oil out in Oklahoma, we were always scared some enviro type would find a little bird or a mouse or something, and shut us down. It could be a real pain in the ass. I heard plenty of stories – not that I would ever condone such a thing – that sometimes those critters just mysteriously disappeared before anybody from the government had a chance to find 'em."

The hypocrisy of certain so-called sportsmen never ceased to amaze me – immersing themselves in the pleasures and beauty of the natural world on the one hand, and jerking it around to satisfy their own greed on the other. Up until now I hadn't put Bryce Wickstrom in that particular camp, but in my book he'd just qualified himself.

"Well, Bryce, I don't suppose anybody is planning to drill for oil over there on Schwimley Key. Are they?"

He laughed at that. "Not that I know of. I'm just sayin' is all."

I wasn't sure what he *was* saying, but it seemed like a good idea just to drop the subject. That, and make sure I never took the man fishing again.

~ ~ ~

We actually had a pretty good day. The tidal flows were strong, the barracuda chum did it's thing, and by quitting time we'd hooked and landed four nice fish above the qualifying four-foot size limit – three lemon sharks and one five-foot bull shark. It wasn't nearly enough to win or even place in the tournament, because of our big zero on the first day. But still, I felt I'd earned my fee.

As soon as Bryce left I hurried inside to check for messages, hoping against hope there might be one from Katie. Something had fallen through, she wasn't moving to Atlanta after all, or she'd come to her senses and figured out that Stuart Brodsky was a jerk.

There was a message, but it was from Stella. She said there was news, and would I call her asap. Geez, I hoped she hadn't heard about Katie and me, because I wasn't ready to talk about it yet, not with her or anybody else except Snooks.

I cleaned up the boat, fed the last of the barracuda chum to a handful of pelicans circling around my dock, and then went inside and took a shower. After that I got a Yuengling out of the refrigerator and took it and my phone out on the deck, and called Stella.

She came on right away. "Hi, Sam. Thanks for calling back. Where were you today? I tried your cell and your land line a bunch of times."

"Sorry. I was out with Bryce Wickstrom on the second day of that shark-fly deal, and forgot to charge my cell. What's up?"

"Three things, actually, and I think you'll find all of them interesting. First, we got preliminary autopsy results back for Peter Donovan. Looks like he died of a ruptured aorta."

"No signs of any other trauma?"

"Nothing except the snakebite and the missing leg, which we already knew about. Looks like it could have been natural causes."

"Yeah, if by 'natural causes' you mean getting bitten by an everglades diamondback and than chased by a crocodile."

Stella laughed. "What I mean is, I don't think we're looking for a killer, or at least not a human one."

"Good point. What else?"

"Better luck there. We got a match between your blood and hair sample and the material attached to the Perkins cousins' hatchet. It looks like they're going down for sure on an assault charge."

This was good news, not that it got us any closer to finding out who killed Mabel Schwimley. "You said there were three things?"

"Team Mabel is going inside Pelican Pete's Emporium tomorrow at 9 AM. We're assuming you'd like to be in on it?"

"Wouldn't miss it."

"Good. Ostensibly we're just looking for evidence that might link to his death, but as long as we're in there..."

"Got it. I assume the place has been closed up since we found Pete's body?"

"Oh you bet. Locked, and I arranged for a guard."

"And his home?"

"Yeah, he has an upscale place over in Port Antigua. Penny Raintree and I went in there yesterday, but we didn't find anything interesting. That's why I'm really banking on today's search."

"What about relatives? Was Pete married?"

"Divorced. The ex lives up in Orlando. Didn't seem all that interested when we got in touch with the news. Of course she might get that way, depending on the value of his inventory and whether she's in line to inherit any of it."

"Which value could be considerable, if the place is as full of Native American artifacts and contraband wildlife products as we suspect. What about employees?"

"Three that we know of, all young and part-time. One of them's his girlfriend. They claimed not to know anything about the man's business."

"Even the girlfriend?"

"Yep."

"Huh. Well okay then, see you in the morning."

~ ~ ~

I couldn't sleep that night. A lot of it was because of Katie, I'm sure. Maybe even all of it, but I also was thinking about the case. In between all that tossing and turning, a couple of ideas popped into my head. Around two in the morning I got up, turned on my computer, and went to one of those on-line dictionaries. Then I looked up the word 'epiphany.' Silly thing to do, but I couldn't get the word off replay, and I knew there was little chance of sleep until I got it unstuck.

According to Webster an epiphany is a 'sudden manifestation or perception of the essential nature or meaning of something.' It turned out I'd actually had three of them earlier that night. If epiphanies came in sizes, I decided two of the three were especially big ones. Unfortunately, none of them had to do with Katie, but each of them had to do with Schwimley Key and Mabel. After we'd finished with Pelican Pete's Emporium the next day, and whatever happened there, it was time for another gathering of the team. Most likely we would need to meet at the Park, with Rhonda Wilcox in charge again, but that was fine with me.

CHAPTER 44

Pelican Pete's Emporium occupied three-fifths of a little strip mall on the ocean side in central Islamorada. At one time it had included five separate business outlets, but that was before Pete started gobbling things up for his ever-expanding empire. He'd knocked out the interior partitions between the three adjacent storefronts, but dedicated each to a different assortment of offerings. The ceilings were low throughout, which would have made the place feel cramped even without all the stuff.

But stuff there was. The northern room was the clothing section, mostly rack upon rack of tacky t-shirts, but there also were various items of beach attire. The central of the three rooms was devoted to household things like insulated beer cozies, plastic coffee mugs, coasters, greeting cards, and cocktail napkins with cute sayings printed on them. The southernmost room was the largest of the three, and it had two doors. The one on the street side was double swinging glass, and it was the only entrance for customers. The other door was centered on the back wall, and we soon discovered that it led to a big back room that ran the full length of the place. Yard ornaments filled up most of the space in the third room, including things like pink flamingos and little fountains shaped like turtles and frogs that you could plug into your garden hose for instant outdoor ambiance. A pair of glass-topped counters flanked the door on the back wall, and these were filled with jewelry. The counters were set out from the wall far enough for employee access from behind, and the one on the left had a cash register sitting on top of it. I assumed this was the vantage point from which Pelican Pete Donovan or one of his employees held court when he was open for business.

It was a real battle fighting through all the crap before we got to any of the good stuff. Dave Ackerman headed straight for the back room, thinking this was where Pete might have kept some of his wildlife artifacts or, for all we knew, some of the wildlife itself. Mike focused on the jewelry because he was most interested to learn if the man had been selling Native American artifacts. I wandered up through the household and clothing rooms, looking for any items that seemed out of place.

Eventually we all ended up in the back room, because nobody found anything of particular interest or value out in front. The jewelry counter looked promising at first, but Mike quickly discovered it held mostly junk except for a few items in turquoise and silver that clearly were contemporary. The storage room was mostly that, except for a small office area just inside and to the right of the door. The whole place was a mess, stacked high with cardboard boxes and plastic bins of every size and shape. It was going to take hours for us to search through all of it, but we all agreed it had to be done.

About mid-day Dave announced that he was hungry, and then he went outside to call for a delivery of pizza and soft drinks. He hadn't had much luck anyway. There were no living turtles or crocodilians on the premises, nor any facilities for keeping them. And even in terms of finished products, we found only one pair of boots and a single purse that looked to have been made from crocodile hide.

Native American artifacts and wildlife-related jewelry were another matter. By the end of the morning's search we had unearthed better than two dozen items of potential interest, and Mike assembled them out on one of the counters for us to inspect while we drank soft drinks and ate our pizzas. Several objects clearly had been made from sea turtle shells, including three pairs of earrings and a large pendant. There also were three small but fully intact shells. The shells were stained and corroded. It was easy for me to imagine they had been dug out of the mound on Schwimley Key, but of course we had no way of knowing that. There were coral pieces carved into stylistic representations of fish, birds, and crabs, and one object that Mike identified as a likely game piece. These too looked very old, and Mike felt certain they were genuine examples of Indian art.

If nothing else, we definitely had Pelican Pete Donovan for trafficking in Native American artifacts and in products made from illegally-obtained wildlife. And although none of it pointed specifically at Schwimley Key, it was hard to conclude otherwise given our solid evidence that he had been out there and that somebody, most likely him, had been looting the shell mound. But none of this got us any closer to understanding just what had been his relationship, if any, with Mabel. And since he was now the *late* Pelican

Pete Donovan, the next logical steps in our investigation were far from clear.

It was Stella who got lucky, to the degree any of us did that day. While Mike, Dave, and I were polishing off the last of the pizzas, she excused herself and returned to the back room. In about five minutes she came back out carrying an old-fashioned ledger book, which she laid out on a section of counter not already cluttered with artifacts, empty pizza boxes, or soda cups.

"While the rest of you were sorting through the merchandise, I decided to take a look in a pair of filing cabinets and the old wooden desk that apparently served as Donovan's corner office. At first I thought it was a dry hole, just a bunch of old sales receipts and such, but then I found this thing tucked in behind one of the desk drawers. I almost missed it."

She flipped the ledger open, and we all gathered around for a look. "Unless I am mistaken, this is where the man kept sales records for his behind-the-counter stuff, all hand-written."

Each page included four columns. The handwriting was small and tidy, and always in the same black ink. The first column was headed 'Item,' and the entries were descriptions, like 'shell' or 'fish totem.' The second column was titled 'Date Found.' The last column was 'Date Sold,' but the entries in this column also included a dollar amount. From what I could see on the pages that Stella was thumbing through, the amounts ranged from as little as $50 to as much as $1,000. The third column, titled 'Source,' was by far the most interesting. Entries in this column included various letter combinations, and each was followed by another dollar amount, always less than the amount in the 'Date Sold' column. Most of the letter combinations meant nothing to me, but there was one that occurred more often than any other: 'M. S'

Was 'M. S.' in fact Mabel Schwimley? Everybody agreed it seemed likely, maybe even close to certain. Dave Ackerman asked to see the ledger. "Okay if I take a look at something? There may be a pattern here." He began skimming through more pages, stopping occasionally to write something in a little spiral-bound notebook he had pulled out of his shirt pocket. After about five minutes he put down his ballpoint pen and said, "huh."

"Huh what?" asked Stella.

"Two things, or maybe three actually. First, while the dates in the ledger go back a decade, the entries with 'M.S.' only started in the last couple of years. Second, the most recent 'M. S.' entry is dated five weeks ago. Isn't that about the time Mabel disappeared?"

I agreed, but only up to a point. "That was about when we found her blue shoes, but we can't know for certain how long she had been missing before that. You said there were three things in that ledger that caught your attention?"

Dave nodded. We gathered in close as he pointed to an example. "Look at this "M.S." entry. The dollar amount next to those initials is exactly one half the dollar amount under the 'Date Sold' column. And it's the same for every one of them. Looks like Pelican Pete was paying Mabel a commission of fifty percent."

I was curious about some of the other entries in the

ledger, particularly the different sets of initials, and asked to take a look. A quick thumb-through revealed maybe a half-dozen combinations in addition to "M.S.", but only one of them clicked. It was "H.M." Could this have been Hector Morales? I'd been wondering if they were partners ever since the night I'd seen the two of them together at the Safari Lounge. Maybe we could get something out of Hector about that, assuming he ever got willing to talk.

I had noticed a laptop computer on Pete's desk, and asked Stella about it.

She shook her head. "I tried that of course, but everything is password protected. My guess is he linked it to the cash register, which is the kind that keeps tabs on inventory while ringing up sales. We probably should take it back to headquarters and let one of our techies have at it. But I'll make a prediction right now that we're only gonna find his legitimate stuff in there, that he didn't want to take any chances on having electronic files around with records of his black market business."

~ ~ ~

We gathered up the contraband, the ledger, and the computer, and headed back to the Sheriff's Department for a post-mortem. Mike spread all the material out on a table in the detective's bullpen, because there wasn't room in Stella's office. She made the offer of coffee and then pointed to a pot that smelled stale even from half way across the room. None of us took her up on it.

Mike started things off. "Good job out there, everybody, and especially to you Stella for finding that ledger. Now, where do we go from here?"

Dave Ackerman laughed and shrugged his shoulders. "We've got a dead guy nailed for dealing in illegal stuff, at least some of it from Schwimley Key. And it doesn't take a genius to figure out that 'M.S.' in the ledger stands for Mabel herself, and that Pelican Pete had been paying for things he or she found in that shell mound."

"And," added Mike, "given some of those dollar amounts, it's not hard to imagine he got tired of handing Mabel all those big commissions."

Stella shrugged and looked skeptical. "A possible motive for murder? Could be. But what do we have for hard evidence?"

"Not one thing," Mike agreed. "And it's the same with Hector Morales and the Perkins' cousins. Just like Pelican Pete Donovan, they were up to their elbows in mischief out on Schwimley – in their case it was about crocodiles – but we haven't got a shred of evidence they had anything to do with Mable's disappearance. How do we get out of this jam?"

It had been a long and busy day, but those midnight epiphanies had kept circling around in the back of my head the whole time. "We may have overlooked another possibility."

"What's that?" asked Mike.

"I'm not quite ready to say yet, because I need to check out a couple of things first. Mike, do you still have a copy of the press release you first sent out about Mabel's shoes?"

"Yeah, I think so."

"If you could e-mail me a copy, I'd appreciate it.

And Stella, do you still have those objects I found under Mabel's floorboards?"

"Of course. They're secured in our evidence room."

"Good. I'd like to take a look at them." I turned to Mike. "And then it's probably going to be time for another meeting with Rhonda Wilcox up at the Park. Can you set that up? Maybe for tomorrow?"

He didn't like it. "Can do, but why all the secrecy? I thought we were a team."

"I just need to be sure about some things before I start raising false hopes, especially with the press and Investigative Services breathing down our necks."

Mike still didn't like it, and I didn't entirely blame him, but something told me to hold off.

~ ~ ~

When I got home that afternoon there was a silver Toyota pickup parked on the street, one house down from mine. I knew I'd seen it before, but couldn't remember where or when. I retrieved the day's mail from my box, and started sorting through it as I walked up the front steps. A big fat manila envelope stood out from the usual assortment of junk mail. It was from the law offices of Schindler, Munoz, and Griebe, with a Fort Lauderdale street address. Uh-oh.

I walked inside, so pre-occupied with tearing open the envelope and examining its contents that at first I failed to notice the woman sitting out on my deck. It was only after she tapped on the window that I looked outside. I had been expecting something from Katie's lawyers. I wasn't expecting Flo.

I walked over, pulled back the sliding door, and said hello. Then I just stood there.

"Hello, Sam. May I come in?"

"Uh, sure, of course." I stood aside and pointed to the leather couch in the living room, the same place where all our trouble had begun. "Please have a seat." It was an awkward moment to say the least, and one that I was handling badly. But the combination of having divorce papers in my hands and Flo in my house at the same time was a bit overwhelming.

She must have sensed my unease. "Sorry for the surprise visit. I was just on my way to work, and ... well, we need to talk."

I sat down across from her in one of two ancient La-Z-Boys left over from when my aunt and uncle had owned the house. "Okay, what?"

"I heard about you and your wife, and I'm really, really, sorry."

I shrugged. "It's just one of those things. But how did you find out?"

"Snooks. He was over at the Safari last night, by himself, and we got to talking."

"Damn that guy. I asked him not to tell you, or anybody else for that matter. And then he went and blabbed anyway."

"I know, Sam, but it's not his fault, it's mine."

"Yours how?"

"Because I knew something was wrong by the way he was acting, and I just kept pushing until he finally blurted things out."

"I didn't want you dragged into this, Flo. And Snooks betrayed my trust."

She shook her head, and color rose in her cheeks. "No Sam, don't say that. Snooks is your friend, can't you see that?" She paused briefly and looked down at her hands. "We both are."

I couldn't think what to say, so I just sat there pretending to watch something interesting outside.

"I'm not talking about the other night. That was just ... the other night. But now I'm thinking maybe your breakup with Katie was all my fault, and I'm really sorry about that."

"No, you're wrong Flo. Whatever we had – or have – it has nothing to do with Katie and me. As far as I am aware she doesn't even know about our, ... uh..."

"You can't even say it, can you? It was an affair, Sam, that's what it was. And it happened that night because I was lonely and drunk. And I feel like shit about it."

This had to stop. "The divorce business between me and Katie? It's her choice, not mine. Not that I necessarily blame her, since I was the one that walked out of our lives up in Lauderdale in the first place. And I still have a little hope – well damn little, but a little – that we can work things out."

Flo stood up and walked over to the window, but she didn't do it fast enough for me to miss a lone tear that was making its way down her right cheek. Something told me to stay where I was and keep quiet. After a while she turned back in my direction, sniffed a couple of times, and started wiping away the tear. "I gotta go, or I'll be late for work."

"Stay for a beer?"

"No, I really..."

"Sure? Not even a half?"

She managed a half-smile to go with the half beer.

I poured hers in a glass, kept the bottle for myself, and led her out into the deck. We sat together in the half-light of evening, drank our beer, and listened as a night bird called somewhere back in the mangroves across the canal.

After Flo left, I went back in the house, found a pair of latex gloves, and pulled them on. Then I went back outside with an evidence bag and placed her empty beer glass inside it.

CHAPTER 45

"I'm guessing and hoping we're all here for something new? What have you got?" Rhonda Wilcox sounded a bit bored, as if the whole Mabel Schwimley affair had begun to slide downwards on her priority list. It may have had something to do with the fact that we weren't getting much of anywhere.

We had assembled once again at Park headquarters, and the ball was squarely in my court because I was the one who had requested the meeting. "Regarding the disappearance and likely demise of Mabel Schwimley, I have some ideas. Everybody's thinking about Pete Donovan and the Perkins cousins, and I understand that we cannot rule any of them out as suspects. But just for the moment at least, let's consider some other possibilities."

Joe Rossini put up his hand. "Such as who?"

I resisted the urge to correct the man's grammar. "For starters, such as Ed Grimes. At our last meeting, Inspector Wilcox suggested that he might be fronting for some shadowy group with designs on developing Schwimley Key. Right?"

Rhonda finished rearranging a stack of papers before she replied. "Right. And so?"

"Last week I ran into Ed out on Schwimley Key, and he offered a day's pay each for as many Cuban todies as I could show him on the island."

Dave Ackerman was the only one who got it. "Why would he want to do that? For a bird watcher interested in nothing but the length of his life list, all todies after the first one would be irrelevant. If you've seen one, you seen 'em all, right?"

I nodded. "Exactly my thinking, Dave. The only reason he might pay me to find more than one was so he could come back later and blow 'em all off the face of the earth." I explained things further, in case Rhonda still didn't see the point. "Even one of those birds left on the island would threaten any possible future development. Finding any endangered species out there, let alone one that had never been seen before outside Cuba, you can imagine the consequences."

Apparently Rhonda still wasn't impressed. "So maybe this guy wanted to take lots of pictures or something. That's all you've got?"

"No, it's not. Ed and I were on a birding trip back in the glades a couple of weeks ago, and he asked if we were anywhere close to the spot where they'd found those blue shoes with the feet inside. I asked where he'd heard about that and he said it was all over the news. I didn't think anything about it at the time. But then the other night I remembered reading the press release the Park put out right after our discovery, and it didn't say anything about the color of the shoes. Right, Mike?"

"Right. We withheld that deliberately, for just this sort of reason."

Stella Reynard looked straight at Rhonda Wilcox and raised her hand. "Let's assume for the sake of argument that Ed Grimes had set about gunning all the todies on Schwimley Key. I can buy that. But on whose behalf?"

The Park Service Investigator stiffened. "Like I said

before, that's all conjecture, and we are in no position to speculate."

Stella didn't flicker. "Horseshit."

Color rose in Rhonda's face. "I beg your pardon?"

"You heard me." Stella paused, but only briefly. "Stop me when I get off track. You told us the other day that Ed Grimes might be part of a conglomerate trying to get their hands on Schwimley Key as some sort of high-end resort. But then you got real vague about it. In light of Sam's new evidence, I think we deserve better than that."

Once again, Rhonda Wilcox took time to shuffle the papers in front of her before she responded. Eventually she stopped shuffling and looked up. "All right, fair enough. Believe me, you're not the only one who's frustrated here. It's just that we have no solid proof. And in light of the possibilities, we just can't dump it all out there and wait to see what happens."

Stella dug in again. "Dump all what?"

"Whose money might be behind this whole thing."

Mike Nunez had stayed out of the conversation up until this point, which I could understand. But evidently now he'd had enough. "The story we're getting is that at least some of the money behind the Schwimley Key development could be coming from one of the biggest names in Florida real estate."

Stella still wasn't satisfied. "But that person or conglomerate or whoever it is would need world class connections, wouldn't they? After all, we're talking about an inholding in a National Park. Who has that kind of clout?"

Rhonda Wilcox slapped shut the manila folder that

had been open on the table in front of her. She was red in the face, and clearly agitated. "For god's sake Stella, listen to me for once. We're just not going there. Period!"

A stunned silence followed, broken eventually by Rhonda herself. "I want you all to keep looking at Donovan and the Perkins boys as our prime suspects. And please stay away from Ed Grimes for the time being. You have my word that Investigative Services will keep after that angle. Now let's get back to work, okay?"

Everybody said okay except me, because there was another reason I had asked for the meeting.

"When this whole thing first came up, Mike mentioned that by written agreement Schwimley Key would go to the Park when the last heir died. And since Mabel was that person, it wouldn't make sense for somebody interested in developing the island to have a hand in her disappearance or death. But then I had another thought. What if there were another Schwimley heir out there someplace? And what if he or she was more interested in development than Mabel?"

"Is this more than just speculation?" asked Rhonda.

"Yes. I think we need to take a look at a man named Bryce Wickstrom. He claims to be a retired oilman from Tulsa. I've had him out fishing three times, and during the first two he insisted on using an ancient Hardy Brothers fly reel. Said it was a family heirloom. I thought it was odd at the time, because the thing barely worked."

Puzzled looks began spreading around the room.

"And then the other night I made a connection. That particular reel was identical to one I found under the floorboards of Mabel's Schwimley's cabin. I confirmed that yesterday when Stella let me take a second look at it down in their evidence room."

Rhonda Wilcox wasn't buying it. Apparently skepticism was one of her specialties. "That's hardly solid proof. What's the big deal about a couple of old reels?"

"Nothing maybe, but think about the coincidence here. Mabel and Bryce had these identical old reels, and they both treated them in special and unusual ways. In Mabel's case it was part of a collection of family treasures that she kept hidden under the floorboards in her cabin. And Bryce refused to fish with any other reel until a couple of days ago when it finally fell apart."

"What else have you got?"

"That's pretty much it, I suppose, except that right from the start Wickstrom seemed more interested in Schwimley than just an ordinary fisherman. He keeps asking me questions about the place, and about our investigation."

"But still..."

"I know, I know. But all I'm suggesting is that we check into the man's background. Stella, you were able to track down Mabel's family history, right?"

"Right. She was an only child, as far as we know. But we didn't go back any farther than that. There could be some other relatives out there. Want me to look into it?"

We all agreed it was a good idea, and with that

Rhonda Wilcox brought the meeting to a close.

~ ~ ~

Later that night I was having an after-dinner Maker's Mark and reading for a second time the divorce papers sent along by Katie's lawyers. They had included a self-addressed stamped envelope "for my convenience," but I still hadn't done anything about it. Notarized signatures were required in a couple of places, and that was all the excuse I needed to keep stalling. The terms were simple enough, and I had to admit they were fair. She got the condo and her Prius, I got the jeep and the house in Islamorada, and we would split a small joint savings account. There would be no alimony, since we were both gainfully employed. Like I said, simple. And simply awful.

The telephone rang, and once again my hopes rose that it was Katie and that she had changed her mind.

Of all the people who might have called me that night, perhaps the one I least expected was Bryce Wickstrom. But it was the man himself.

"Evening, Sam, how are ya'?"

"Good."

"Good. And listen, the reason I'm calling is I've heard the fishing's really hot right now back in the everglades. And since the tide's gonna be just right on Sunday, I was hoping we might be able to head out that way with your canoe."

Snooks and I hadn't firmed up a date for our own backcountry trip, but I decided right then it would be Sunday, the day after tomorrow.

"Sorry, Bryce. I'm already booked up."

"Probably got another fisherman with the same

thing in mind?"

"Yep. Sorry."

"Then what about Monday?"

"Busy then too. I guess you should find somebody else."

"I already tried Snooks. Turns out he can't go either. And then by Tuesday the tide's gonna be wrong. Damn."

Good old Snooks.

CHAPTER 46

We left the dock at 8:30, with my canoe strapped in its usual place along the port side of the Hell's Bay. The cooler was full of ice and beer, we had two good eight-weight rods on board, and Snooks' vest was filled with the right kinds of flies. I couldn't remember a time when I had looked forward to a day on the water with greater anticipation. The wind blew fresh in my face as we made out way out toward the Rabbit Key Basin. The sky was clear, and on board with me was one of the best fishermen – maybe *the* best fisherman – in all of the Florida Keys. It was a chance to forget all about Mabel Schwimley, and maybe even push Katie to the back of my mind, at least for a day.

We worked our way north and west through various channels until we broke out into open water up near the mainland. Then we turned west and ran parallel to the coast, heading for the East Cape Canal. It was familiar territory all the way. Based on what he'd been hearing, Snooks recommended that we follow the same route we had taken five weeks earlier to the spot where he'd found Mabel's blue shoes, "unless that bugs you too much."

It *was* a little creepy, but I said okay. After all, good fishing was good fishing.

We were about half way down the coast when I noticed that another boat had fallen in behind us. It closed to within about a hundred yards and stayed there. It was a center console Mako, something over twenty feet, with a light blue hull. There appeared to be two people on board. When we turned up into the East Cape Canal, the other boat turned with us. I began to think maybe they had seen our canoe, decided we knew what we were doing, and thought they could follow us to a secret hot spot. Neither Snooks nor I were exactly unknown among local fishermen. But when we made a right turn into the creek that would take us back up into the glades, the other boat kept on going west toward Lake Ingraham, and so I forgot all about it.

I drove up the creek until we came to the sign that marked the beginning of the no-motor zone, where we tied up and transferred our gear into the canoe. I took the first turn paddling while Snooks strung up his rod and started casting. We had agreed ahead of time that we would take turns, switching off about every hour or so depending upon the availability of a good place to beach the canoe and trade places.

The incoming tide was strong, and I didn't have to do much except keep the canoe in the middle of the creek as we drifted upstream. Tarpon rolled here and there, and Snooks managed to hook two and land one before we broke out into the first of a series of three lakes we hoped to fish that day. At that point he suggested we switch places, and pointed to a sandy beach about fifty yards down the shore.

Once out of the canoe, we both took the opportunity to relieve ourselves and stretch as bit before getting back on the water. Snooks was fiddling with the rubber band holding his ponytail. Naturally I knew something was bothering him.

"Good fishing out there. What's wrong?"

He hesitated a bit, then shook his head. "Oh hell, Sam, I did it again. Shot my mouth off about your personal life, even when you asked me not to."

I already knew what he was talking about. "That's all right. Flo told me all about it. Said it wasn't your fault."

"She did, huh. And just why wasn't it my fault?"

"She claims she pushed you into it."

"Yeah, I guess maybe that's the way it happened. But still, I'm damned sorry. Anyway, how's it going with you and Katie?"

"Her lawyers sent me the divorce papers."

"Shit. Did you sign?"

I really wanted to end this conversation. "Not yet. And anyway, I thought we were here to get away from my personal soap opera, as you put it the other night. So let's get back to fishing before we lose the tide."

And fish we did. We traded places three more times that day, working pockets and points around the shore of that lake and one more before it was time to head back out. Snook were on the prowl, along with a handful of redfish, and the action was steady enough that I could keep my mind off Mabel and even Katie most of the time.

What had started out as a great day went all to pieces when we got back to my Hell's Bay, because it had sunk. The creek was shallow enough that most of the center console was still above water, and I couldn't see any obvious damage, but that was little consolation.

"Shit! First the fire, and now this. It just isn't my year for boats."

"Any chance you forgot the drain plug?"

Snooks had asked a legitimate question. Draining the bilge was part of the ritual when you pulled your boat out of the water to clean it. And most of us had forgotten at least once to put the plug back in afterwards.

"Don't think so. And besides, she'd have gone down on the ride over if that was it."

"Yeah, but maybe it was just loose or something."

"Possible, I suppose. Anyway, you got a signal? Maybe we can call for help."

We checked our phones, but both came up empty. The only thing to do was start paddling until one of us got a signal or ran into somebody who would give us a tow. The nearest marina was at Flamingo, about fifteen miles east and at least a half-day's canoe trip away.

As things turned out, it didn't take nearly that long. We hadn't been at it more than fifteen minutes, and we weren't even back to the East Cape Canal, when up the creek came the blue Mako that had been following us earlier. Bryce Wickstrom was behind the wheel, and sitting right next to him was Ed Grimes. They made a big wake and seemed in a hurry. I started to get an uneasy feeling about things.

Snooks apparently didn't share my concern. And after all, why would he? Instead he waved and shouted as the boat pulled up along side our canoe. "Boy are we glad to see you guys! You wouldn't believe what just happened." He pointed back over his shoulder. "Our boat sank back up there a little ways, and we sure could use a tow."

Bryce gave Snooks a big smile, said he was glad to help, and invited us on board. "Lucky thing we came along, huh? Ed, why don't you find a rope and help these guys tie up their canoe off our stern. Then we'll get started."

As soon as we were settled Wickstrom gunned the big Mako and continued on upstream. At first I thought he was just looking for a place to turn around, but when that didn't happen my initial unease got a whole lot worse. I rose from where Snooks and I had been sitting on the stern, and walked up beside Bryce. At the same time Ed moved back and took my place beside Snooks.

"Maybe you didn't understand, Bryce. My Hell's Bay is on the bottom. There's no way we can get it going. Please just drive us back to Flamingo, where we can get come help."

He shook his head. "That's not the plan."

"Look, I don't know what's going on here, but..."

"Sam, he's got a gun!"

I turned in time to see Ed Grimes lift a black automatic and put it against Snooks' temple.

Wickstrom's voice was icy, and he never took his eyes off the water ahead as he maneuvered the Mako up through the winding creek channel. "Now we're going on a little boat ride, just the four of us, during which I want you to sit still and shut the hell up. Otherwise, you're not gonna like what happens to your old buddy Snooks there."

We went past the spot where my Hell's Bay lay on the bottom and right on up into the no-motor zone. Like either of us gave a damn at this point about who was or wasn't following the Park rules.

It was another twenty minutes before Wickstrom slowed the boat to a stop and dropped the power pole anchor. We were next to a stretch of beach along the south shore of a good-sized lake. The place looked familiar.

"Say, isn't this the spot where..."

"Where you guys found Mabel Schwimley's blue shoes and got us into this mess in the first place? The very same. Right, Mr. Ed?"

Grimes might have moved the automatic an inch or two, but otherwise he held steady. "I told you not to call me that. But yeah, this is the place." He kept the gun at Snooks' temple, but turned and stared at the beach like he was remembering something. "That old lady was bat crazy. I could have made her rich."

"Lucky thing I came along," said Wickstrom.

Grimes shook his big round head. "You didn't just come along. I found you, remember? Hell, you didn't even know about Schwimley Key until I clued you in."

I sensed that Ed Grimes and Bryce Wickstrom were reluctant partners, who maybe didn't like each other all that much. Was there a way of turning that to my advantage? I couldn't think of one. The only plan I could come up with was to stall for time.

"Which one of you clowns tried to blow up my boat?"

Wickstrom grinned and didn't say anything.

"What are we doing here, Bryce?"

"We're here to talk about a pair of fishing reels."

I decided to play dumb. "What fishing reels?"

"If that's the way you want it." He nodded at Ed Grimes, who responded by moving his pistol away from Snooks temple and around to the back of his head. Then he pulled the trigger and blew a hole through my

326

friend's right ear.

Snooks screamed and grabbed at the pain. Ed took a handkerchief out of his back pocket, and handed it to Snooks. "Here, hold that on it. You're gonna survive, at least for a little while."

So much for the dumb act.

Bryce spun me around and stuck a finger in my face. "You know, Sam, your big mistake – or at least one of them – was showing Ed here the contents of that box you dug up under my cousin Mabel's floorboards. As soon as he told me about that, I knew that sooner or later you were going to put two and two together. Apparently those Hardy reels were something of a tradition in our family. I guess she had one just like mine."

He stopped talking long enough to reach into the center console and pull out his own pistol, an ugly black German Luger. "You want to know why we're here? For starters, we're here to find out if you already told your buddies in law enforcement about those reels."

It did not take the proverbial rocket scientist to realize they had no plans to let us go. Maybe I could buy some time by withholding information, but to what ultimate end?

He must have read my mind. "If you're looking for a reason to cooperate, then try this. Snooks' ear was just the first step. Ed likes to play with guns, and he'll be taking his time. Next he'll do a hand. Then maybe a knee. I understand that really hurts."

Snooks had heard it all, even with only one good ear. "Don't play along, Sam, that's what the man wants."

But I just couldn't do it. Would he back off if he knew the cat was out of the bag, or might he at least spare Snooks? It was a chance worth taking, under circumstances where we had nothing to lose. We still didn't have any solid proof that either he or Ed had actually killed Mabel Schwimley, which meant all Stella or Mike could make stick at this point was their assault on Snooks and me. Was Bryce rational enough to figure that out?

"I told them about the reels two days ago."

That stopped him, at least for the time being. I looked over at Snooks. Ed Grimes still had the gun at his head, but Snooks caught me eye and then glanced sharply up to his right, in the direction of the gun. His head didn't move, just his eyes. I tried to read the message, and then I thought I had it.

During the law enforcement training I had taken with the Park Service, we were taught to keep a suspect talking in order to delay violence for as long as possible. I wasn't sure if that rule applied in cases where the bad guys held all the cards. But I never had a chance to find out, because Snooks had other ideas. His elbow came up so fast into Ed Grimes' jaw he never saw it coming. The gun flew out of his hand and went overboard, followed immediately by Ed himself.

Wickstrom was distracted, if only for an instant, but I took the opportunity and made a grab for his gun. He held on and we fell to the deck, fighting for control of the weapon. We rolled twice, then there was a deafening retort and I felt a searing pain in my side. We continued to grapple and tumble around on the deck, until suddenly he grunted and went limp in my arms. I looked up to find Snooks standing over us, with a big red fire extinguisher in his right hand.

"You okay?"

I reached down to touch my side, and brought up a bloody hand. "Apparently not. Looks like he got me."

"Can you get up?"

The unconscious body of Bryce Wickstrom had me pinned to the deck. Snooks bent down and rolled him off, then helped me to my feet. "Now pull up your shirt and let me take a look at that."

We had been so busy dealing with Wickstrom and my gunshot that neither of us had been paying any attention to Ed Grimes, who was splashing around in the water trying to get back in the boat. Apparently he wasn't much of a swimmer.

Something else had seen the commotion. I glanced up just in time to spot a pair of mud-colored eyes and a row of shiny scales heading in our direction. Then they sank out of sight. The last thing we saw of Ed Grimes was the top of his oversized head as it disappeared under the water. The last sounds we heard were the fragments of a scream, escaping from his final bubbles as they rose to the surface.

I read somewhere that American crocodiles are disinclined to take down very large prey. But Ed Grimes was a little guy, and I guess he must have come in just under the limit.

Snooks was still bleeding from the bullet hole in his ear, and I had taken a hit in my left flank. He poked around my wound, and then sounded the optimistic note that the slug had gone all the way through my flank, apparently without penetrating my abdominal cavity. He found a first aid kit, and we set about patching each other up as best we could. Snooks also unearthed a role of duct tape, and we used that to bind Wickstrom's hands and feet before he had time to wake up. Based on the size of a red welt growing on the side of his head, it was going to be a while.

Once we had Wickstrom secured, it was time to get the hell out. We had no phones and no radio, but we had a boat that floated, with a motor that ran. And we almost certainly had the killer of Mabel Schwimley tied up on the deck, or at least one of them. The other one had just become crocodile food.

CHAPTER 47

We didn't encounter a single fisherman on our boat ride over to the marina at Flamingo, not that it would have mattered very much. My phone got a signal as soon as we were back out in the East Cape Canal, and I called Park headquarters to tell them we were coming in hurt, with a prisoner on board. Park Rangers and an ambulance already were on the scene by the time we pulled up at the dock. The EMTs tended to our wounds and also had a look at Bryce Wickstrom, who by then had started to come around. There was only one ambulance, which meant the three of us got to share a ride along with a medic and one of the Rangers.

Wickstrom lay on a gurney inside the ambulance, glassy-eyed but awake. He showed no inclination to talk, but I decided to probe a little, hoping he might give up something in his weakened condition. I even had the Ranger read him his rights, just in case.

"Why Mabel?"

"You think you're gonna get me to talk, just like that? Bullshit."

Apparently his condition wasn't as weak as I thought. I decided to try a different tack. "Then why Schwimley Key?"

He didn't answer right away, and I thought at first maybe he'd passed out. But then he stirred and turned his head in my direction. "Because it was mine, that's why. And with Ed's plans, we were gonna be millionaires. Until those damned little birds came

331

along."

"The todies?"

"Yeah, whatever. Ed said they hadda go. He's dead, isn't he?"

"Yeah, Bryce, he's dead. Just like your plans for Schwimley Key."

~ ~ ~

They put Snooks and me in rooms right across the hall from each other at the hospital up in Homestead, while they attended to his ear and my side. Wickstrom was someplace else, under guard. We were told he was being treated for a severe concussion.

Like I cared.

As for Snooks and me, our prognoses were good but they wanted to keep us for a couple of days as a precaution. For one thing, we'd both lost a fair amount of blood by the time we'd made our way back to the marina at Flamingo.

We had lots of visitors before the doctors let us go home from the hospital. Stella and Mike and Dave all came at the same time that first afternoon. They brought balloons and cards, just as if Snooks and I were little kids who'd just had our tonsils out. They also brought news.

I raised my bed up into a sitting position. Stella found a chair and carried it over to my bedside, while Mike and Dave sat across the room on a couch.

It turned out Stella had been working her on-line magic again, and she'd begun to piece together the life story of Bryce Wickstrom. His father Aldous Wickstrom had been a wildcatter in the Oklahoma oil fields, and he hit it big back in the 1940s. But the story before then was the interesting part. It turned out Aldous was born in Pennsylvania, where he'd met and courted one Audrey Schwimley, who was the daughter of Gustav Schwimley. Gustav and his wife had two children, Audrey and Harold. Harold was Mabel Schwimley's father, which made Bryce and Mabel first cousins. This meant Bryce Wickstrom was a rightful heir to Schwimley Key, and likely the only one if Mabel was out of the way.

By the time Stella finished explaining all this my head had started to hurt. But even in my weakened condition, I realized that some pieces of the puzzle were still missing.

"So why didn't the Park know about Bryce, if his claim to Schwimley Key was as strong as Mabel's?"

This was one of the pieces Stella had put together, or at least some of it. "We know for sure that Bryce's father Aldous was a grunt laborer on one of Gustav Schwimley's railroads. My guess is that Gustav wouldn't countenance a relationship between Aldous and his daughter, and so the two of them ran off to Oklahoma."

"And if they were estranged, that explains why Bryce grew up without knowing any of his Schwimley relatives, right?"

Stella nodded. "Seems likely, doesn't it?"

"But then he must have found out, not only about his family but about the key as well?"

"Again, that seems likely. I'm hoping that's something we'll get out of Bryce as soon as we can talk to him, because at this point we have no idea how he might have figured it out."

I knew we didn't have to wait that long. "He didn't figure it out. Ed Grimes made the connection. He said as much when we were back there in the glades."

"I wonder how Ed Grimes put it all together."

"Too bad we can't ask him."

Mike Nunez stood up and walked over next to Stella. He reached down and put his hand on my shoulder. "I think that's enough for one day. It's time for Team Mabel to get out of here and let you get some rest. Oh, and on the way out we're gonna drop in on Bryce Wickstrom and find out if by some miracle he's gotten himself into a chatty mood."

I was starting to feel a little groggy, but I couldn't let them go without one final question. "How do you suppose Mabel Schwimley ended up all by herself out on that key?"

None of them had any ideas about that.

As soon as Team Mabel walked out of my room, Snooks appeared at the door and knocked. "Okay if I come in?"

"Yeah, of course. You think you really need to ask? And how's the ear?"

Snooks came inside. He was wearing a hospital-issue bathrobe, and fingering a big white bandage that covered the whole right side of his head. "Numb, thanks to some very fine drugs they keep around here. The docs are telling me it's gonna be fine. Actually, I'm thinking of asking them to leave the bullet hole. Maybe I'll hang a big pirate earring from it. Whatcha think?"

We had a good laugh, and after a while Snooks went back to his own room, claiming he was beat and needed to take a nap. It sounded like a good idea, so I found the control that lowered my bed down into a horizontal position, and let myself doze off.

It must have been a long sleep, because it was dark outside the window when I finally woke up. Someone had dimmed the lights in my room, but I had no trouble recognizing a face that was hovering over me. I was still groggy from the painkillers they had given me, and at first I thought it might have been a dream.

"Katie?"

"In the flesh. How are you feeling?"

"Okay, I guess. How did you... ?"

"Somebody from the Sheriff's Department called, a woman named Stella I think, and told me that you'd been shot. I came as soon as I could."

The after-nap fog was lifting, and I thought I could detect real concern in her eyes. But then something else occurred to me. "Listen, if it's about those divorce papers, I was just about to find a notary when ... all *this* happened."

"Burn 'em."

"What?"

"Things have changed. I was gonna call you."

"Changed how?"

She went across the room, brought back a chair, and sat down beside my bed. "Well for one thing, Atlanta is off. I'm not going."

That sounded promising. "What about Stu or Stuart or whatever he's called?"

"He's not going either."

That sounded less promising, but then it wasn't after she cleared things up.

"He may be out of a job altogether, depending on how

the paternity suit comes out."

By now I was wide awake. "You're not...?"

This actually got a laugh. "Oh hell no, Sam, not me. It's somebody else in the office. It turns out there was a whole line of somebodies. The guy's a world-class serial philanderer. I was the latest in a very long line."

I wasn't the least bit sorry to hear that Stu the wonder boy had crashed and burned, but if there ever was a right time to say so, this wasn't it. "Sorry for your troubles, Katie."

She shrugged and looked away.

I reached out and put my hand on her shoulder. "This was partly my fault. Maybe even mostly. After all, I was the one who moved out in the first place."

"Don't beat yourself up over it. I was the idiot in this family." She paused long enough to pull a tissue from the box next to my bed and blow her nose. "Maybe it's time to figure out what happens next, instead of dwelling on how we got here?"

"And you really mean it about the divorce?"

"Yeah, I really mean it."

Perhaps we both knew there was an elephant in the room, but I was the one to point it out. "I'm not sure I could move back up to Lauderdale."

She surprised me with her answer. "And I'm not sure I want you to."

That sounded like progress. Or was it?

Katie rose to leave, but I put my hand out to stop her. "What happens next?"

"You get yourself well, and I'll be back in a couple of days. There's somebody I need to talk to."

And with that she was gone.

CHAPTER 48

They let Snooks and me out of the hospital two days later. Our wounds were healing well, and the doctors decided they could treat us on an outpatient basis from here on. Snooks might need some plastic surgery at some point, whether or not he opted for the pirate earring.

I hadn't heard anything more from Katie, not even a call, but something told me not to push things. If she was making up her mind about something hard, sticking my nose in might only make it worse.

There was one piece of very good news. Mike Nunez had arranged for a salvage crew to rescue my boat. It actually was waiting for me at the dock when I got home, a little droopy around the edges, but all there. Evidently either Ed Grimes or Bryce Wickstrom had dived down and unscrewed the drain plug, but otherwise they had done no damage. All that time in salt water had messed up my outboard and some of the wiring, but Billy Nelson thought he could fix things up in a couple of days.

~ ~ ~

It would be good to get back to fishing full-time, but before that could happen there was one thing left to do about the Mabel Schwimley affair. Stella Reynard held the key, which explains why I was in her office early the next week. We were each working on a cup of hot black Sheriff's Department coffee, and sitting on opposite sides of her desk.

She started by catching me up on Bryce Wickstrom. Like Snooks and me, he was out of the hospital. Unlike us, he was completing his recovery in the county jail instead of at home.

"He's lawyered up, and we're not getting much out of him. He's been arrested and charged with attempting to murder you and Snooks. I'm positive that part will stick. We're sure he and Ed Grimes did away with Mabel Schwimley, and I'm pleased to report we have our first piece of solid physical evidence."

Stella stopped talking and made a big show about fiddling with her coffee cup. So of course I had to bite.

"And...?"

She looked up and grinned. "My forensics people went over the Mako that Wickstrom and Ed Grimes used to drive you back into the glades? Turns out it is registered to Grimes, which we more or less expected. There was fresh blood on the deck, some yours and some probably from Snooks, although we're gonna need a sample from him to be sure. But there was a third spatter of blood, old and dried, up under one of the seats. And here's the cool part. The DNA matches the samples we got from the blue shoes and from Mabel's cabin."

"How did Wickstrom react to that news?"

"We haven't told him yet. So we'll see."

"Do you need anything from me at this point?"

Stella drank some coffee and shook her head. "Not yet. I'll let you know."

"Where was Wickstrom living? Have you done a search?"

"Sure, but nothing much turned up." She paused

for another swallow. "There was one interesting thing. His place turned out to be an old doublewide down in Marathon, which seemed odd for somebody who was supposed to be a wealthy retired oilman from Tulsa. We had a look at his bank account and it was a real eye-opener. Retired oilman? Yes. Wealthy? Not so much. The guy was practically broke."

"I guess that explains why he was desperate to get his hands on Schwimley Key. And speaking of which, what's become of the real estate group supposedly trying to develop the place?"

Stella laughed and rolled her beautiful black eyes. "Vanished like the wind, apparently."

"You asked Rhonda Wilcox about that?"

"Sure, and she stonewalled me just like before. All she said was the developers were 'no longer in the picture,' and we should forget about it."

Stella's eyes drifted momentarily to the window and then back. "But that's not really why you're here, is it? You're here because you want to know what we picked up on that glass you brought in the other day, right?"

"Right. Any results?"

"Uh huh." She opened a file folder that had been sitting on her desk. "We got good DNA off the glass, both nuclear and mitochondrial, and there's no doubt. Most likely none of it belonged to Mabel Schwimley herself, but somebody out there must be a close relative. Did Bryce Wickstrom handle that glass?"

"Nope."

"And you're not going to tell me who did?"

"Not yet. Give me a little time."

She didn't like that until I told her it had nothing to do with a crime, or at least none that we knew of. Then I thanked her for the information, and left.

~ ~ ~

The Safari Lounge beckoned that night, but I broke with tradition and didn't invite Snooks. There was business to be done, and he might have gotten in the way.

The place was jammed when I got there, and both Flo and Burt were working behind the bar. I found an empty stool, asked Burt to bring me a Maker's on the rocks, and then waited for a chance to catch Flo's eye. It was another five minutes before she made it over.

"Hi Sam, how's the wound?"

"You heard about that?"

"Yeah, Snooks was here a couple nights ago. He told me all about it, but even if he hadn't, that big white bandage on his ear would have gotten my attention."

"You got a minute?"

"I'm here, aren't I?"

"No, I mean is there someplace we can talk?"

Her green eyes focused right on mine, and she raised one eyebrow. "I'm about due for a break. It's a warm night, so why don't you go outside and find an empty table. I'll see you there in five minutes."

I didn't blame Flo for being suspicious, given our history. When she came outside she was carrying a glass ashtray, a pack of unfiltered Camels, and a lighter. She sat down at my table and lit up. I had never seen her smoke before.

I tried to put her mind at ease. "This is not about us."

She took a puff, blew smoke in my direction, and picked a bit of tobacco off her lower lip. "No? Then why are we here?"

"You told me once that you were adopted as an infant, and never knew your biological parents?"

"That's right. Why?"

"I may have some information about one of them. In fact I'm sure I do. It's about your mother."

Another puff, even bigger than the first. "Yes?"

"I think she was Mabel Schwimley."

Flo stubbed out the remains of her cigarette. "You're kidding."

I told her about the DNA she'd left on a glass the last time she was over at my house, and about the photograph I'd seen from Mabel's high school yearbook, and how I finally figured out why it looked familiar.

She didn't say anything for a while, just looked out in the direction of a flock of laughing gulls circling over the beach. Their crazy calls must have added to her sense of unreality.

"You're sure about this?"

"Yes."

"Well then god-*damn* it, Sam! How could she do that to me!" It wasn't a question.

I tried to find something comforting to say. "Sometimes people aren't in a position to keep their babies, Flo. And didn't you say your adoptive parents loved you?"

She lit up another smoke and shook her head. "That's not what I mean."

"Then what is it?"

"She was *here*, Sam. She came here all the time. Why didn't she ever say anything?"

I could think of two reasons, but there was no way of proving either one. "Maybe she was afraid. Or maybe she didn't even know."

It seemed likely that Flora Delaney would never get all the answers, and there was little I could do to ease her pain. But I did think of one thing that might help.

"There may be an upside to all this."

She raised an eyebrow. "There'd better be. What?"

"I think you're about to become the owner of a big chunk of land right in the middle of Florida Bay."

CHAPTER 49

Fishing was good over the next four months. Tarpon season kept Snooks and me busy through most of the summer. For the most part we had good clients, and we made some good money. Dave Ackerman asked me to help Fish and Wildlife take down a guy selling illegal Florida conch steaks down in Big Pine, and later we busted somebody digging up turtle eggs in the State Park on Long Key. But that was it for crime-fighting.

I checked in with Stella a couple of times for updates on the Wickstrom case, including once when we met for beers at the Safari Lounge. Bryce and his lawyers had kept playing hardball, with no confessions or plea deals in sight. His trial for murder and attempted murder was scheduled for December, and I would be spending plenty of time on the witness stand. The D.A. was confident he would go down for trying to kill me and Snooks, but she was less certain about the murder of Mabel Schwimley. Bryce certainly had plenty of motive, and the blood spatter evidence put Mable in Ed Grimes' boat, either dead or injured. But Wickstrom's defense was that Ed must have acted alone, and that he knew nothing about how Mabel's blue shoes ended up way over there in the Everglades. We all knew it was bullshit, but ultimately that would be up to a jury and not us to decide.

They had dug a little deeper into Ed Grimes' background, and it turned out he was a real piece of work. Lots of his real estate deals involved shadowy groups of investors and borderline financial doings, but as far as they could tell none except Schwimley had risen to the level of murder. They searched his house and found a room full of guns. Apparently he had one obsession in addition to bird-watching, and it had almost gotten me and Snooks killed.

In the end it all worked out for Flo Delaney. A judge finally declared Mabel officially dead, and then ruled that Flo was a rightful heir to Schwimley Key. He would rule on any claim Bryce Wickstrom chose to make, once his trial had ended. In the mean time Flo was at liberty to dispose of the property as she saw fit.

And that was how things also worked out for Florida Bay and a handful of Cuban todies, because Flo decided to sell Schwimley Key to the Park Service. They settled on $300,000, which everybody agreed was a modest but fair price. Best of all for me and a whole lot of other people, the Dead Animal Bar had come up for sale and she used part of her windfall to make a down payment. She also hired Snooks to tend bar when he wasn't on the water, which was more often than it used to be. I was surprised at first, because I knew how much he loved fishing. But it all made sense once I figured out that Snooks and Flo had become an item.

Katie and I got back into the routine we'd been following before Stu and Flo got in the picture. She usually came down to Islamorada on weekends, and I managed reciprocal visits to Lauderdale with about the same frequency. And there were bigger and better things on the horizon. The day after Katie had visited me in the hospital, she'd made an appointment with her Dean and arranged for a sabbatical leave the following spring semester. She would spend it in Islamorada, working on a book about forensic plant science. Or at least that was the official justification. We also filled out the necessary paperwork for the creation of Sawyer & Sawyer, LLC, and we anticipated expanding our services beyond forensics to include any sort of zoological or botanical fieldwork.

It seemed like good times were ahead. Then, around the end of August, we started hearing news stories about a tropical storm that was growing into a hurricane out over the southern Atlantic. Ten days later, everything changed.

===

Thank you for reading.
Please review this book. Reviews help others find
Absolutely Amazing eBooks and inspire us to keep
providing these marvelous tales.

If you would like to be put on our email list to receive
updates on new releases, contests, and promotions,
please go to AbsolutelyAmazingEbooks.com and sign
up.

ACKNOWLEDGMENTS

Our thanks to the following individuals for their advice, encouragement, and assistance:

– To Billy Dahlberg and Steve Friedman, who taught us all we know about fishing the skinny water;

– To John Helzer, a good fisherman and a better boat mechanic; without him we'd probably still be stuck out there someplace;

– To the late Sandy Sprunt of the National Audubon Society, who first introduced us to the birds and ecology of Florida Bay;

– To fellow members of the Red Herrings writers' group, Beth Eikenbary, Milt Mays, and Jean McBride, for their encouragement and editorial skills, and for helping us get better at the writing craft;

– To Beth Steele and Brandon Fies, who have made our stays in the Keys more comfortable than we have a right to expect;

- To our family: Laura, Larry, Anthony, Chris, Dominic, Kaylee, Bryce, and Benson;

- To Shirrel Rhoades and Chuck Newman of Absolutely Amazing eBooks.

ABOUT THE AUTHORS

Carl and Jane Bock are retired Professors of Biology from the University of Colorado at Boulder. Carl received his PhD in Zoology from the University of California at Berkeley, while Jane holds three degrees in Botany, a B.A. from Duke, and M.A. from the University of Indiana, and a PhD from Berkeley. Carl is an ornithologist and conservation biologist. Jane is a plant ecologist and an internationally recognized expert in the use of plant evidence in criminal investigations. She is co-author with David Norris of *Forensic Plant Science* (Elsevier-Academic Press, 2016). The Bocks have co-authored numerous articles and two books based on their fieldwork in the Southwest: *The View from Bald Hill* (University of California Press, 2000), and *Sonoita Plain: Views from a Southwestern Grassland* (with photographs by Stephen Strom; University of Arizona Press, 2005).

Now largely retired from academic life, the Bocks have turned their creative efforts toward fiction writing, and are co-authors of two ongoing mystery series, the Arizona Borderlands Mysteries, and the Florida Swamp Guide Mysteries, both published by Absolutely Amazing eBooks and Whiz Bang, LLC, of Key West.

Coronado's Trail (Arizona Borderlands Mystery Number 1) was published in 2016, and *Death Rattle*

(Arizona Borderlands Mystery Number Two) in 2017. *The Swamp Guide* is the first of their series set in the Florida Keys.

Today the Bocks divide their time between Colorado, Arizona, and Florida, mostly fly fishing (Carl), fighting crime (Jane), and writing.

ABSOLUTELY AMA⚡ING eBOOKS

AbsolutelyAmazingEbooks.com

or AA-eBooks.com

Made in the USA
San Bernardino, CA
14 August 2018